Witold Gombrowicz

Bacacay

Translated from the Polish by Bill Johnston

archipelago books

Library of Congress Cataloging-in-Publication Data
Gombrowicz, Witold.
[Bakakaj. English]
Bacacay / by Witold Gombrowicz ;
translated from the Polish by Bill Johnston.
p. cm.
ISBN 0-9728692-9-8
I. Johnston, Bill.   II. Title.
PG7158.G669B313 2004
891.85373—dc22   2004012573

Archipelago Books
239 West 12th Street, 3C
New York, NY 10014
www.archipelagobooks.org

Distributed by
Consortium Book Sales and Distribution
1045 Westgate Drive
St. Paul, Minnesota 55114
www.cbsd.com

BAKAKAJ
Wydawnictwo Literackie, Krakow 2002
Copyright © Rita Gombrowicz and Institut Litteraire
All rights reserved

English Translation © 2004 Bill Johnston

Jacket art: *Déjeuner d'affaires*, Jean Dubuffet, 1946
Copyright © 2004 Artists Rights Society (ARS), New York / ADAGP, Paris
Indiana University Art Museum: Gift of Dr. and Mrs. Henry R. Hope
Photograph by: Michael Cavanagh, Kevin Montague

Book Design by David Bullen Design
Printed by The Stinehour Press, Lunenburg, Vermont

*This publication is made possible with a regrant from the
Council of Literary Magazines and Presses, supported by public funds
from the New York State Council on the Arts, a state agency.*

Table of Contents

Bacacay

Lawyer Kraykowski's Dancer

➤⭇

I was on my way to see the operetta "The Gypsy Princess" for the thirty-fourth time—and, since it was late, I bypassed the line and went straight to the lady at the ticket window: "My dear madam, please just quickly give me my usual, in the balcony"—when suddenly someone took hold of me from behind, and coldly—yes, coldly—dragged me away from the window and pushed me back to my proper place, i.e., the end of the line. My heart began pounding, I was short of breath—is it not a murderous thing when a person is suddenly taken by the collar in a public spot?— but I looked around: He was a tall, vigorous, fragrant individual with a short, trimmed mustache. He was conversing with two fashionably dressed ladies and one gentleman, and checking the tickets he had just bought.

They all looked at me—and I had to say something.

"Was it you who did me the honor?" I asked in a tone that might have been ironic, perhaps even sinister, but since I suddenly came over weak, I said it too quietly.

"Say what?" he asked, leaning toward me.

"Was it you who did me the honor?" I repeated, but once again too quietly.

"Yes, I did you the honor. Back there — at the end. We need order! This is Europe!" And, turning to the ladies, he remarked: "We must teach, teach indefatigably; otherwise we shall never cease to be a nation of Zulus."

Forty pairs of eyes and all kinds of faces — my heart was beating, my voice dried up, and I turned toward the exit — at the last moment (I bless it, that moment) — something shifted within me and I came back. I stood in line, bought my ticket, and just made it for the first bars of the overture; but this time I did not become engrossed in the show. While the Gypsy Princess was singing and tapping her castanets, twisting at the waist and panting, and the young elegants with their wing collars and top hats were parading before her raised arm — I was staring at a blond, brilliantined head just visible in the front of the orchestra, and repeating to myself: "Aha, so that's how it is!"

After the first act I went downstairs, leaned lightly on the orchestra rail, and waited a short while. All at once I bowed. He didn't respond. And so I gave one more bow — then I gazed up at the boxes a little, and again — I bowed when the appropriate moment came. I went back upstairs trembling; I was exhausted.

Leaving the theater, I stopped on the sidewalk. He soon appeared — he was bidding farewell to one of the ladies and her husband: "Goodbye, my dear friends; then we must — if you please! — ten o'clock tomorrow at the Polonia; good evening." After which he helped the second lady into a taxicab and was about to get in himself when I walked up. "I'm sorry to impose, but would you be so kind as to drop me off? I do like a good ride."

"Please stop bothering me!" he exclaimed.

"Perhaps you would back me up, sir," I said calmly to the driver. I felt an uncommon calm within me. "I do like . . ."— but the automobile was already moving off. Though I don't have much money, barely enough for the most basic necessities, I jumped into the next cab and gave the order to follow them. "Excuse me," I said to the doorman of the brown, four-story apartment building, "that was Engineer Dziubiński who came in a moment ago, was it not?"

"Oh no, sir," he replied, "that was Lawyer Kraykowski and his wife."

I went back home. That night I couldn't get to sleep — dozens of times I went over the whole incident in the theater, and my bows, and the lawyer's departure — I tossed and turned in a state of alertness and increased activeness that wouldn't allow me to sleep, and that at the same time, thanks to a repeated spinning about in the same place, became a sort of second, waking sleep. The very next morning I sent a magnificent bouquet of roses to Lawyer Kraykowski's address. Opposite the building where he lived there was a small milk bar with a verandah; I sat there the whole morning and finally spotted him around three, in a stylish gray suit, with a walking cane. Ah, ah — he was walking along and whistling and occasionally waving his cane, waving his cane . . . I immediately paid the check and followed him—and, admiring the slightly sinuous motion of his back, I reveled in the fact that he knew nothing of it, that this was my own, inside. He trailed behind him the scent of eau de toilette; he was fresh—it seemed impossible to draw close to him in any manner. But for that too a way was found! I decided: If he turns left, you'll buy that book, London's *The Adventure*, that you've wanted for such a long time; if he turns right, you'll never have it, never, even if someone were to give it to you for free you won't read a single page! It'll be wasted! Oh, I could have stared for hours at the place where his hair ended in an even line and his pale neck began. He turned left. In other circumstances I would have run to the bookstore at once, but this time I continued to follow him—only now with a feeling of unutterable gratitude.

The sight of a flower seller gave me a new idea—certainly I could, right away, immediately—it lay within my power—to arrange an ovation for him, a discreet homage, something he might not even notice. But what did it matter that he wouldn't notice! That was even more beautiful—to worship in secret. I bought a posy, overtook him—and as soon as I came within the orbit of his gaze a regular, indifferent step became an impossibility for me—and I unobtrusively tossed a couple of timid violets beneath his feet. And in this way I had found myself in a most curious situation: I was walking on without knowing whether he was behind me, or whether he had turned onto a side street, or had entered a gateway; and I didn't have the strength to look around—I wouldn't have looked around whatever had depended on it, even if everything had depended on it—and when I finally got the better of myself, pretended my hat was blowing off, and looked back—he was no longer behind me.

Till the evening I lived only with the thought of the Polonia.

I entered the glittering room right behind them and took a seat at the next table. I had a presentiment that this was going to cost me dearly, but when it came down to it (I thought) it was all the same to me and perhaps—perhaps I wouldn't live longer than a year, and so I had no need to spare myself. They noticed me at once; the ladies were even indelicate enough to start whispering, whereas he—he did not disappoint my expectations. He didn't pay me the slightest attention; he devoted himself to the ladies, leaning toward them, then looked about, scrutinizing the other women there. He spoke slowly, with relish, looking through the menu:

"Hors d'oeuvre, caviar . . . mayonnaise . . . poularde . . . pineapple for dessert—black coffee, Pommard, Chablis, brandy and liqueurs."

I ordered:

"Caviar—mayonnaise—poularde—pineapple for dessert—black coffee, Pommard, Chablis, brandy and liqueurs."

It took a long time. The lawyer ate a great amount, especially of the poularde—I had to force myself—I truly thought that I wouldn't be able to manage, and I watched anxiously to see if he would have another helping. He kept taking more and he ate with gusto, in big bites, he ate mercilessly, washing it down with wine, until in the end it became a veritable torment for me. I don't think I shall ever be able to look at another poularde or that I shall ever be able to swallow mayonnaise again, unless—unless we go to a restaurant again together one day; that would be a different matter entirely, in such a case I know for sure that I'll hold out. He also drank volumes of wine, till my head started to spin. The mirror reflected his figure! How magnificently he leaned forward! How ably and skillfully he made himself a cocktail! How elegantly he joked, a toothpick between his teeth! He had a concealed bald spot on the crown of his head, pampered hands with a signet ring on one finger, and a deep baritone voice that was soft and caressing. The lawyer's wife was nothing remarkable, she was, it might be said, unworthy; whereas the doctor's wife! I noticed at once that when he addressed the doctor's wife his voice took on a softer and more rounded tone. Aha! Of course! The doctor's wife seemed made for him, narrow, serpentine, refined, indolent, a kitten with a marvelous womanly capriciousness. And in his mouth the word "talons" for fingernails sounded perfect; it was obvious that he liked it, that he knew how. Talons, dame, binge, swell, wolf, toper —"Ha ha, you're quite the toper, my dear doctor!" And—"if you please," that "if you please" so emphatic and compelling, so cultured yet authoritative, like a three-word chronicle of all possible triumphs. And his nails were rosy, one in particular, on his little finger. It was around two when I finally returned home and threw myself on the bed in my clothing. I was sated, filled to bursting, overwhelmed; I had the hiccups, my head was ringing, and the delicate dishes had upset my stomach. It had been an orgy! An orgy and a delight, a carousal! "A night in a restaurant," I whispered, "a nighttime carousal! Because of him—and for him!"

From that time on, every day I would sit on the verandah of the milk bar, waiting for the lawyer, and would follow him when he appeared. Another person might not have been able to devote six or seven hours to waiting. But I had time to spare. Sickness, epilepsy, was my only occupation, and furthermore it was an occupation for special occasions only, one on the margins of the string of days; aside from that I had no responsibilities, and my time was free. Unlike other people, I was not distracted by relatives, friends and acquaintances, women, or dancing; other than one dance— St. Vitus'—I knew no dances and no women. My modest income sufficed for my needs; besides, there were indications that my debilitated organism would not last long—then why should I scrimp and save? From morning to evening the day was free, unoccupied, like an endless holiday; there were unlimited amounts of time; I was a sultan and the hours were my houris.

Oh, come at last, death!

The lawyer was something of a gourmand, and it's hard to convey how beautiful it was: On his way home from the courthouse he would always stop off at a confectioner's, where he would consume two napoleons—I would watch surreptitiously through the display window as, standing at the buffet, he would put them in his mouth, careful not to spill cream on himself, and then delicately lick his fingers or wipe them with a paper napkin. For a long time I thought about this, then in the end—one day I entered the confectioner's.

"Do you know Lawyer Kraykowski, miss? He always has two napoleons here. You do? Then I'd like to pay for his napoleons for one month in advance. When he comes in, please don't accept any money from him, but just smile and say: 'It's already taken care of.' It's nothing; you see, miss, I lost a bet, that's all.'"

The next day he came as usual, ate, and wished to pay—his money was refused—he became irritated and threw the money in the charity box. What did it matter to me? An empty formality—he could give as much as he wanted to the homeless children, it wouldn't alter the fact that he ate my two napoleons. But I'm not going to describe everything here; besides, it is possible to describe everything? It was an ocean—from morning to evening, and often in the night too. It was wild, for instance, when we once sat opposite one another, eye to eye, in the tram; and sweet, when I was able to perform some service for him—and sometimes funny too. Funny, sweet, and wild?—yes, there's nothing so difficult and delicate, so sacred even, as human individuality; nothing can equal the rapacity of secret connections that arise, faint and purposeless, between strangers, only to bind imperceptibly with a terrible chain. Imagine the lawyer coming out of a public lavatory, reaching for fifteen groszy, and being told that it had already been paid. What does he feel at such a moment? Imagine that at every step he comes across indications of a cult, he meets homage and service all around, loyalty and an iron sense of duty, remembrance. But the doctor's wife! I was fearfully tormented by her behavior. Did his advances not move her? Did the toothpick and the cocktail in the Polonia make no impression on her whatsoever? She evidently did not accept them—once, I observed, he left her apartment furious, his necktie awry . . . What kind of woman was she! What could be done, how could she be prevailed upon, how could she be convinced, so that she should fully comprehend at once, so that she should thoroughly understand, just as I understood, that she should feel it? After hesitating for a long time, I decided that the best thing would be an anonymous letter.

Madam!
How is this possible? Your conduct is incomprehensible; behavior such as yours cannot be countenanced! Are you insensitive to those shapes, movements, modulations; to that scent? Do you not grasp that perfection? In what way are you a woman? In your place I would know what was expected of me if he should deign even to glance at my small, paltry, indolent woman's body.

A few days later (this was on a deserted street in the late evening) Lawyer Kraykowski stopped, turned around, and waited with his cane. It did not behoove me to retreat, and so I walked on, though a faintness overcame me; then he seized me by the arm and shook me, banging his cane against the ground.

"What's the meaning of these idiotic libels? What are you after?" he shouted. "Why are you trailing around after me? What is all this? I'll take my cane to you! I'll break your bones!"

I was unable to speak. I was happy. I received it into myself like a communion, and I closed my eyes. In silence I merely bent over and offered my back. I waited—and experienced some of those perfect moments known only to one who truly has but a few days ahead of him. When I straightened up he was walking quickly away, tapping his cane. My heart full, in a state of grace and beatitude, I returned home through the empty streets. Too little, I was thinking; too little! Too little of everything! More—ever more!

And contrition mingled with gratitude. Of course! She had read my letter as if it were some pitiful claptrap, a stupid joke, and she had shown it to the lawyer. Instead of helping I had hindered, and all because I was too selfish, too lazy, and gave too little of myself —I wasn't sufficiently serious and responsible, and I had been unable to inspire understanding.

Madam!
In order to make you aware, to appeal to your conscience, I declare that starting today I shall apply various forms of self-denial (fasts and so on) until it comes about. You are insolent! What words can I employ to explain the necessity, the obligation, the bounden duty? Will it go on much longer? What could be the meaning of this resistance? What is the source of this pride?!

And the next day, remembering an important detail, I wrote:

Only "Violette" perfume. That's what he likes.

From this moment the lawyer stopped visiting the doctor's wife. I agonized; I could not sleep at night. I am not naïve. In many matters I have an understanding that no one would suspect in me —I'm well aware, for example, of the impression such a letter might make on a polished, worldly person like the doctor's wife. I'm able even at the heights of ecstasy to give a sudden composed smile—but what of it? Did this make my suffering less intense, or the torments I imposed upon myself less painful? Was my indignation less fundamental? My adoration of the lawyer less genuine? No! What is fundamental? Life, health? And so I swear that with the same sudden composed smile I would give up both life and health if only she would . . . if only she would comply. Or perhaps this woman had ethical scruples? What are foolish ethics in the face of Lawyer Kraykowski? Just in case, I resolved to reassure her in this respect too!

Madam, you must! The doctor is a zero, a nobody.

But with her it wasn't ethics, it was simply pride, or even non-sensical female sulkiness, and a failure to grasp sacred elemental matters. I walked to and fro beneath her windows—what was going on in there behind those drawn curtains (for she usually rose late), in what phase did she find herself? Women are too superficial! I tried magnetism—"You must, you must," I repeated over and again, staring at her window. "Today, this evening, if your husband goes out." Then suddenly, all at once, I remembered that the lawyer had wanted to beat me; that since he had not done so at that time, on the street—then perhaps it was for lack of time? And so I dropped everything and rushed to the courthouse, from which, I knew, he would emerge in a moment. And, in fact, a few minutes later he came out in the company of two gentlemen, and I went up to him and, in silence, offered him my back.

The astonishment of the two gentlemen hovered over me, but I paid them no heed—the entire world meant nothing to me! I half-closed my eyes, clasped my arms, and waited trustfully—but no blow fell. In the end I murmured, stammering into the flagstones of the sidewalk:

"Maybe now? Always, always, always . . ."

"It's just some idiot," his voice drifted over me. "How absentminded of me! I quite forgot that I have a meeting! We'll speak another time; goodbye, gentlemen. Here's a few pennies, my man. Good afternoon!"

And he hurriedly got into a cab. Oh, those cabs! One of the gentlemen reached into his pocket. I stopped him with a gesture.

"I'm neither a beggar nor an idiot. I have my dignity; and I accept charity only from Lawyer Kraykowski."

I conceived a plan of hypnosis, a constant, unwavering pressure with the aid of a thousand little facts, mystical signs that, without penetrating the consciousness, would create a subconscious state of necessity. On the wall of the building in which she lived I drew in chalk an arrow and a large K. I won't enumerate all my intrigues, some more adroit than others; she was enwrapped in a web of strange occurrences. A shop assistant in a fashion boutique referred seemingly by mistake to "her husband, the lawyer." The concierge, encountered on the steps, said that Judge Krajewski had asked if the umbrella had been returned. Krajewski-Kraykowski, judge-lawyer: Caution was needed; dripping water wears away a boulder. It was unclear how on earth she could have returned from the city with the lawyer's fragrance on her dress—his invigorating scent of violet soap and eau de cologne. Or, for example, such an incident: Late at night the telephone rings—she's awoken from her sleep, she hurries to pick up and she hears a stranger's voice saying peremptorily: "At once!"—and nothing more. Or a slip of paper stuck in her door with nothing on it but a line of poetry: "Hush, my child, and don't you *kray*."

But I was gradually losing hope. The lawyer had stopped visiting her; it seemed that all my efforts had come to nothing. I could already foresee the moment of final capitulation, and I was afraid: I felt I would be unable to reconcile myself to this. The affront to the lawyer in this regard was something I could not bear, even if he himself were untroubled by it. For me it would be the ultimate outrage, an injury and a disgrace. Ultimate—yes, ultimate, that is the right word. Unable to believe it, I nevertheless trembled before the inevitable end that was approaching.

And indeed . . . but there is after all such a thing as mercy! And oh, how artful they were—and incidentally, I'm angry at the lawyer for keeping it secret—did he not know that I was suffering? Was it by chance? Oh no, it wasn't chance, it was the heart! I was on my way home one evening, walking along the Aleje, when something prompted me to step into the park. I really should have gone to bed early that night, because the next morning at dawn I was going to attach a little gilt plate to the lawyer's door with the inscription LAWYER KRAYKOWSKI; but something prompted me to enter the park. I did so—and right at the far end, beyond the pond, I saw . . . ah! ah! I saw her large hat and his bowler. Oh, the naughty so-and-sos, the rascals, the little rogues! So while I'd been tiring myself out, they had been meeting here in secret from me— and so cleverly! They must have made use of taxicabs!—They turned into a side path and sat on a bench. I hid in the bushes. I expected nothing, I was thinking about nothing—there was nothing I wanted to know; I just crouched behind a bush and quickly counted leaves, without a second thought, as if I weren't there at all.

And suddenly—the lawyer embraced her, held her close and whispered:

"Here — nature . . . Do you hear? The nightingale. Now, quickly — while it's singing. . . . To its music, to the rhythm of its song . . . if you please!"

And then . . . oh, it was cosmic, I couldn't stand it any longer — as if all the forces of the world had gathered within me in a great frenzy, as if a terrible pile, an electrical pile, the pile of the vertebral column, or the pile of a funeral pyre, had given me a mighty jolt — I jumped up and began shouting at the top of my voice, across the whole park:

"Lawyer Kraykowski gave her . . . ! Lawyer Kraykowski gave her . . . ! Lawyer Kraykowski gave her . . . !"

The alarm was raised. Someone was running, someone was fleeing, people suddenly appeared from every direction; and I was seized once, twice, three times, I was knocked off my feet and I danced like never before, with foam on my lips, in twitches and convulsions — a bacchic dance. I don't recall what happened next. I woke up in the hospital.

My health is deteriorating. My recent experiences have exhausted me. Lawyer Kraykowski is leaving tomorrow in secret from me (though I know about it) to a small mountain village in the eastern Carpathians. He wants to disappear in the mountains for a few weeks and he thinks that maybe I'll forget. I'll follow him! Yes, I'll follow him! Everywhere I shall follow that guiding star of mine! But it's unclear whether I'll return alive from the journey; these emotions are too strong. I may die suddenly on the street, by the fence, and in such a case — a card must be written — they should send my body to Lawyer Kraykowski.

The Memoirs of Stefan Czarniecki

→‹

I

I was born and raised in a most respectable home. It is with great emotion that I run toward you, my childhood! I see my father, a handsome man of lofty stature, with a face in which everything—gaze, features, and gray-tinged hair—all combined into the very image of perfect noble breeding. I see you too, mother, in spotless black, with no other adornment than a pair of antique diamond earrings. And I see myself, a small, solemn, thoughtful lad, and I feel like weeping at those shattered hopes. Perhaps the only imperfection in our family life was the fact that my father hated my mother. Actually, "hate" is the wrong word; rather, he could not abide her, though why—I was never able to say; and this was the beginning of the mystery whose vapors led me in my adult years to moral ruination. For what am I today? An upstart—or better, a moral bankrupt. What do I do, for example? When I kiss a lady's hand I lick it moistly, after which I quickly take out my handkerchief: "Oh, pardon me," I say, and wipe it with the handkerchief.

I noticed early on that my father avoided my mother's touch like the plague. More, even—he avoided her eyes, and when he spoke to her he would most often look to the side or study his fingernails. There was nothing sadder in its way than that lowered gaze of my father's. Sometimes, on the other hand, he would look askance at her with an expression of boundless disgust. For me it was incomprehensible, since I felt no aversion whatsoever toward my mother; quite the opposite, though she had put on considerable weight and was spreading in every direction, I liked to cuddle up to her and lay my little head on her lap. But in such conditions how is it possible to explain the fact of my existence, how I had come to be? I must have been created, as it were, by force, with gritted teeth, in contravention of natural impulses; in a word, I suspect that for some time, in the interest of marital duty, my father suppressed his repugnance (for he placed the honor of his manhood above all else) and that the fruit of this heroism was myself—a little child.

After this superhuman and in all probability one-time exertion, my father's revulsion flared up with elemental power. I once heard him shouting at my mother as he cracked his fingers: "You're losing your hair! Before long you'll be as bald as a coot! A bald woman; do you understand what that means to me—a bald woman! A bald spot on a woman . . . a wig . . . no, I can't take it!"

And he added more calmly, in a quiet voice laden with suffering: "Oh, how awful you are. You have no idea how awful you are.

Besides, the bald spot is just a detail, the nose too; one detail or other can be awful, that can happen in the Aryan race too. But you're awful through and through; you're imbued with hideousness from head to toe; you're hideousness itself. . . . If there were at least one part of you free from the element of hideousness I'd at least have a starting point, some base, and I swear I'd concentrate upon it all the feelings I vowed to you at the altar. Oh dear Lord."

For me this was beyond comprehension. How was my mother's bald spot worse than my father's bald spot? And my mother's teeth were even better; there was one white eye-tooth with a gold filling . . . And why for her part was my mother not disgusted by my father, but quite the opposite, she liked to caress him — in the presence of guests, for it was only then that my father would not shudder. My mother was replete with majesty. To this day I can see her, sponsoring a charitable raffle, or at a dinner party, or leading the servants in an evening meditation in her private chapel.

My mother's piety was unparalleled; it was not so much ardent as voracious — a voracity for fasting, prayer, and good works. At the appointed hour we would appear, myself, the valet, the cook, the chambermaid and the concierge, in the pall of the black-lined chapel. After prayers had been said the lesson began. "Sin! Hideousness!" my mother would declare forcefully, and her chin would sway and tremble like the yolk of an egg. Perhaps I am not speaking with the respect owed to those dear shades? Life has taught me this language, the language of mystery. . . . But let us not get ahead of events.

Occasionally my mother would summon me, the cook, the valet, and the maid at an unusual time. "Pray, you poor child, for the soul of that monster your father; all of you, pray for the soul of your master, sold to the devil!" On some occasions, we would sing litanies till four or five in the morning under her direction, until the door opened and my father appeared in a tailcoat or a tuxedo, with an expression of supreme distaste on his face. "On your knees!" my mother would exclaim, swinging and undulating toward him, her outstretched finger pointing at the image of Christ. "Off with you, to bed, to sleep!" my father would order the servants imperiously. "These are my servants!" my mother would reply, and my father would leave hurriedly, to the accompaniment of our supplicatory lamentations before the altar.

What did this mean, and why would my mother speak of his "filthy deeds"? Why was she disgusted by my father's deeds since my father was disgusted by my mother? A child's innocent mind is lost in such secrets. "He's a libertine!" my mother would say. "Remember, all of you—don't stand for it! Whoever does not cry in outrage at the sight of sin should tie a millstone round their neck. One cannot feel enough disgust, contempt, and hate. He took a vow, and now he's disgusted? By hell's fires! He's disgusted by me—but I'm disgusted by him too! The Day of Judgment will come! In the next world we shall see which of us is better. A nose! —A spirit! A spirit has no nose, nor bald spot, and zealous faith opens the gates of future heavenly delights. There will come a time when your father will be writhing in torments and will implore me as I sit at the right hand of Jehovah, that is, I mean, of the Lord God, to give him my moistened finger to lick. We'll see then if he will be disgusted!"—In fact, my father was also devout and regularly went to church, but never to our chapel at home. Often, in his perfect elegance, he would say with that aristocratic narrowing of his eyes: "Believe me, my dear, it's a faux pas on your part, and when I see you before the altar with that nose and those ears and lips of yours — I'm convinced that Christ himself feels ill at ease. I don't deny your natural right to piety," he added, "quite the contrary — from the religious point of view a neophyte is a beautiful thing; but there's no getting away from it! Nature cannot be won over by pleading; and remember the French saying: *"Dieu pardonnera, les hommes oublieront, mais le nez restera."*

In the meantime I was growing up. Sometimes my father would take me on his knee and, at length, anxiously inspect my countenance. "The nose so far is mine," I would hear him whisper. "Thank the Lord! But here in the eyes and the ears . . . the poor child!"— and his noble features would fill with pain. "He's going to suffer terribly when he grows to awareness; I wouldn't be surprised if at that point something happens within him along the lines of an inner massacre."— What awareness was he speaking of, and what massacre? And in general — what ought to be the coloration of a rat born of a black male and a white female? Ought it to be mottled? Or was it also possible, when the opposing hues were of exactly equal strength, that such a union could produce a rat without hue, without color . . . but again I see that with my impatient digressions I am getting ahead of things.

2

In school I was diligent, a model student, yet I did not enjoy universal popularity. I remember the first time I stood before the principal, willing, earnest, filled with resolve, with the eagerness that always characterized me, and the principal took me benevolently by the chin. I thought that the better I worked, the more I would earn the approval of my teachers and schoolmates. But my good intentions shattered against the impassable wall of a mystery. What mystery? Bah! I did not know, and in fact I still do not — I only felt I was encircled on all sides by a mystery that was alien and hostile, yet charming, and which I was unable to penetrate. For is it not charming and mysterious, that little rhyme— "One, two, three, every Jew's a flea, all the Poles are orioles, you are it, not me"—with which my schoolmates and I would count each other out on the playground? I sensed that it was charming—I recited it with relish and deep feeling—but why it was charming, that I was unable to comprehend, and it even seemed to me that I was completely unnecessary, that I ought to stand to the side and merely watch. I compensated with assiduity and good behavior, but my assiduity and good behavior earned me the antipathy not only of the students but also, and this was stranger and more unjust, of the teachers too.

I also remember:

Who are you? A little Pole.
What's your sign? The eagle bold.

And I remember my late lamented teacher of history and Polish literature—a quiet, rather torpid old man who never raised his voice. —"Gentlemen," he would say, coughing into a great silk kerchief or cleaning his ear with a finger—"What other nation was the Christ of nations? The bulwark of Christianity? Which other had Prince Joseph Poniatowski? As concerns the number of geniuses, especially precursors, we have as many of them as the whole of Europe combined." And without a moment's notice he would begin: "Dante?" — "I know, sir!"— I would jump up right away — "Krasiński!" — "Molière?" — "Fredro!" — "Newton? — "Copernicus!" — "Beethoven?" — "Chopin!" — "Bach?" — "Moniuszko!"—"You can see for yourselves, gentlemen," he would conclude. "Our language is a hundred times richer than French, which is supposedly the most perfect tongue. What does the Frenchman have? Petit, petiot, très petit at the most. But what riches we have: small, little, titchy, tiny, teeny, teeny-weeny, teensy-weensy, and so on." Despite the fact that I answered the best and the fastest, he didn't like me. Why not? That I did not know, though he once said, coughing, in an odd, knowing, and confidential tone: "The Poles, gentlemen, were always lazy, for laziness is inseparably associated with great ability. Poles are able but lazy rogues. The Poles are a strangely likable nation." From that moment my enthusiasm for learning was somewhat dampened, but this too failed to win me the favor of my pedagogue, even though in general he had a weakness for lazy rascals.

At times he would close one eye, and then the whole class would prick up their ears. "Hm?" he would say. "Springtime, eh? It goes through your bones, draws you out into the meadows and the woods. The Pole was always, as they say, a good-for-nothing and a wild one. He wouldn't stay in one place, not a bit of it . . . that's why the women of Sweden, Denmark, France, and Germany are so fond of us, but we prefer our own Polish women, for their good looks are famous the world over." This speech and others like it had such an effect on me that I fell in love — with a young lady who used to do her homework on the same bench as me in the Łazienki Park. For a long time I had no idea how to begin, and when I finally asked: "Will you permit me, miss? . . ."—she didn't even respond. The next day, however, I consulted with my pals, got a grip on myself, and pinched her, upon which she narrowed her eyes and started giggling . . .

It had worked—I returned in triumph, exhilarated and sure of myself, but also curiously perturbed by that to me incomprehensible giggling and narrowing of the eyes. "You know what?" I said on the playground. "I'm also a wild one, a rogue, a little Pole; it's a pity you couldn't have watched me yesterday in the park, or you'd have seen a thing or two . . ." And I told them everything. "Moron!" they said, but for the first time they listened to me with interest. Then one of them shouted: "A frog!" "Where? What? Smash the frog!" They all rushed off, and I followed them. We set about lashing it with sticks till it died. In a fever of excitement, proud that I had been admitted to their most exclusive pastimes and seeing in this the beginning of a new era in my life: —"You know what!" I exclaimed. —"There's a swallow too. A swallow's gotten into the classroom and it's banging against the windows— just wait a minute . . ." I brought the swallow and, to stop it flying away, I broke its wing, and then picked up my stick. Meanwhile everyone had gathered round. "The poor thing," they said, "the poor little bird; give it some bread and milk." And when they saw me raising my stick, my classmate Pawelski narrowed his eyes till his cheekbones stood out distinctly and smacked me painfully in the mug.

"He got it in the mug!" they shouted. "You've got no honor,

Czarniecki, don't let him, fight back, smack him in the mug."—
"How can I?" I replied. "I'm the weaker one. If I try to fight back
I'll get smacked again and I'll be doubly humiliated."—Then they
all descended on me and beat me up, showering me with mockery
and malicious taunts.

Love! What bewitching, incomprehensible absurdity—pinching, squeezing, even snatching in an embrace—how much it contains! Bah! Today I know what to hold onto; I see here the secret
affinity with war, because in war too the purpose is in fact to pinch,
to squeeze, or to seize in an embrace; but at that time I was not yet
one of life's bankrupts—quite the opposite, I was full of goodwill.
To love? I can say boldly that I was drawn to love because I hoped
in this way to break through the wall of the mystery; and with
enthusiasm and faith I bore all the eccentricities of this most
bizarre of emotions in the hope that I would nevertheless eventually understand what it was all about.—"I desire you!"—I would
say to my beloved. She would fob me off with generalizations.
"You're nothing but a nothing, Mr. Czarniecki!" she would say
enigmatically, staring into my countenance. "A daddy's little pet, a
mama's boy!"

I shuddered: a mama's boy? What did she mean by that? Could
she have guessed . . . because I myself had already guessed to some
extent. I had understood that if my father was well-bred to the
marrow of his bones—my mother was also well-bred, but in a different sense, in the Semitic sense. What had inclined my father,
that impoverished aristocrat, to marry my mother, the daughter of
a rich banker? I now understood his anxious looks as he inspected
my features, and the nocturnal excursions of this man who, going

to waste in his abominable symbiosis with my mother, was following the higher dictates of the species in seeking to pass on his race to worthier loins. I understood? In truth I did not understand, and here once again there rose the bewitching wall of the mystery — I knew in theory, but I personally felt no aversion toward either my mother or my father; I was a devoted son. And today too I do not entirely comprehend; not knowing the theory, I do not know the color of a rat born of a black male and a white female; I imagine only that I constituted an exceptional case, an unheard-of instance, namely, that the antagonistic races of my parents, being of precisely the same strength, were so perfectly neutralized in me that I was a rat without color, without hue! A neutral rat! This is my fate, this is my mystery, this is why I was always unsuccessful and, taking part in everything, I was unable to take part in anything. And it was for this reason I was overcome by unease at the sound of the phrase: mama's boy — the more so because it was accompanied by the slight lowering of the eyelids by which I had been burned a number of times already in life.

"A man," she would say, narrowing her beautiful eyes, "a man ought to be bold!"

"Fine," I would reply; "I can be bold." She would have whims. She would order me to jump over ditches and carry heavy weights. "Go trample on that flower bed — but not now, rather when the groundsman is looking. Go break some branches off that bush, go throw that gentleman's hat into the water!" I refrained from reasoning, mindful of the incident in the school playground; and besides, when I asked for a reason or a purpose, she would reply that she herself did not know, that she was an enigma, an elemental force. "I am a sphinx," she liked to say, "a mystery . . ."—when I failed she was concerned, and when I succeeded she rejoiced like a child and as a reward permitted me to kiss her on her little ear. But she would never respond to my "I desire you."—"There's something about you," she would say embarrassedly—"I don't know what it is—some kind of unpleasant taste."—I was well aware what that meant.

All this, I confess, was strangely charming, strangely lovely— yes, lovely, that's exactly it; but it was also strangely unconvincing. Yet I never lost heart. I read a lot, especially the poets, and acquired as best I could the language of mystery. I remember an assignment—The Pole and Other Nations. "Of course, it is unnecessary even to mention the superiority of the Poles over the Africans and Asians, who have repulsive skin," I wrote.

"But the Pole is also unquestionably superior to the nations of Europe. The Germans are uncouth, violent, and flatfooted; the French are petty, undersized, and depraved; the Russians are hairy; the Italians have bel canto. What a relief it is to be Polish, and it is no wonder everyone envies us and wants to wipe us from the face of the earth. Only the Pole does not arouse our disgust." I wrote thus, without conviction, but I felt that this was the language of mystery, and it was precisely the naïveté of my assertions that was sweet to me.

3

The political horizon darkened, and my beloved betrayed an odd agitation. Oh, those great, fantastical days of September! They smelled, as I once read in a book, of heather and mint; they were airy, bitter, fiery, and unreal. On the streets there were crowds, songs, and processions; there was consternation, madness, and ecstasy, captured in the rhythmic step of the endless battalions. Here — an old man who had taken part in the uprising, tears, and a blessing. Elsewhere — mobilization, the farewells of newlyweds. Elsewhere still — bunting, speeches, outbursts of zeal, the national anthem. Oaths, consecrations, tears, posters, outrage, noble-mindedness, and hatred. Never before, if the artists were to be believed, had the women been so handsome. My beloved ceased to pay any attention to me; her gaze deepened and darkened and became expressive, but she looked only at the men in uniform.— I wondered what I should do. The world of the enigma had suddenly intensified to an extraordinary degree, and I had to be doubly on my guard.

I cheered with everyone else and expressed my patriotism, and a few times I even took part in the summary lynching of spies. But I sensed that this was merely a palliative. In the eyes of my Jadwisia there was something that led me as quickly as possible to sign up, and I was assigned to an uhlan regiment. And right from the beginning I realized that I was on the right path, for at the army medical commission, standing naked with my papers in my hand, in the presence of six clerks and two physicians who instructed me to lift my leg and then studied my heel — I encountered the same scrutinizing, grave, as it were contemplative, and coldly evaluative gaze I had seen in Jadwisia, and I was only surprised that back then, in the park, when she accused me of various shortcomings, she had not taken a look at my heel.

And here I was — a soldier, an uhlan; and I sang along with the others: "Uhlans, uhlans, bright-colored boys, there's many a maiden will make you her choice." Indeed, though individually speaking none of us was a boy—yet when a host of us passed through a town singing that song, inclined over our horses' necks, with our lances and the peaks of our caps, a most curiously wonderful expression appeared on the mouths of the women and I felt that this time hearts were beating for me too. . . . Why, I do not know, since I was still Count Stefan Czarniecki, whose mother's maiden name was Goldwasser, only in high-topped boots and raspberry-red facings on my collar. My mother, appealing to me not to stand for anything, blessed me for battle with a holy relic in the presence of all the servants, among whom the chambermaid was the most affected.—"Cut, burn, kill!" cried my mother, inspired. "Let no one pass! You are an instrument of the wrath of Jehovah, that is, I mean, of the Lord God. You are an instrument of wrath, abhorrence, revulsion, hatred. Wipe out all the libertines who feel disgust even though they swore at the altar not to feel disgust!" My father, on the other hand, an ardent patriot, wept discreetly. "Son," he said, "with blood you can wash away the stain of your origins. Before battle think always of me, and avoid the memory of your mother like the plague—it could be your downfall. Think of me and have no mercy! No mercy! Wipe out all those villains to the last man, so all other races perish, and there remains only my race!"—And my beloved gave me her lips for the first time; it was in the park, to the sounds of a café quartet, on an evening scented with heather and mint—just like that, without any introduction or any explanation she gave me her lips. It was profoundly beautiful! It made one want to cry! Today I understand that it was a matter of compensating in terms of corpses; that since we men had begun the slaughter, they, the women, had set about the job from their side; but at the time I was not yet a bankrupt, and that idea, though I was familiar with it, was for me empty philosophy and could not stem the tears flowing from my eyes.

O war, o war, what lady are you? Pardon me for returning once again to the mystery that troubles me so. A soldier at the front flounders in mud and in flesh; he is prey to fungus and filth, and in addition, when his belly is blown open by a shell, often his guts spill out . . . How is it then? Why is a soldier a swallow and not a frog? Why is it that the soldier's profession is beautiful and longed for on all sides? No, that's the wrong word; it's not beautiful but lovely, lovely to the highest degree. Precisely this—the fact that it is lovely—gave me strength in my struggle with the abominable traitor of the soldier's soul—fear; and I was almost happy, as if I were already on the other side of that impassable wall. Each time I managed to shoot my rifle accurately, I felt that I was suspended on the inscrutable smiles of women and on the bars of an army song, and after many attempts I was even able to win the good graces of my horse—the pride of an uhlan—who up till then had only bitten and kicked me.

4

But then came an incident that propelled me into an abyss of moral depravation from which to this day I have been unable to extricate myself. Everything was going splendidly. War was raging across the entire world, and with it—the Mystery; people stuck bayonets in each other's bellies, hated one another, were disgusted by one another, despised one another, loved and adored one another; where previously a peasant had quietly threshed his corn, now there lay a heap of rubble. And I did what others did! I was in no doubt about how to act or what to choose; strict military discipline was for me a signpost toward the Mystery. I rushed into the attack, or lay in the trenches amid the asphyxiating gases. — Already hope, the mother of fools, was showing me joyful visions of the future, how I would return home from the army, liberated once and for all from my disastrous ratlike neutrality . . . But alas, it happened otherwise . . . In the distance the cannon rumbled . . . On the ravaged field before us night was falling; tattered clouds raced across the sky; there was a cold, driving wind, and we, more lovely than ever, for the third day were stubbornly defending a hill on which there stood a broken tree. Our lieutenant had just ordered us to remain to the death.

Suddenly an artillery shell flew over, burst its sides, and exploded, blowing off both of Uhlan Kacperski's legs and tearing open his stomach; and Kacperski was at first confused, not grasping what had happened; then a moment later he also exploded, but in laughter; he was also bursting his sides, but with laughter! — holding his stomach, which was gushing blood like a fountain, he squealed and squealed in his comical, loud, hysterical, farcical high-pitched voice — for minutes on end! How infectious that laugh was! You have no idea what such an unexpected sound can be like on the field of battle. I barely managed to survive till the end of the war. — And when I returned home I realized, my ears still ringing with this laughter, that everything by which I had lived up till then had crumbled into dust; that my dreams of a happy new existence with Jadwisia had all been laid to waste; and that in the wilderness that had suddenly opened up there was nothing left for me but to become a communist. Why a communist? But first—what do I understand by "communist"? By this term I do not refer to any precise ideological meaning nor any particular program or ballast; quite the opposite, I employ it for what it contains that is alien, hostile, and incomprehensible, forcing the most serious individuals to shrug their shoulders or emit wild cries of revulsion and horror.

But if a program must be discussed, then please: I demand and require that everything—fathers and mothers, race and faith, virtue and fiancées—everything be nationalized and distributed with the aid of ration cards in equal and sufficient portions. I demand, and maintain such a demand in the face of the whole world, that my mother be cut into little pieces and that anyone who is not fervent in prayer be given a piece, and that the same be done with my father in relation to individuals devoid of race. I also insist that all half-smiles, all charms and graces be provided only on explicit request, while unjustified disgust should be punished by incarceration in a correctional facility. This is my program. And as for a method, it involves above all shrill laughter, and also narrowing of the eyes.—With a certain contrariness I rely on the principle that war destroyed all human feelings in me. And I maintain furthermore that I personally did not sign a peace treaty with anyone and that the state of war—for me—has not been suspended at all. —"Ha,"—you will exclaim—"it's an unrealistic program and a foolish and unintelligible method." Fine, but is *your* program truly more realistic, are *your* methods more intelligible?

Besides, I do not insist either on the program or the method—and if I chose the term "communism" it was only because "communism" is a mystery as inscrutable for minds opposed to it as are for me all your poutings and half-smiles.

That is how it is, ladies and gentlemen; you smile and narrow your eyes; you cherish swallows and torment frogs; you find fault with a nose. There is constantly someone that you hate, someone you find disgusting; then again you tumble into an incomprehensible state of love and adoration—and everything on account of some Mystery. But what would happen if I were to acquire my own mystery and impose it on your world with all the patriotism, heroism, and devotion I was taught by love and by the army? What will happen if I in turn smile (with a rather different smile) and narrow my eyes with the bluntess of an old warrior? I may have acted most wittily with my beloved Jadwisia. "Is woman an enigma?" I asked. (After my return she had greeted me with boundless effusiveness; she took a look at my medal and we went straight to the park.) "Oh yes," she replied. "Am I not enigmatic?" she said, lowering her eyelids. "An elemental woman and a sphinx." "I am an enigma too!" I said. "I too have my own language of mystery and I demand that you speak it. Do you see that frog? I swear on my honor as a soldier that I'll put it under your blouse if you don't say immediately, with complete gravity and looking me in the eye, the following words: cham—bam—bue, mue—mue, bah—bih, bah—beh—no—zar."

She wouldn't do it for anything. She wriggled out of it as best she could with the excuse that it was stupid and pointless, that she *could not*; she went scarlet trying to turn everything into a joke, and in the end she began to cry. "I can't, I can't," she repeated through her sobs. "I'm embarrassed; how it is possible . . . such nonsensical words"? And so I took a great fat toad and did what I had said I would. It seemed as if she would go mad. She thrashed about on the ground like one possessed, and the squawk she emitted I can only compare to the comical shriek of a man hit by an artillery shell who has lost both legs and part of his stomach. It may be that this comparison, like the joke with the frog, is distasteful; but please remember that I, a colorless rat, a neutral rat, neither white not black, am also distasteful to the majority of people. And is it really the case that the same thing should be tasteful and lovely to everyone? What seemed to me most lovely, most mysterious, and most redolent of heather and mint in this entire adventure was the fact that in the end — unable to free herself of the toad squirming about beneath her blouse — she lost her mind.

Perhaps I am not in fact a communist; perhaps I am only a militant pacifist. I wander around the world, sailing across that abyss of inexplicable idiosyncrasies, and wherever I see some mysterious emotion, whether it is virtue or family, faith or fatherland, I always have to commit some villainy. This is my mystery, which for my part I impose upon the great enigma of being. I simply cannot calmly pass by a pair of happy lovers, or a mother and child, or a respectable old man — but at times I am seized by a longing for you, my dear Father and Mother, and for you, my sacred childhood!

A Premeditated Crime

><

In winter of last year I was obliged to visit Ignacy K., a landed gentleman, to conduct certain property-related business. I took a few days' leave, left a junior judge in charge and telegrammed: "Tuesday, 6 pm, please send horses." Yet when I arrived at the railroad station there were no horses. I checked and found out that my telegram had been properly delivered. The addressee himself had signed for it the previous day. Like it or not, I had to hire a primitive wagonette, load it up with my suitcase and my toiletry case — the latter containing a small bottle of eau de cologne, a vial of Vegetal, almond-scented soap, a nail file, and nail scissors — and spend four hours bumping across the fields by night, in the quiet, during a thaw. I was shivering in my city overcoat, my teeth chattering, as I stared at the driver's back and thought — turning one's back like that! Permanently, often in secluded places, to be turned the other way and exposed to the whims of those sitting behind!

We finally pulled up in front of a wood-built country manor — it was in darkness, the only light coming from a window on the second floor. I knocked at the door — it was locked; I knocked harder — nothing, silence. I was set on by yard dogs and had to beat a retreat to the cart. There, in turn, my driver started to accost me.

"This isn't exactly hospitable," I thought.

At last the door opened and there appeared a tall, frail-looking man of about thirty with a blond mustache and a lamp in his hand.

"What is it?" he asked, as if he had been awoken from sleep, as he raised the lamp.

"Did you not receive my wire? I'm H."

"H.? What H.?" He stared at me. "Leave with God's blessing," he suddenly said in a quiet voice, as if he had spotted some special sign — his eyes looked away, and his hand closed more tightly around the lamp. "With God's blessing, with God's blessing, sir! God guide your way!" — and he hurriedly stepped back into the house.

I said more sharply this time:

"Pardon me. Yesterday I sent a wire concerning my arrival. I am investigating magistrate H. I wish to talk with Mr. K. — and if I wasn't able to get here sooner it's because no horses were sent to the station for me."

He set the lamp down.

"That's right," he said after a moment, pensively, my tone having made no impression on him whatsoever. "That's right . . . You cabled . . . Please, do come in."

What had happened? It turned out, as I was told in the entryway by the young man (who was the owner's son), that quite simply . . .

they had completely forgotten about my arrival and about the cable that had been received the previous morning. Explaining myself and apologizing politely for the incursion, I took off my overcoat and hung it on a peg. He led me into a small sitting room whereupon seeing us a young woman sprang up from the sofa with a soft "Oh." "My sister." "It's a pleasure to meet you." And it was indeed a pleasure, for femininity, even without any incidental intentions, femininity, I say, is always welcome. But the hand she gave me was perspiring—who gives a man a perspiring hand?— and the femininity itself, despite a charming little face, seemed somehow, how shall I put it, perspirational and indifferent, devoid of reaction, unkempt, and disheveled.

We sat down on the old-fashioned red furniture and began an introductory conversation. But the very first courteous common-places came up against an indefinable resistance, and instead of the fluidity that one wished for, things kept breaking off and get-ting stuck. I: "I expect you were surprised to hear a knock at the door at this hour?" They: "A knock? Oh, that's right . . ." I, politely: "I'm very sorry to have alarmed you, but otherwise I think I would have had to roam the fields all night, like Don Quixote, ha ha!" They (awkwardly and softly, not seeing fit to respond to my little joke even with a conventional smile): "Not at all, you're wel-come."—What was this? It looked truly bizarre—as if they were offended by me, or they were afraid of me, or they felt sorry for me, or they were embarrassed for me. . . . Planted in their arm-chairs, they avoided my gaze, nor did they look at each other; they bore my company with the greatest discomfort—it seemed that they were preoccupied exclusively with themselves, and the whole time they were worried only that I might say something to insult them. In the end it begin to irritate me. What were they afraid of, what was it about me? What sort of reception was this, aristocratic, timid, and proud? And when I asked about the purpose of my visit, in other words about Mr. K., the brother looked at the sister as if each were letting the other go first — in the end the brother swallowed and said distinctly, distinctly and solemnly, as if it were I don't know what: "Yes, he is indeed at home."

It was exactly as if he had said: "The King, my Father, is at home!"

Supper was also somewhat eccentric. It was served carelessly, not without scorn for the food and for me. The appetite with which I in my hunger devoured the gifts of the Lord appeared to arouse the indignation even of the solemn butler Szczepan, not to mention the brother and sister, who attended in silence to the noises I made over my plate — and you know how hard it is to swallow when someone is listening — against one's will every mouthful descends into the throat with a terrible gulping sound. The brother's name was Antoni, and the sister was called Miss Cecylia.

All at once I looked up — who was this coming in? A dethroned queen? No, it was their mother, Mrs. K., approaching slowly; she gave me a hand cold as ice, looked at me with a hint of dignified surprise and sat down without a word. She was a small, corpulent, even fat individual, one of those old country matrons who are implacable when it comes to all sorts of principles, especially social ones — and she eyed me sternly, with boundless surprise, as if I had an obscene saying written on my forehead. Cecylia made a gesture in an attempt to explain, or to justify — but the gesture died in midair, and the atmosphere became even more artificial and oppressive.

"I expect you're rather disappointed on account of . . . this futile journey," said Mrs. K. suddenly—and in such a tone! A tone of indignation, the tone of a queen to whom someone has failed to bow for the requisite third time—as if eating chops constituted a crime of *lèse majesté*!

"The pork chops here are excellent!" I replied in anger, since despite myself I was feeling ever more vulgar, foolish, and uncomfortable.

"Chops . . . chops . . ."

"Antoś still hasn't said anything, Mama," the timid Cecylia burst out all of a sudden, quieter than a mouse.

"What do you mean, he hasn't said anything? What do you mean, you haven't said anything? You *still* haven't said anything?"

"What for, Mama?" whispered Antoni; he turned pale and gritted his teeth, as if he were about to sit in the dentist's chair.

"Antoś . . ."

"I mean . . . What for? It makes no difference . . . there's no point —there'll always be time," he said and fell silent.

"Antoś, how can you? What do you mean it makes no difference? What are you saying, Antoś?"

"No one could be . . . It's all the same . . ."

"You poor thing!" whispered his mother, stroking his hair, but he brushed her hand aside roughly.—"My husband," she said dryly, turning to me, "died last night."—What?! So he was dead? So that was it! I interrupted my meal—I set down my knife and fork —I hurriedly swallowed the morsel I had in my mouth.—How could this be? It was only yesterday that he had picked up my telegram from the station! I looked at them: all three of them were waiting. They were modest and grave, but—they were waiting, with stern, reserved faces and pursed lips; they were waiting stiffly —what on earth were they waiting for? Oh, that's right, condolences had to be offered!

It was so unexpected that to begin with I was completely put out of countenance. In my confusion I rose from my chair and mumbled something indistinctly along the lines of: "I'm terribly sorry . . . I'm very . . . I'm sorry."—I fell silent, but they did not respond whatsoever, for this was still too little for them; with lowered eyes and unmoving faces, their clothes untidy, he unshaven, the women with disheveled hair, their fingernails dirty—they all stood without saying anything. I cleared my throat, desperately thinking of where to begin, the right expression, but it so happened that my head was completely empty, a void, as I'm sure has happened to you too, while they—they were waiting, immersed in their suffering. They were waiting without looking—Antoni was drumming his fingers lightly on the tabletop, Cecylia was embarrassedly picking at the hem of her dirty gown, and their mother stood motionless, as if turned to stone, with that stern, unyielding matronly expression. All at once I began to feel uneasy, despite the fact that as an investigating magistrate I had dealt with hundreds of deaths in my time. But that was just it . . . how shall I put it—an unsightly murdered corpse covered with a blanket is one thing; quite another is a worthy fellow who has died of natural causes and is laid out on a catafalque; a certain unceremoniousness is one thing, while quite another is a death that is above board, accustomed to considerations, to manners—death, you could say, in all its majesty. No, I repeat, I would never have been so perturbed if they had told me everything at once. But they were too uncomfortable. They were too afraid. I don't know whether it was simply because I was an intruder, or whether they were perhaps in some way embarrassed by my profession in such circumstances, because of a certain . . . matter-of-factness that my many years of practice must have formed in me; but in any case—this embarrassment of theirs embarrassed me terribly, embarrassed me, in fact, entirely disproportionately.

I stammered something about the respect and affection I had always felt for the deceased. Recalling that since our schooldays I had never met him once, a fact that could have been known to them, I added: "During our schooldays." They still made no reply, and I had after all to finish somehow, to round things off; and finding nothing else to say, I asked: "Could I see the body?"—and the word "body" somehow came out most unfavorably. Yet my confusion evidently appeased the widow; she burst into painful tears and gave me her hand, which I kissed humbly.

"In the night," she said dazedly, "last night . . . I got up this morning . . . I went in . . . I called—Ignaś, Ignaś—but there was no response; he was lying there . . . I fainted . . . I fainted . . . And from that moment my hands haven't stopped trembling—see for yourself."

"What's the point, Mama?"

"They're trembling . . . they haven't stopped trembling"—she raised her arms.

"Mama," Antoni repeated from the side, in a half-whisper.

"They're trembling, trembling—of their own accord; see, they're trembling like aspen leaves . . ."

"No one is . . . no one will be . . . it makes no difference. It's embarrassing!" he burst out violently and suddenly turned his back and walked away. "Antoś!" his mother called in fright. "Cecylka, go after him . . ." And I stood there and looked at her shaking hands; I had absolutely nothing to say and felt at a loss, growing more and more disconcerted.

All at once the widow said softly: "You wanted . . . Then let us go . . . there . . . I'll show you the way."—In principle I believe—today, when I consider the matter dispassionately—that at the time I had a right to myself and my pork chops; that is, I could and even should have replied: "At your service, ma'am, but I'll just finish these pork chops, since I've not had a bite to eat since midday." Perhaps, if I had replied in this vein, many tragic events would have been averted. But was it my fault she had terrorized me so much that my pork chops, and I myself, seemed to me something trivial and unworthy of mention, and I was so ashamed all of a sudden that even today I blush at the thought of that embarrassment?

On the way, on the second floor, where the deceased was to be found, she whispered to herself: "A terrible misfortune . . . A blow, an awful blow . . . The children said nothing. They're proud, difficult, reserved; they won't allow just anyone into their hearts, but rather prefer to worry on their own. They got that from me, from me . . . Oh, I only hope Antoś doesn't do himself any harm! He's tough, stubborn, he won't even let his hands twitch. He wouldn't let anyone touch the body—yet something has to be done, arrangements have to be made. He didn't cry, he didn't cry at all . . . Oh, if only he had cried at least once!"

She opened a door—and I had to kneel down with my head bowed, with a look of concentration on my face, while she stood to the side, solemn and still, as if she were showing the Blessed Sacrament.

The deceased lay on the bed—just as he had died—the only thing they had done was to turn him on his back. His livid, swollen face betokened death by asphyxiation, as was usual in the case of heart attacks.

"Asphyxiated," I murmured, though I could clearly see that it was a heart attack.

"It was his heart, his heart, sir . . . He died because of his heart."

"Oh, the heart can sometimes asphyxiate . . . it can," I said lugubriously. She was still standing and waiting—and so I crossed myself, said a prayer, and then (she was still standing there) I said quietly:

"Such noble features!"

Her hands were shaking so much that I decided I ought to kiss them again. She did not react with the slightest movement, continuing to stand like a cypress, gazing painfully away toward the wall—and the longer she stood there, the harder it became to avoid showing at least a little heart. This was required by common decency; there was no getting out of it. I rose from my knees, unnecessarily removed a piece of lint from my suit, gave a low cough—and she went on standing. She stood fanatically, silent, with staring eyes, like Niobe, her gaze fixed on her memories, crumpled, disheveled; and a tiny droplet appeared at the tip of her nose and dangled there, and dangled . . . like the sword of Damocles—and the candles smoked. After a few minutes I tried to say something softly—she flinched as if she'd been bitten, took a few steps and again stood still. I knelt down. What an intolerable situation! What a dilemma for a person as sensitive, and above all as irritable, as I am! I do not accuse her of deliberate malice; nevertheless, no one will deny that there was malice in this. No one will convince me! It was not she herself, but her malice that gloated insolently at the way I was simpering before her and the corpse.

Kneeling two paces away from that corpse, the first one I was not able to touch, I stared vacantly at the bedspread that covered him smoothly up to the armpits, at his hands laid carefully over that bedspread—potted plants stood at the foot of the bed, and the face loomed palely from a depression in the pillow. I gazed at the flowers, then I gazed back at the dead man's face, but nothing came into my head except for one pesky thought, strangely persistent—that this was some kind of prearranged, theatrical scene. Everything looked as if it had been staged—over there the corpse, proud and untouchable, looking indifferently through closed eyes at the ceiling; next to it the grieving widow; and here—I myself, the investigating magistrate, on my knees, like a bad dog forced to wear a muzzle. "What would happen if I were to rise, go up, pull off the bedspread and take a look—to touch at least—to touch with the tip of my finger?" I thought these things—but the grave integrity of death pinned me to my place; pain and virtue kept me from profanation.—Down! That's forbidden! Hands off! On your knees!—"What is it," I thought slowly to myself. "Who staged all this? I'm an ordinary, regular fellow — I'm not the right person for such performances . . . I wouldn't advise . . . Dammit!" I suddenly decided, "What nonsense! Where did this come from? Could I be acting a part? Where did this artificiality, this affectation come from in me — I'm usually completely different — have they infected me? What is it — ever since I arrived, everything in me has been coming out artificially and pretentiously, as if it were being performed by a third-rate actor. I've completely lost myself in this house — I'm acting up most terribly. Hmm," I murmured, and once again not without a certain theatrical pose (as if I were already sucked into the game and I could no longer return to normality) — "I wouldn't advise anyone . . . I wouldn't advise anyone to make a demon of me, because I'm prepared to take up the invitation . . ." In the meantime the widow had wiped her nose and moved toward the door, talking to herself and clearing her throat as she waved her hands about.

When I finally found myself alone in my own room, I took off my collar, and instead of placing it on the table, I hurled it to the floor and crushed it with my foot. My face was contorted and infused with blood; my fingers closed convulsively in a manner that was entirely unexpected for me. I was quite clearly in a fury. "They've made a fool of me," I whispered. "That wretched woman . . . How they've arranged everything so cleverly. They make people pay homage to them — kiss their hands! They demand sentiments from me! Sentiments! They demand to be humored! And I — let's say, I hate that. And, let's say — I hate it when they use trembling to make me kiss their hands, when they compel me to mumble

prayers, to kneel, to produce false, revoltingly sentimental noises
— and above all I hate tears, sighs, and droplets at the tips of noses;
whereas I like cleanliness and order.

"Hmm"—I cleared my throat thoughtfully after a pause, in a
different tone, cautious and somehow probing—"they make me
kiss their hands? I ought to kiss their feet; isn't it obvious what I
am in the face of the majesty of death and of this family's pain? . . .
A coarse, unfeeling police informer, nothing more—my nature
has been exposed. Yet . . . hmm . . . I don't know if this has been
done too hastily; yes, in their place I personally would have been a
little more—circumspect . . . a little more—modest . . . Because
some allowance ought to have been made for this abject character
of mine, and if not for my . . . private character, then . . . then . . . at
least for my official character. This they forgot about. When it
comes down to it, I am after all an investigating magistrate, and
here after all there is a corpse, and the idea of a corpse somehow
rhymes in a not entirely innocent way with the idea of an investigating magistrate. And if for instance I were to look at the course
of events from precisely the perspective . . . hmm . . . of an investigating magistrate," I thought slowly, "what would transpire then?"

If you please: A guest arrives who—by chance—is an investigating magistrate. They don't send horses, they don't open the
door—in fact they make difficulties for him, and so someone
must be unwilling to let him into the house. Then he's received
reluctantly, with poorly disguised anger, with fear—and who on
earth is afraid, who on earth is angry at the sight of an investigating magistrate? Something is hidden from him and covered up—
and in the end it turns out that what was being covered up is . . .

a corpse that has died of asphyxiation in an upstairs room. How base! When the corpse comes to light, attempts are made by hook or by crook to make him kneel and kiss hands, on the pretext that the deceased died a natural death!

If anyone, however, should call this notion preposterous, laughable even (for after all, to speak frankly, how can anyone deceive so crudely), they should bear in mind that a moment ago, in my anger, I crushed my collar underfoot—my soundness of mind was impaired, my consciousness dimmed as a result of the resentment I felt, and so it was clear I was not fully responsible for my antics.

Looking straight ahead, I said with gravity:

"Something's not right here."

And I began with considerable perspicacity to link the chain of facts, to create syllogisms, spin threads, and search for evidence. But soon, wearied by the fruitlessness of this endeavor, I fell asleep. Yes, yes . . . The majesty of death is in every regard worthy of respect, and no one could say that I had not rendered to it the necessary honors—but not every death is equally majestic, and, before elucidating this circumstance, if I were them I would not be so sure of myself, the more so because the matter is murky, complex and dubious . . . hmm . . . hmm . . . all the evidence points to this.

The next morning, as I drank my coffee in bed, I noticed that the serving boy, a thickset, sleepy lad who was lighting the stove, kept glancing at me out of the corner of his eye with a faint glimmer of curiosity. He probably knew who I was—and I spoke to him:

"So your master died?"

"That he did."

"How many servants are there here?"

"There's Szczepan and the cook, your honor. Not counting me. And counting me there's three of us."

"Your master died in that upstairs room?"

"Yeah, upstairs," he said indifferently, puffing out his fleshy cheeks as he blew on the fire.

"And you, where do you sleep?"

He stopped blowing and looked at me—a sharper look this time.

"Szczepan and the cook sleep in the kitchen, and I sleep on my own in the pantry."

"That's to say, from where Szczepan and the cook sleep there's no other access to the rest of the house except through the pantry?" I asked further, as if by the by.

"Only through there," he answered, and looked at me very sharply now.

"And where does the lady of the house sleep?"

"She used to share a room with the master—but now she sleeps next door, in the neighboring room."

"Since the master died?"

"Oh no, she moved before that—it must have been a week or so ago."

"And you don't know why your mistress moved out of the master's room."

"Couldn't say . . ."

I asked one more question:

"And where does the young master sleep?"

"Downstairs, next to the dining room."

I got up and dressed with care. Hmm . . . hmm . . . So, if I was not mistaken, here was one more thought-provoking piece of evidence—a curious detail. Whatever one might say, it was intriguing that a week before her husband's death his wife should move out of their shared bedroom. Could she possibly have been afraid of being infected with heart disease? That would have been an extravagant fear, to say the least. But there must be no premature conclusions, no rash moves—and I went down to the dining room. The widow stood by the window—with folded arms she was staring at her coffee cup—and she was murmuring something in a monotone, earnestly shaking her head, with a wet handkerchief in her hands. When I approached, she suddenly moved around the table in the opposite direction, still murmuring, and waving her hand, as if she had lost her reason—nevertheless, I had already recovered the poise I had lost the previous day and, standing to the side, I waited patiently until at last she noticed me.

"Ah, farewell, farewell," she said absently, seeing that I was bowing—"It's been a pleasure . . ."

"Pardon me," I whispered, "I . . . I . . . I'm not leaving just yet; I'd like to stay a while . . ."

"Oh, it's you, sir," she said. She mumbled something about a funeral procession, and even favored me with a wan question about whether I would stay for the service.

"It would be a great honor," I replied piously. "Who could refuse that final duty? Might I be allowed to visit your husband one more time?" Without answering and without looking back to see if I was following, she mounted the creaking stairs.

After a short prayer I rose to my feet and, as if meditating on the enigma of life and death, I looked around. "That's strange!" I said to myself; "that's interesting! Judging from appearances, this man undoubtedly died of natural causes. True, his face is swollen and livid like someone who has been asphyxiated, but there are absolutely no signs of a struggle anywhere, either on the body or in the room — it really would seem that he died peacefully of a heart attack." Nevertheless — I suddenly went up to the bed and touched his neck with my finger.

This slight movement had an electrifying effect on the widow. She started.

"What are you doing?" she cried. "What are you doing? What are you doing? . . ."

"My poor lady, don't be so upset," I replied, and without further ceremony I conducted a thorough investigation of the corpse's neck and the entire room. Ceremony is good up to a point! We wouldn't get very far if ceremony stood in the way of carrying out a detailed inspection when the need arose. Alas! — there were still literally no signs either on the body or on the chest of drawers, or behind the wardrobe, or on the rug next to the bed. The only noteworthy thing was an immense dead cockroach. On the other hand, a certain sign appeared on the widow's face — she stood motionless, watching what I was doing with a look of befuddled consternation.

At this point I asked as circumspectly as I could: "Why did you move into your daughter's room a week ago?"

"I? Why? I? Why did I move? How did you . . . My son persuaded me to . . . So there would be more air. My husband used to suffocate in the night. But what do you want? . . . What do you actually want? Why are you . . . ?"

"Please forgive me . . . I'm sorry—but . . ." I finished my sentence with an eloquent silence.

She seemed to understand somewhat—as if she had suddenly realized the official character of the person with whom she was talking.

"But still . . . How is it? Surely—surely you can't have . . . you haven't noticed anything?"

In this question fear could distinctly be heard. I responded merely by clearing my throat. "Be that as it may," I said dryly, "I'd like to request . . . I believe you mentioned something about a funeral procession . . . I'd like to request that the body remain here until tomorrow morning."

"Ignaś!" she exclaimed.

"Exactly!" I replied.

"Ignaś! How can that be? It's not possible, it's out of the question," she said, staring dully at the body. "Ignaś!"

And—curious!—all at once she broke off in mid-sentence, went stiff, crushed me with a look, and then left the room in high dudgeon. I ask you—what could there possibly have been to offend her? Is a husband dying of unnatural causes a source of offense to a wife if she didn't have a hand in it? What could possibly be offensive about death from unnatural causes? It may be offensive for the killer, but surely never for the corpse or his family? However, for the moment I had something more urgent to do than pose such rhetorical questions. Left alone with the corpse, I once again set about conducting a scrupulous investigation—yet the longer I worked, the more my face betrayed my astonishment. "Not a thing," I whispered. "Nothing aside from the cockroach behind the chest of drawers. It truly might be concluded that there's no basis whatsoever for further action."

Ha! Now here was a stumbling block—in the form of the corpse, who loudly and clearly confirmed to the expert eye that he had died of an ordinary heart attack. All these appearances, the horses, the animosity, the dissembling, argued for something suspicious, whereas the corpse gazed at the ceiling and proclaimed: I died of a heart attack! It was physically and medically self-evident, it was a certainty—no one had murdered him for the simple and conclusive reason that *he had not been murdered at all*. I must confess that at this point most of my fellow magistrates would have closed the investigation. But not I! I was too ridiculed, too vengeful, and I had already ventured too far. I raised my finger and frowned. "A crime does not come of its own accord, gentlemen; it must be worked upon mentally, thought through, thought up—dumplings don't cook themselves.

"When appearances testify against there having been a crime," I said wisely, "then let us be cunning, let us not be taken in by appearances. Whereas when logic, common sense, the obvious finally become advocates for the criminal, and appearances argue against him, then let us trust appearances, let us not be deceived by logic and the obvious. Very well . . . but with all these appearances, how on earth—as Dostoevsky says—can we make rabbit stew with no rabbit?" I stared at the corpse, and the corpse stared at the ceiling, announcing his innocence with an unblemished neck. Now here was a difficulty! Here was a stumbling block! But

what can't be removed must be jumped over—*hic Rhodus, hic salta!*
Which is to say, could this dead object with human features which
I might, if I wished, have taken in my hand—could this frozen
face present any real resistance to my own mobile and changing
physiognomy, which was capable of finding an expression suitable
for any occasion? And while the corpse's visage remained the same
—calm, if a little swollen—my face expressed solemn cunning,
foolish arrogance and self-confidence, just as if I had said: you
can't teach your grandmother to suck eggs!

"Yes," I said with gravity, "it's an obvious fact: the dead man was
asphyxiated."

The lawyer with his prevarications might try to suggest that he
was asphyxiated by his heart? Hmm, hmm . . . Not for us such
legal maneuvers. "Heart" is a very flexible term—symbolic, even.
Who, springing to their feet on hearing that a crime has been committed, would possibly be satisfied to hear the reassuring reply
that it was nothing—that his heart had asphyxiated him? I'm
sorry, but which heart? We know how tangled and ambiguous the
heart can be—the heart is a sack into which a great deal can be put
—the cold heart of a murderer; the ashen heart of a libertine; the
faithful heart of a lover; a warm heart, an ungrateful heart, a heart
that is jealous, envious, and so on.

The crushed cockroach seemed not to be directly related to the
crime. For the moment one thing had been established—the dead
man was asphyxiated, and this asphyxiation was connected with
the heart. It could also be said, bearing in mind the lack of any
external injuries whatsoever, that the asphyxiation was of a typi-
cally internal character. Yes, that was all . . . nothing more—inter-

nal, connected with the heart. No premature conclusions—and now it would be good to walk around the house a little.

I went back downstairs. Entering the dining room, I heard the sound of light, quickly fleeing footsteps—probably Miss Cecylia? —Now then, running away is not a good idea, young lady—the truth will always catch up with you! Passing the dining room— where the servants setting the table watched me surreptitiously— I slowly looked in on the other rooms, and at one point, some-where through a door, I caught a glimpse of Mr. Antoni's retreat-ing back. "Since it's now a matter of internal, heart-related death," I reflected, "then it must be admitted that this house couldn't be better suited for it. Strictly speaking, there may not be anything clearly incriminating here—and yet . . ." I sniffed—"nevertheless there is consternation, and in the atmosphere there is an odor, a characteristic odor—an odor of the kind that is bearable when it is your own, like the odor of sweat—an odor that I would describe as the odor of family affection . . ." Still sniffing, I noted certain tiny details that, though small, seemed not to be entirely without sig-nificance. Thus—faded, yellowed lace curtains—hand-embroi-dered cushions—an abundance of photographs and portraits— chairs worn by the backs of many generations . . . and in addition to this: an unfinished letter on lined white paper—a pat of butter on a knife on the windowsill in the drawing room—a glass of med-icine on the chest of drawers—a blue ribbon behind the stove—a cobweb, lots of cupboards—old smells . . . All this together created an atmosphere of special solicitude, of great warm-heartedness— at every step the heart found sustenance for itself—yes, the heart could make use of butter, lace curtains, a ribbon, smells (and bread was carried, I noticed). And it also had to be acknowledged that the house was exceptionally "internal," a quality that manifested itself principally in the window filling, and in a chipped saucer, and in a dried-up sheet of flypaper left over from the summer.

But, so it should not be said that I was set pig-headedly on one internal direction and had ignored all other possibilities, I took the trouble to check whether indeed from the servants' quarters there was no access to the family rooms other than through the pantry—and I ascertained that there was not—and I even went outside and, pretending to take a stroll, I walked slowly all around the house in the wet snow. It was unthinkable that through the door, or through the windows, which had heavy shutters, someone could have entered the house in the night. From which it followed that if any act had been committed in this house in the night, then no one could be suspected except possibly the serving boy, Stefan, who slept in the pantry. "Yes," I said shrewdly, "it must have been Stefan the serving boy. No one else but him, the more so because he has a bad look about him."

Saying this, I pricked up my ears—because through an open casement I heard a voice that was oh-so-different from the voice I had heard not long before, and so exquisite, so full of promise, the voice no longer of a woebegone queen, but one that was wracked with dread and unease, atremble, weakened, a woman's voice—a voice that, it seemed, raised my spirits, wishing to help me out.— "Cecylka, Cecylka—look outside . . . Has he gone yet? Look outside! Don't lean out, don't lean out—he might see you! He might come in here—poke around—have you put away your underwear? What's he looking for? What has he seen? Ignaś! Oh Lord, what can he have been looking at that stove for, what did he want with the chest of drawers? It's awful, all over the house! It doesn't matter about me—with me he can do whatever he wants; *but for Antoś, for Antoś it'll be too much.* For him this is sacrilege! He went terribly pale when I told him—*oh, I'm afraid that he won't have the strength.*"

Yet if the crime, as could be considered established in the course of the investigation, was internal (I thought on)—then duty forces one to confess that murder committed by the serving boy, probably with a view to robbery, could in no manner be regarded as a crime of an internal nature. Suicide is a different matter—when people kill themselves and everything happens internally—or parricide, when, whatever else one might say, blood kills its own. As for the cockroach, the murderer must have crushed it in his haste.

As I reflected on these remarks I took a seat in the study and lit a cigarette—then all at once Mr. Antoni came in. On seeing me he offered a greeting, though a little more modestly than on the first occasion; he even appeared somewhat out of countenance.

"Your family has a beautiful house," I said. "It's exceptionally cosy, hearty—a real family home—warm . . . I'm reminded of my childhood—I'm reminded of my mother, my mother in her dressing gown, of chewed fingernails, of lacking a handkerchief . . ."

"Our home? Our home—of course . . . There are mice. But that's not why I'm here. My mother was telling me—apparently you . . . that is . . ."

"I know an excellent remedy for mice—Ratopex."

"Yes, I really must start dealing with them more vigorously—

more vigorously, much more vigorously . . . Apparently this morning you visited . . . my father . . . or rather, pardon me, his body . . ."

"I did."

"Ah!—And . . . ?"

"And? And what?"

"Apparently you . . . found something there . . ."

"Actually I did—a dead cockroach."

"There are lots of dead cockroaches too; that is—just cockroaches . . . I mean to say—cockroaches that aren't dead."

"Did you love your father very much?" I asked, picking up an album with views of Kraków that lay on the table.

This question clearly took him by surprise. No, he was not prepared for it; he bowed his head, looked to the side, swallowed—and muttered with inexpressible constraint, almost with repugnance:

"I suppose."

"You suppose? That's not very much. You suppose! Only so much?"

"Why do you ask?" he said in a muffled voice.

"Why are you so artificial?" I replied sympathetically, leaning toward him in paternal fashion, the album in my hands.

"Me? Artificial? Why do . . . you . . . ?"

"Why did you just turn pale?"

"Me? Turn pale?"

"Oh yes! You're scowling . . . You don't finish your sentences . . . You expatiate about mice and cockroaches . . . Your voice is too loud, then too quiet, hoarse or somehow shrill, so it pierces the ears," I said solemnly, "and such nervous movements . . . In fact, all of you here are somehow—nervous and artificial. Why is that, young man? Wouldn't it be better just to grieve in a straightforward way? Hmm . . . You . . . 'suppose' you loved him?! And why did you persuade your mother to move out of your father's bedroom a week ago?"

Utterly paralyzed by my words—not daring to move hand or foot—he was barely able to stammer out:

"Me? What do you mean? My father . . . My father needed . . . fresh air . . ."

"On the night in question you slept in your room downstairs?"

"Did I? Of course, in my room . . . in my room downstairs."

I cleared my throat and went to my bedroom, leaving him on a chair with his hands on his knees, his mouth tightly shut and his legs pressed stiffly together. Hmm—he obviously had a nervous nature. A nervous nature, bashfulness, excessive sensitivity, excessive heartfeltness . . . But I was still keeping a tight rein on myself, not wishing to frighten anyone prematurely. As I was in my room washing my hands and preparing for dinner, Stefan the serving boy slipped in and asked if I didn't need anything. He looked like a different person! His eyes darted about, his figure displayed a servile cunning, and all his mental powers were aroused to the highest degree! I asked: "So then, what can you tell me that's new?"

He answered in a single breath: "Well, your honor, you were asking if I slept in the pantry the night before yesterday? I wanted to say that on that night the young master locked the pantry door on the dining room side." I asked: "Has he ever locked that door before?" "Never. This one time he locked it, and he probably thought that I was already asleep, because it was late—but I wasn't sleeping yet and I heard him come up and lock it. When he unlocked it, that I couldn't say, because I dropped off—it was only at dawn that he woke me to say the master was dead, and by then the door was already open."

And so in the night, for unexplained reasons, the deceased's son locks the pantry door! He locks the pantry door?—What could this mean?

"Only please, your honor, don't say that I told you."

I was not wrong to have labeled this death an internal one! The door had been locked so no outsider should have access to the death! The net was closing in; the noose tightening around the murderer's neck was ever more visible.—Yet why, instead of manifesting triumph, did I only give a rather foolish smile?—For the reason that—alas, it must be acknowledged—something was missing that was at least as important as the noose around the murderer's neck, and that something was the noose around the neck of the victim. True, I had jumped over this stumbling block, I had leapt naively over his neck, which glowed with an immaculate whiteness; but nonetheless it's not possible to be permanently in a state of absolving passion. Very well, I agree (speaking aside), I was in a fury; for whatever reason hatred, repulsion, resentment had blinded me and forced me to persist in the face of a glaring absurdity—this is human, this anyone will understand; yet the moment will come when one must—settle down, there will come, as the Scriptures say, the Day of Judgment. And then . . . hmm . . . I'll say—he is the murderer, and the corpse will say—I died of a heart attack. And then what? What will Judgment say?

Let's suppose Judgment will ask: "You claim the dead man was murdered? On what basis?"

I will reply: "Because his family, your honor, his wife and children, and especially his son, are behaving suspiciously; they're behaving as if they had murdered him—there's no doubt about it."

"Very good—but by what earthly means could he have been murdered, since he was *not* murdered, since it's blindingly obvious from the forensic report that he simply died of a heart attack?"

And then the defense lawyer, that hired prevaricator, will stand up and in a long speech, waving the sleeves of his gown, will set about proving that there has been a misunderstanding rooted in my own base way of thinking, that I have confused crime and mourning—for that which I took as a sign of a guilty conscience was only a sign of the timidity of feelings which retreat and contract at the cold touch of a stranger. And once again there will appear the exasperating, unbearable refrain—how could he possibly have been murdered when he was absolutely not murdered? Since there are not the slightest marks of asphyxiation on his body?

This stumbling block so troubled me that at lunch—simply for myself, to quell my distress and bring relief to my nagging doubts, for no other reason—I began to explain that crime in its essence is not physical, but mental *par excellence*. I believe I am right in saying that apart from me, no one else spoke. Mr. Antoni did not say a word—I don't know whether it was because he regarded me as unworthy, as he had the previous evening, or because he was afraid his voice might come out a little hoarse. The widowed mother sat pontifically, still mortally offended, it seemed, and her hands trembled, striving to secure immunity for themselves. Miss

Cecylia was quietly swallowing the scalding liquids. While I, for the aforementioned inner motives, and oblivious to the faux pas I was committing, or of certain tensions in the air, discoursed eloquently and at great length. "Believe me, ladies and gentlemen, the physical shape of the act, the mistreated body, the disorder in the room, all the so-called evidence—these are entirely secondary details, a supplement, to be precise, to the real crime, a forensic formality, a tip of the hat by the criminal toward the authorities, nothing more. The real crime is always committed in the soul. The external details . . . oh my Lord! Take for instance the following case: A charitable uncle is suddenly stabbed in the back—with an old-fashioned hat pin—by a nephew whom he has been showering with kindnesses for thirty years. And if you please!—such a huge mental crime and such a small, imperceptible physical sign, a tiny little hole from a pinprick. The nephew subsequently explains that he absentmindedly mistook his uncle's back for his cousin's hat. Who is going to believe him?

"Yes indeed, physically speaking crime is a triviality; it is mentally that it is hard. Given the extreme fragility of the organism, it's possible to murder by accident, like that nephew, by absentmindedness—out of nowhere, all at once, bang, there's a corpse.

"One woman, the most upright person in the world, head over heels in love with her husband—this was right in their honeymoon period—notices on her husband's plate of raspberries an elongated white worm—and you should know that her husband hated these revolting grubs more than anything else. Instead of warning him, she watches with a playful smile, and then says: 'You ate a bug.' 'No!' the horrified husband exclaims. 'Oh yes,' replies the wife, and describes it—it was like so, fat and white. Much laughter and banter; the husband, pretending to be angry, raises his hands in the air at his wife's mischievousness. The matter is forgotten. Then, a week or two later, the wife is most surprised when the husband starts to lose weight and waste away; he rejects any kind of food, he's repulsed by his own arms and legs, and (please excuse the expression) he spends all his time on his knees praying to the porcelain god. Progressive disgust at oneself—a terrible illness! And one day there's great weeping and great moaning—he's died suddenly—he threw himself up, only his head and throat remained, he expelled the rest into a bucket. The widow is in despair—only in the crossfire of questions does it come to light that in the most hidden depths of her being she felt an unnatural fondness for the large bulldog her husband had beaten shortly before eating the raspberries.

"Or in one aristocratic family there was a son who murdered his mother by continually repeating the grating phrase: 'Please sit down!' At the hearing he acted innocent to the very end. Oh, crime is so easy it's a wonder that so many people die of natural causes—especially if one throws in the heart, the heart—that mysterious link between people, that twisting underground passageway between you and me, that lift-and-force pump which knows so perfectly how to lift and so wonderfully forces . . . It's only later that there comes the mourning, the graveside faces, the dignity of grief, the majesty of death—ha, ha—and all for the purpose of 'respecting' suffering and not accidentally looking too closely into that heart, which has quietly, cruelly murdered!"

They sat quiet as mice, not daring to interrupt!—Where was

that pride from the previous evening? All of a sudden the widow threw down her napkin and, pale as death, her hands trembling twice as much, stood up from the table. I spread my hands apologetically. "I'm terribly sorry. I didn't mean to offend. I'm merely speaking in general terms about the heart, about the heart sac, in which it's so easy to hide a body."

"Despicable man!" she blurted out, her breast heaving. Her son and daughter jumped up from the table.

"The door!" I exclaimed. "Very well—I'm despicable! But tell me please, why was the door locked that night?"

There was a pause. All at once Cecylia burst out in nervous, plaintive sobs and said through her tears:

"The door wasn't Mama. I was the one who locked it. It was me!"

"That's not true, Cecylka—I was the one who ordered the door to be locked! Why are you humiliating yourself in front of this man?"

"Mama ordered it, but I wanted to . . . I wanted to . . . I also wanted to lock the door and I locked it."

"I'm sorry," I said, "just a moment . . . What's this?" (After all, it was Antoni who had locked the pantry door.) "Which door are you talking about?"

"The door . . . the door to Daddy's bedroom . . . I locked it!"

"No, I locked it . . . I forbid you to talk like that, do you hear? I ordered it!"

What was this?! So they had also locked a door? On the night when the father was to die, the son locked the pantry door and the mother and daughter locked his bedroom door!

"And why did the two of you lock that door?" I asked abruptly, "Exceptionally, on that particular night? For what purpose?"

Consternation! Silence! They did not know! They bowed their heads! A theatrical scene. Suddenly Antoni's perturbed voice was heard:

"Are you not embarrassed to explain yourselves? And to whom? Be quiet! Let's go!"

"Then perhaps you'll tell me why on that night you locked the door of the pantry, cutting the servants off from the other rooms?"

"Me? I locked it?"

"What then? Perhaps you didn't lock it? There are witnesses! It can be proved!"

More silence! More consternation! The women looked up, terrified. Finally the son, as if remembering something that had happened long ago, declared in a whisper:

"I locked it."

"And why was that? Why did you lock it? Was it perhaps to prevent drafts?"

"That I am unable to explain," he answered with indescribable haughtiness — and left the room.

I spent the rest of the day in my bedroom. For a considerable time I walked to and fro, from wall to wall, without lighting a candle. Outside, the darkness was gathering — snowflakes could be seen increasingly bright in the falling shadows of night, while the house was surrounded on all sides by the tangled skeletons of the trees. — What a fine house this was! A house of murderers, a monstrous house where cold, dissembling, premeditated murder was on the prowl; a house of asphyxiators! The heart?! I had known right away what to expect from that well-fed heart, and what parricide it was capable of, swollen as it was with grease, butter, and familial warmth! I knew, but I did not wish to speak too soon! And they put on such airs! They demanded such homage! Feelings? Rather let them explain why they locked the doors.

Yet why at that moment — when I already held all the threads in my hand and could point my finger at the criminal — did I needlessly waste time instead of acting? The stumbling block, the stumbling block — the white neck, untouched, resembling the snow outside — the darker things were, the whiter it became. The corpse was evidently in league with the band of murderers. Once again I made an effort and attacked the corpse, head on this time, with raised visor — calling things by their names and clearly indicating the guilty party. It was just as if I had been wrestling with a chair. However I strained my imagination, my intuition, my logic, the neck remained a neck, and whiteness remained whiteness, with the obstinacy characteristic of lifeless objects. Nothing remained, then, but to play the part to the very end, to abide in my vengeful blindness and wait, and wait — counting naively on the notion that since the corpse was unwilling, perhaps — perhaps — the crime itself would rise to the surface like olive oil. Was I wasting time? Yes, but my steps sounded throughout the house; everyone could hear that I was constantly pacing, and they, downstairs, were probably not wasting time.

Suppertime had passed. It was almost eleven o'clock, yet I had not stirred from my room, and went on cursing them all for villains and criminals, exulting, and at the same time hoping with my remaining strength that my stubbornness and persistence would be rewarded — that the situation could after all be won over by so many different facial expressions, made with so much passion, that in the end it would be unable to resist, that, intense, brought to extremities, it would have to resolve itself somehow, give birth to something, give birth to something no longer from the realm of fiction but something real. After all, we couldn't go on like this forever — with me upstairs and them downstairs — someone had to call out "pass," and everything depended on who would be the first to do so. It was quiet and still. I looked out into the hallway, but nothing could be heard from below. What could they be doing down there? Could they possibly be doing what they ought to be doing; if I was exulting here because of the locked doors, were they for their part sufficiently afraid, conferring among themselves, straining their ears to catch the sounds of my footsteps; were their souls not too lazy to work this out within themselves? Oh, I breathed a sigh of relief when around midnight I finally heard steps in the hallway and someone knocked. "Come in," I called.

"I hope you'll forgive me," said Antoni, sitting in a chair to which I gestured. He looked bad — sallow and pale — and it was clear that eloquent discourse would not be his strong point. — "Your behavior . . . and lately — those words. . . . In a word — what does all this mean? Either leave . . . and right away! . . . or say what you have to say! This is extortion!" he exclaimed.

"At last you're asking," I said. "It's late! And even this you're asking in a very general way. What am I in fact to say? But very well — since you ask: Your father was . . ."

"What? Was what?"

"Was asphyxiated."

"Asphyxiated. Good. Asphyxiated."—He tossed his head with a certain bizarre satisfaction.

"You're glad?"

"I'm glad."

I waited a moment, then said:

"Was there anything else you wished to ask?"

He burst out:

"But no one heard any cries or commotion!"

"First of all, in the vicinity only your mother and your sister were sleeping, and they had shut their door for the night. Secondly, the criminal could quickly have throttled a victim who . . ."

"All right, all right," he murmured, "all right. Fine. One more thing: Who in your opinion . . . with this act, who do you . . ."

"Suspect, no? Who do I suspect? What do you think—in your opinion, could someone from outside have entered the house when it was locked up tight and guarded by a night watchman and by vigilant dogs? You'll no doubt say that the dogs fell asleep along with the watchman, and out of forgetfulness the front door was left unlocked? Eh? A terrible series of coincidences?"

"No one could have gotten in," he replied proudly. He sat erect and it could plainly be seen that—motionless—he despised me, he despised me with all his soul.

"No one," I agreed with alacrity, reveling in advance at the sight of his pride. "Absolutely no one! And so there remains only the three of you and the three servants. But the servants too had their way blocked, since you . . . for some unknown reason . . . locked the door from the pantry. Or perhaps now you'll claim that you did not lock it?"

"I did!"

"And why, for what purpose did you do so?"

He jumped up from his chair. "Don't play games!" I said, and with that short remark I put him firmly in his place. His anger was paralyzed and died away, breaking off in a squeak.

"I locked it—I don't know—without thinking," he said with difficulty, and whispered twice: "Asphyxiated. Asphyxiated."

A nervous nature! They were, all of them, deep, nervous natures.

"And since your mother and sister also . . . unthinkingly locked the door of their bedroom (and besides, it's hard to imagine, is it not?), then that leaves . . . you know who that leaves. You were the only one with free access to your father that night. 'The moon is up, the dogs asleep, and someone's clapping in the wood.'"

He burst out:

"And so this is supposed to mean . . . that I . . . that I . . . ha, ha, ha!"

"And that laugh is supposed to mean that it wasn't you," I observed, and his laughter ended after a few attempts on a protracted false note.

"It wasn't you?—But in that case, young man," I continued more quietly, "please explain to me—why did you not shed a single tear?"

"Tear?"

"Yes, tear. That's what your mother whispered to me, right at the beginning, yesterday, on the stairs. It's normal for mothers to compromise and betray their own children. And now, just a moment ago—you laughed. You declared that you were glad about your father's death!" I said with such triumphant obtuseness, catching him in his words, that he wilted and looked at me as if I were an instrument of torture.

Yet, sensing that the matter was becoming serious, he exerted all his powers of will and attempted to stoop to an explanation—in the form of an *avis au lecteur*, a footnote, which he could barely spit out.

"That was . . . . It was irony . . . . You understand? . . . The opposite . . . on purpose."

"Being ironic about your father's death?"

He was silent, and then I whispered confidentially, almost in his ear:

"Why are you so embarrassed? Surely there's nothing embarrassing about one's father's death."

Looking back on this moment I'm glad I came through uninjured—though he did not move a muscle.

"Or perhaps you're embarrassed because you loved him? Perhaps you really did love him?"

He stammered with difficulty—with abhorrence—with despair:

"Very well. If you absolutely must . . . if . . . then yes, so be it . . . I loved him."

And throwing something on the table, he cried:

"Here! This is his hair!"

It was indeed a lock of hair. "All right," I said, "now take it away."

"I don't want to! You can take it away! I'm giving it to you!"

"Why these outbursts? Fine—you loved him—agreed. Just one more question (because, as you see, I don't understand a thing about these romances of yours). I admit you almost had me convinced with the lock of hair, but—you see—above all there's one thing I don't understand."

Here again I lowered my voice and whispered in his ear.

"You loved him, very good, but why was there so much shame, so much scorn in that love?"

He turned pale and said nothing.

"So much cruelty, so much disgust? Why do you conceal it like a criminal concealing a crime? You don't answer? You don't know? Perhaps I will know for you.

"You did love him—yes indeed—but when your father fell ill . . . you mentioned to your mother the need for fresh air. Your mother —who incidentally also loved him—listens and nods. That's right, that's right, good air won't hurt, and so she moves next door to her daughter's room—'I'll still be close enough to come whenever the sick man calls.' Or perhaps that wasn't how it was? Perhaps you'll set the record straight?"

"That's how it was!"

"Exactly! I know a thing or two, as you see. A week passes. One evening your mother and sister lock the bedroom door. Why? God alone knows! Does one need to deliberate about every turn of a key in a lock? They just turned it, without thinking, then one two three they're in their beds. Yes, and at the same time you lock the pantry door downstairs. Why? Can every trivial action of that kind be justified? One might just as well demand an explanation for why at this particular moment you're sitting and not standing."

He leapt to his feet, then sat down again and said:

"Yes, that's how it was! It was just the way you said!"

"Then it occurs to you that—your father may need something. And maybe—you think—your mother and sister have fallen asleep, and your father needs something. And so quietly, so as not to wake up those who are sleeping, quietly you go to your father's room up the creaking stairs. And then, when you're already in his room—the rest requires no commentary—then, without thinking now—full steam ahead."

He listened, unable to believe his own ears, but suddenly—it was as if he roused himself and groaned with a note of desperate frankness that only great fear is capable of inspiring:

"But I wasn't there at all! I was downstairs in my room the whole time! I didn't only lock the pantry door, I also locked my own door —I also locked myself in my room . . . There's been some mistake!"

I exclaimed:

"What?—so you locked yourself in too?—so everyone was locked in? . . . Then in that case who on earth . . . ?"

"I don't know, I don't know," he replied aghast, rubbing his forehead. "It's only now that I'm beginning to understand—that perhaps we were expecting something—perhaps we were waiting for something—perhaps we had an inkling of something and— out of fear, out of shame"—he burst out vehemently all of a sudden —"everyone was locked in their room . . . because we wanted father, we wanted father—to take care of it by himself!"

"Aha, so having an inkling that death was drawing close, you locked yourselves in to keep death away as it approached? So—you were all waiting for the murder after all?"

"We were waiting?"

"Yes. But in that case who could possibly have murdered him? Because he was murdered, and you were all simply waiting, and there's absolutely no way an outsider could have come in."

He was silent.

"But I really was locked in my room," he whispered, sagging under the weight of irrefutable logic. "There's been some mistake."

"But in that case who could possibly have murdered him?" I said assiduously. "Who could possibly have murdered him?"

He lost himself in thought—as if he were taking terrible stock of his conscience—he was pale and motionless, his gaze withdrawn deep below his half-closed eyelids. Had he glimpsed something there, deep within himself? What had he glimpsed? Perhaps he had seen himself rising from his bed and cautiously walking up the treacherous stairs, his hands ready for the deed? And perhaps for just a moment he was seized by doubt that after all, who knew whether such a thing . . . would be completely unthinkable. Perhaps in that one second hatred appeared to him as the complement of love, who knows (this is only my conjecture) if in that twinkling of an eye he had not glimpsed the terrible duality of every emotion—that love and hatred are two sides of the same thing. And this blinding though momentary revelation must have instantly laid waste to everything within him—and he with all his pity became unbearable to himself. And though this lasted only a second, it was enough, for he had been forced to grapple with my suspicions for twelve hours now, for twelve hours he had felt someone senselessly, stubbornly pursuing him, and he had probably ruminated on the absurdity of thought a thousand times—he bowed his head like a broken man, and then raised it, looked at me from close by with boundless determination and said distinctly, right to my face:

"It was me. I—steamed out."

"What do you mean, you steamed out?"

"I steamed out, I say, because as you remarked, it was—without thinking—full steam ahead."

"What?! It's true! You're confessing? It was you? It was you—really?"

"It was me. I steamed out."

"Aha—just so. And the whole thing lasted no longer than a minute."

"No longer. A minute at most. And I don't know if we're not overestimating at a minute. Then afterward I returned to my room, got into bed, and fell asleep—and before I fell asleep I yawned and thought to myself—I remember vividly—that oho, tomorrow I'll have to get up in the morning!"

I was astonished—he had confessed to everything so smoothly; or rather not so much smoothly, for his voice was hoarse, as fiercely, with extraordinary relish. There could be no doubt! No one could deny it! Yes—but what about the neck, what was to be done with the neck, which was in the bedroom dully sticking to its story? My mind worked feverishly—but what can a mind do when faced with the mindlessness of a corpse?

I looked despondently at the murderer, who seemed to be waiting. And it's hard to explain, but at this moment I realized that nothing was left to me but a frank confession. There was no point in continuing to beat one's head against the wall, that is, against the neck—further resistance or evasion was useless. And the moment I realized this, I immediately acquired great confidence in him. I realized that I had gone too far, that I had gotten up to a little too much mischief—and, in deep waters, tired, exhausted by so much effort, so many faces made, I suddenly became a child, a helpless little boy, and I had a wish to confess to my big brother my mistake and the trouble I had caused. It seemed to me that he would understand . . . and surely he wouldn't refuse me some advice . . . "Yes," I thought, "nothing remains but a frank confession. . . He'll understand, he'll help! He'll find a way!" But in any case I rose and moved unobtrusively toward the door.

"You see," I said, and my lips were a little out of control, "there's a certain stumbling block here . . . a certain obstacle—of a purely formal character, as it happens—nothing of significance. The thing is"—I already had my hand on the door handle—"that actually the body shows no signs of asphyxiation. Physically speaking —he wasn't asphyxiated at all, but rather died of an ordinary heart attack. The neck, you know, the neck! . . . The neck was untouched!"

Having said this, I ran for it out the open door and rushed as fast as my legs would carry me along the hallway. I dashed into the room where the dead man lay and hid in the wardrobe—and with some degree of confidence, though with fear too, I waited. It was dark, cramped, and stuffy, and the deceased's trousers brushed against my cheek. I waited for a long time, and began to doubt, thinking that nothing would happen and that I had been basely duped, that I had been cheated! All at once the door opened quietly and someone crept in—after which I heard an awful noise, the bed creaked like crazy, and in the absolute silence all the formalities were dealt with after the fact! Then the steps receded just as they had come. When after a long hour I climbed out of the wardrobe, trembling and drenched in perspiration, violence reigned amid the disordered bedsheets; the body was thrown diagonally across a crumpled pillow, and the dead man's neck bore clear imprints of all ten fingers. The forensic experts looked askance at those imprints, it was true, saying that something was not as it should have been in all this—but the imprints, in conjunction with the criminal's unequivocal confession at the hearing, were taken as sufficient proof.

Dinner at Countess Pavahoke's

✦

It is hard to determine with complete certainty what established my closeness with Countess Pavahoke — of course, when I speak of closeness, I am referring to the slight degree of familiarity that can exist between a well-bred person who is every inch an aristocratic member of Society, and an individual from the good, worthy, yet only middle classes. I flatter myself that perhaps a certain loftiness I am sometimes capable of manifesting in favorable circumstances, a deeper gaze, and a certain sense of idealism, had captured for me the fastidious affections of the countess. For ever since I was a child I felt myself to be a thinking reed and I was marked by a fondness for sublime matters; I often spend long hours discussing beautiful and exalted topics.

Thus, disinterested curiosity, nobility of thought, a romantic, aristocratic, idealistic disposition of mind rather anachronistic in today's times gained me, I believe, access to the countess' petits fours and to her extraordinary Friday dinners. Because the countess was one of those higher women — on the one hand evangelical, on the other a Renaissance spirit — she sponsored charitable raffles, and at the same time worshipped the muses. She was admired for her many humanitarian activities — her charity teas and artistic afternoons, in which she took part like some Medici, were widely known — and simultaneously there was the alluring exclusivity of the smaller salon in her palace, in which the countess received only a small handful of truly intimate and trusted guests.

But most famous of all were the countess' meatless Friday dinners. These dinners — as she herself put it — had the quality of a respite in the daily round of philanthropy; they were something along the lines of a holiday and a departure from the usual. "I want to have something for myself too," the countess said with a mournful smile as she invited me for the first time, two months ago, to one of these dinners. "Please come on Friday, sir. There'll be a little singing, music, a few of my closest friends — and you . . . and the reason it's on Friday is so there won't be a single thought of meat" — she gave a slight shudder — "of that eternal meat of yours, and that blood. There's too much carnivorousness! Too many meat vapors! You no longer see any happiness other than a bloody beefsteak; you avoid fasts — you'd devour that revolting offal all day long without a break. I'm throwing down the gauntlet," she added with a subtle narrowing of the eyes, as always meaningful and symbolic. "I wish to convince everyone that a fast is not a diet but — a feast for the soul." What an honor! To be included among the ten, at most fifteen, persons admitted to the countess' meatless dinners!

The upper world always drew me magnetically, the world of these dinners all the more so. It seemed that Countess Pavahoke's unspoken idea was to build, as it were, new earthworks to protect the Fortress of the Holy Trinity from the barbarity of the present day (it was not for nothing that the blood of the Krasińskis flowed in her veins)—it seemed she adhered to the profound conviction that the old aristocracy was called upon not only to add superficial luster to entertainments and receptions, but that in all fields, including the spiritual and the artistic, by dint of its superiority of breeding it is capable of ensuring its own self-sufficiency—that accordingly, to achieve a truly sublime salon, an aristocratic salon suffices in every respect. This was an archaic thought, somewhat amateurish, but in any case—in its venerable archaicness uncommonly bold and profound, such as could unquestionably be expected of a descendant of the historic commanders. And indeed when, at table, in the antique dining room, far from dead bodies and murder and from the millions of slaughtered cattle, under the countess' leadership representatives of the most ancient lines revived memories of Platonic symposia—it seemed that the spirit of poetry and philosophy hovered amid the crystal and the flowers, and that enchanted words formed themselves into rhymes of their own accord.

There was one duke present, for instance, who at the request of the countess took on the role of intellectual and philosopher, and did so in such a ducal style, and uttered such beautiful and noble ideas, that if Plato had heard them he would have been embarrassed and would in all probability have stood behind the duke's chair with a napkin over his arm, ready to bring new dishes. There was a baroness who undertook to grace the company with song, though she had never taken singing lessons before that moment; and I doubt whether Adi Sari herself could have found so much bon ton within. There was something inexpressibly marvelous, marvelously vegetarian — I might say, luxuriously vegetarian — in the gastronomic moderation of those parties; and the immense fortunes modestly bending over a portion of cabbage left an unforgettable impression, especially against the background of the terrible carnivorousness of present-day relations. Even our teeth, the teeth of rodents, seemed in this place to lose the mark of Cain that they bore . . . . While as far as the cuisine was concerned, it was beyond dispute that the countess' vegetarian cuisine had no equal; uncommonly rich was the taste of her tomatoes stuffed with rice, and her asparagus omelettes were phenomenal in their firmness and aroma.

On the Friday in question, after a few months I had once again been honored with an invitation, and it was not without an unavoidable nervousness that I pulled up in a modest dorozhka before the ancient façade of the palace, situated just outside Warsaw. But instead of the dozen or so guests that I expected to find there were only two, and far from illustrious ones at that — a toothless old marchioness who out of necessity ate nothing but vegetables all week long, and a certain baron, namely Baron de Apfelbaum, from a somewhat dubious family who, with numbers in the millions and with his mother — who came from the family of the Pstryczyński dukes — had compensated for the number of his ancestors and his disastrous nose. Also, right from the beginning I sensed an almost imperceptible dissonance . . . a certain discordant quality . . . and moreover the pumpkin paste soup — specialité de la maison — the sweet pumpkin soup, boiled till it was soft, which was served as the first course, turned out to be unexpectedly paltry, watery and insubstantial. Despite this I did not betray the slightest surprise or disappointment (such manifestations would have been appropriate anywhere else, but not at Countess Pavahoke's); instead, with a glowing, rapt expression I managed to produce a compliment:

This soup's deliciously filling —
And made, what's more, without corpses or killing.

As I mentioned, at the countess' Friday parties verse rose to one's mouth of its own accord as a consequence of the exceptional harmony and high-mindedness of those gatherings — it would simply have been unseemly not to intersperse the periods of prose with rhyme. Then suddenly — to my consternation — Baron de Apfelbaum, who as a poet of immeasurable delicacy and an exacting gourmet was doubly an admirer of the inspired gastronomy of our hostess, leaned over to me and whispered in my ear with ill-concealed repugnance and a malice which I would never have suspected in him:

The soup would have been rich and thick
If the cook weren't such a . . .

Startled by his outburst, I gave a cough. What did he mean by this? Fortunately the baron pulled himself together at the last moment. What on earth had happened since my last visit — this dinner seemed a mere spectre of a dinner, the food was mediocre, and everyone had a long face. After the soup the second course was served—a platter of meager, sparse carrots in browned flour. I admired the countess' spiritual fortitude! Pale, clad in a black evening gown and wearing the family diamonds, with utmost courage she was consuming the indifferent dish, forcing the others to follow her lead—and with her customary skill she guided the conversation to exalted regions. She began charmingly, though not without melancholy, fluttering her napkin:

May deeper thoughts among us flow!
Tell me—wherein does Beauty grow?

I responded at once, assuming an appropriate air, the front of my tailcoat gleaming:

Most beautiful is Love, without a doubt,
Which twinkles all about;
On us, and on the birds that wield nor plow, nor sword,
Tiny tailcoated lambs of the Lord.

The countess smiled in gratitude at the immaculate beauty of this notion. The baron—like a thoroughbred stallion seized by the spirit of noble rivalry—replied, wiggling his fingers, scattering sparks from precious stones, and pouring out rhymes the mastery of which he alone possessed:

Beautiful the rose,
Beautiful the snows (etc.),
But more beautiful still is the feeling of pity.
Look now—woe betide!
The rain is still falling outside!

There's been foul weather for three days already;
Wretched are the poor and unsteady.
Yes—a tear of compassion, a raindrop of pity—
That's the secret of what's noble and pretty!

"You expressed that magnificently, my dear sir," the toothless marchioness lisped in delight. "Marvelous! Pity! St. Francis of Assisi! I have my own poor little ones, children suffering from rickets, to whom I've devoted the whole of my toothless old age! We ought always to remember the poor and the unfortunate . . ."

"Prisoners, and cripples who cannot afford artificial limbs," added the baron.

"Old, haggard, retired, emaciated schoolmistresses," the countess said compassionately.

"Barbers with varicose veins and starving miners suffering from sciatica," I put in, touched.

"Yes," said the countess, and her eyes glistened and ran off into the distance, "Yes! Love and Pity, two flowers—*roses de thé*—the tea roses of life . . . But one's obligations toward oneself should not be forgotten either!"—and, thinking for a moment, she paraphrased the famous saying of Joseph Poniatowski: "God entrusted Maria Pavahoke to me; only to Him will I give her up!"

Within me I must stir up ideals, elation,
A flame that burns without cessation!

"Bravo! Incomparable! What an idea!—profound! wise! proud! God entrusted Maria Pavahoke to me; only to Him will I give her up!" everyone exclaimed; while I permitted myself sotto voce to strum a patriotic chord (since Prince Joseph had been mentioned):

And never forget — the White Eagle of our nation!

The manservants brought in an immense cauliflower dressed in fresh butter and marvelously browned — alas, on the basis of my prior experiences it could be surmised that it was a consumptive brown. This was what conversation was like at the countess' — what a feast it was even in such unfavorable culinary circumstances. I flatter myself that my assertion about Love being most beautiful was not the most shallow of assertions; I even believe that it could provide the crowning moment of many a long philosophical poem. But right away another dinner guest, raising the bidding, tosses out an aphorism that says Pity is more beautiful even than Love. Excellent — and true! For indeed, when one thinks more deeply about it, Pity is even more encompassing, and covers more with its cloak, than sublime Love. And that's not the end of it — the countess, our wise Amphitryon, concerned that we should not dissolve without a trace in Love and Pity, mentions our lofty obligations toward ourselves — and then I, subtly exploiting the rhyme on "-ation," add just one more thing: "The White Eagle of our nation." And the form, the manner, the way of speaking, the noble and refined moderation of the feast battles for the upper hand with its substance! "No!" I thought in delight. "Whoever has not attended one of the countess' Friday parties cannot really say that he knows the aristocracy!"

"The cauliflower is excellent," murmured the baron, epicure and poet, all at once, and in his voice there sounded a pleasant surprise.

"Indeed," confirmed the countess, gazing suspiciously at her plate. As for myself, I did not notice anything out of the ordinary in the taste of the cauliflower; to me it seemed as wan as the preceding dishes.

"Could Philip . . . ?" asked the countess, and her eyes shot daggers.

"It should be checked!" said the marchioness mistrustfully.

"Have Philip summoned!" ordered the countess.

"There's no reason to conceal anything from you, my dear friend," said Baron de Apfelbaum; quietly, and not without suppressed irritation, he explained to me what the matter was. It turned out to be nothing less than the following: Two Fridays before, the countess had found her cook Philip seasoning the ideal of the fast with bouillon and the taste of meat! What a scoundrel! I couldn't believe it! I found it impossible to believe! Truly, only a cook was capable of such a thing! Worse still, the recalcitrant cook apparently showed no remorse, and instead had the impudence to defend himself with the bizarre thesis that "he wanted to satisfy all parties." What did he mean by this? (It seemed that he had previously served as cook to some bishop.) It was only when the countess threatened to give him his notice immediately that he swore he would desist! "Booby!" the baron concluded his story angrily. "Booby! He let himself be caught! And that's why, as you see, today the majority of people did not come and . . . hm . . . if it weren't for this cauliflower, I'd frankly be afraid that they made the right decision."

"No," said the toothless marchioness, chewing the vegetable with her gums, "no, this isn't the taste of meat. Mmm, mmm . . .

this isn't the taste of meat; rather—*comment dirais-je*—it's exceptionally refreshing—it must contain a great number of vitamins."

"There's something peppery," declared the baron, discreetly taking a second helping. "Something delicately peppery—mmm, mmm—but meatless," he added hurriedly, "decidedly vegetarian, peppery and cauliflowerish. One can rely on my palate, countess; in questions of taste I am a second Pythia!"

But the countess did not calm herself till the cook appeared—a long, skinny, ruddy individual with a cross-eyed gaze—and swore on the shade of his late wife that the cauliflower was pure and spotless.

"All cooks are like that!" I said sympathetically, and also took more of the popular dish (though I still could not see anything exceptional in it). "Oh, cooks have to be watched!" (I don't know if remarks of this kind were sufficiently tactful, but I was overcome by a euphoria light as champagne bubbles.) "The cook in that hat of his and his white apron!"

"Philip looks so good-hearted," said the countess with a faint note of bitterness and mute resentment, reaching for the melted butter.

"Good-hearted, good-hearted—no doubt," I said, sticking to my ground with perhaps too much stubbornness. "Nevertheless, a cook. . . . A cook, ladies and gentlemen, is a man of the common people, *homo vulgaris*, whose task is to prepare elegant, refined dishes—in this there lies a dangerous paradox. Elegance being prepared by boorishness—what can that mean?"

"The aroma is exceptional!" said the countess, breathing in the smell of the cauliflower through flared nostrils (I could not smell it), and not letting the fork out of her hand, but instead continuing to wield it briskly.

"Exceptional!" repeated the banker, and, so as not to spill butter on himself, he fastened his napkin over his shirt front. "A little more, if I might ask, countess. I'm reviving after that . . . um . . . soup, mmm, mmm . . . Indeed, cooks cannot be trusted. I had a cook who made Italian pasta like no one else—I would simply stuff myself! And imagine if you please, I go into the kitchen one day and in the pot I see my pasta, and it's crawling—simply crawling!—and it was worms—mmm, mmm—worms from my garden, which the villain was serving up as pasta! Since then—mmm, mmm—I've stopped looking into pots!"

"Just so," I said. "Exactly!" And I spoke further about cooks, saying that they were butchers, small-time murderers, that it was all the same to them what and how, all that mattered was adding pepper, adding seasoning, making meals—comments that were not entirely appropriate and rather crass, but I had gotten carried away.—"You, countess, who would never touch his head, in the soup—you are ingesting his hair!" I would have continued in the same vein, since I had suddenly been seized by an access of treacherous eloquence, but all of a sudden—I broke off, for no one was listening to me! The extraordinary sight of the countess, that dogaressa, that patroness, eating in silence and so rapaciously that her ears trembled, terrified and astonished me. The baron accompanied her gallantly, bent over his plate, slurping and smacking his lips with all his might—and the old marchioness did her best to keep up, chewing and swallowing huge mouthfuls, evidently worried that they would take her plate away before she had eaten the best morsels!

This extraordinary, sudden image of guzzling—I cannot put it otherwise—of *such* guzzling, in *such* a house, this awful transition, this diminished seventh chord, shook the foundations of my being to such an extent that I was unable to restrain myself and I sneezed—and since I had left my handkerchief in the pocket of my overcoat, I was obliged to rise from the table and excuse myself. In the hall, falling motionless onto a chair, I attempted to bring my scattered thoughts to equilibrium. Only a person who, like me, had long known the countess, the marchioness, and the baron for their refined gestures, the delicacy, moderation, and subtlety of all their functions, and especially the function of eating, the incomparable nobility of their features—only such a person could appreciate the horrible impression I had received. At the same time I happened to cast a glance at the copy of the *Red Herald* sticking out of my overcoat pocket, and I noticed a sensational headline:

MYSTERIOUS DISAPPEARANCE OF CAULIFLOWER

along with the subtitle:

CAULIFLOWER IN DANGER OF FREEZING

and an article containing the following text:

Stable hand Valentine Cauliflower of the village of Rudka (belonging to the estate of the renowned Countess Pavahoke) reported to the police that his son Bolek, aged 8, has run away from home. According to the police the boy, described as having a snub nose and flaxen hair, ran away because his father was drunk and walloping him with a belt, and his mother was starving him (a common phenomenon, alas, in the current crisis). There is concern that the boy could freeze to death wandering about the fields during the autumn rains.

"Tsk, tsk," I tutted, "tsk, tsk . . ." I glanced through the window at the fields, veiled by a thin curtain of rain. And I returned to the dining room, where the huge silver platter contained nothing but the remains of the cauliflower. The countess' stomach, on the other hand, looked as if she was in her seventh month—the baron's organ of consumption was virtually dangling in his plate—while the old marchioness was chewing and chewing indefatigably, moving her jaws—truly, I must say it—like a cow! "Divine, marvelous," they all kept repeating, "delightful, incomparable!" Utterly disconcerted, I carefully and attentively tasted the cauliflower one more time, but I sought in vain for something that would even partially justify the company's unprecedented demeanor.

"What is it that you see in this?" I coughed timidly, somewhat abashed.

"Ha ha ha, he's asking!" cried the baron loudly, gorging himself and in a capital humor.

"Can you really not taste it . . . young man?" asked the marchioness, without interrupting her consumption even for a moment.

"You're not a gastronome," declared the baron, as if with a hint of polite sympathy, "whereas I . . . *Et moi, je ne suis pas gastronome—je suis gastrosophe!*" And did my ears deceive me—or was it the case that as he pronounced that French platitude, something swelled within him, so that he threw out the last word "*gastrosophe*" from bulging cheeks with an exceptional exaltation he had never shown before?

"It's well seasoned, no doubt . . . very tasty, yes, very . . . but . . ." I mumbled.

"But? . . . But what? So you truly cannot taste it? This delicate freshness, this . . . mmm . . . indefinable firmness, this . . . characteristic pepperiness . . . this scent, this alcohol? But my deah sir" (this was the first time since we had known each other that I had been addressed in the aristocratic manner as 'deah sir') "surely you are pretending? Surely you are meahly attempting to alahm us?"

"Don't talk to him!" the countess interrupted flirtatiously, convulsed with laughter. "Don't talk to him! After all, he'll never understand!"

"Style, young man, is imbibed with one's mother's milk," the marchioness lisped benevolently, reminding me, it seemed, that my mother's maiden name was Turky—may she rest in peace!

And everyone abandoned the continuation of the dinner and dragged their full stomachs into the gilded Louis XVI boudoir, where they sprawled in the softest armchairs they could find and began laughing—and there was no doubt whatsoever it was me they were laughing at, just as if I had given them cause for especial merriment. I had long rubbed shoulders with the aristocracy at tea parties and benefit concerts—but, by my word of honor, I had never seen such behavior, nor such an abrupt change, such a transformation unmotivated by anything at all. Not knowing whether to sit or stand, whether to be serious or rather *faire bonne mine à mauvais jeu* and give a foolish smile, I tried vaguely and timidly to return to Arcadia, that is, to the pumpkin soup:

Returning to the matter of Beauty . . .

"Enough, enough!" exclaimed Baron de Apfelbaum, holding his hands over his ears. "What a tedious fellow! Now it's time to have fun! *S'encanailler!* I'll sing you something better! From an operetta!"

> *This greenhorn is a funny bird!*
> *He doesn't understand a word!*
> *I'll teach him to know the things he should:*
> *What's beautiful's not what's beautiful, what's beautiful is what*
> *   tastes good.*
> *Taste! Taste! Good taste!*
> *That's where Beauty's based!*

"Bravo!" cried the countess, and the marchioness chimed in, baring her gums in a old woman's giggle: "Bravo! *Cocasse! Charmant!*"

"But it seems to me . . . that this . . . that this is not right . . ." I stuttered, yet my stupefied gaze was thoroughly out of keeping with my formal attire.

"We aristocrats"—the marchioness leaned over to me good-naturedly—"in our innermost circle profess a great freedom of manners; at such times, as you have heard, we occasionally even use coarse expressions and we can be frivolous, often even vulgar in our own way. But there is no need to be appalled! You must get used to us!"

"We're not so feahful," added the baron patronizingly, "though our vulgahness is hahder to come to terms with than our refinement!"

"No, we are not fearful!" squealed the countess. "We won't eat anyone alive!"

"We won't eat anyone, apart from . . ."

"Apaht from . . . !"

"*Fi donc*, ha ha ha," they burst out laughing, throwing their embroidered cushions in the air, and the countess sang:

It must be faced—
Everything's a matter of taste!
Everything's a matter of style!
For a lobster to be good you have to torture it,
For a turkey to be fat it has to hurt a bit.
D'you know the taste of my lips awhile?
Whose taste from ours diverges thus
Will never be on first-name terms with us!

"Oh, but"—I whispered—"Countess . . . green peas, carrots, celery, cabbage . . ."

"Cauliflower!" added the baron, seized by a suspicious cough.

"Exactly!" I said in total confusion. "Exactly! . . . Cauliflower! . . . Cauliflower . . . fasting . . . vegetarian vegetables . . ."

"Well, what about the cauliflower—did you like it? Eh? Was it good? Eh? I expect you eventually understood the taste of the cauliflower?" What a tone of voice! The condescension, the barely audible but menacing lordly impatience in that tone! I began to stammer—I didn't know what to reply—how on earth could I deny it—yet how could I confirm it?—and then (oh, I would never have believed that noble, humanitarian individual, that poetical brother was so capable of giving one to understand that lordly favors are fickle)—then, leaning back in his armchair and stroking his long, slim leg, inherited from Duchess Pstryczyńska, he said to the ladies in a tone that literally destroyed me: "Really, my deah countess, it's hahdly worthwhile inviting to dinnah individuals whose taste has nevah risen beyond the uttahly primitive!"

And, paying me no more heed, they began to banter amongst themselves, their glasses in their hands, in such a way that I immediately became a *quantité négligeable*,—about "Alice" and her caprices, about "Gabie" and "Bubie," about princess "Mary," about some "Pheasants" or other, about one fellow who is awful and another woman who is *vraiment impossible*. They exchanged anecdotes and gossip, in a few words, in a higher language, with the aid of expressions such as "crazy," "fantastic," "mahvelous," "fahcical," and even frequently resorting to crude curses such as "bothah!" or "buggah!" till it appeared that this sort of conversation represented the apogee of human ability, while I with my Beauty, my humanity and all the topics of the thinking reed had in some inexplicable fashion been pushed aside like a useless piece of furniture, and had no reason to open my mouth. They were also telling in a few words some aristocratic jokes that caused extraordinary jollity, but at which I—who did not know their genealogy—could barely force myself to smile. Dear Lord, what could have happened?! What a cruel and sudden transformation! Why were they one way over the pumpkin soup, and now completely different? Was it really with them that not so long ago I had been disseminating humanitarian brilliance in the utmost harmony—moments before, over the pumpkin soup? So where had it come from so suddenly and without any visible cause—all this disastrous ingredient, all this alienness and iciness, this ironic humor, this incomprehensible inclination to painful mockery of appearance itself, this distance, this remoteness, rendering them quite unapproachable! I was unable to explain such a metamorphosis — and the marchioness' mention of "our circle" brought to my mind all those awful things that were said in my own middle-class sphere and to which I never lent any credence — about the double face of the aristocracy and its inner life, locked away from undesirable eyes.

No longer able to tolerate my own silence — which with every moment was thrusting me deeper into a terrible abyss — I finally said to the countess out of the blue, like a defunct echo of the past:

"I'm sorry to interrupt . . . Countess, you promised that you would dedicate to me your triolets: 'Musings of my Soul.'"

"How's that?" she asked, not having heard me, and in high spirits. "What was that? You said something?"

"I'm terribly sorry — you promised, Countess, that you would dedicate to me your work entitled 'Musings of my Soul.'"

"Ah, yes, that's right," replied the countess absently, but with her usual courtesy (her usual courtesy? Or was it a different kind? Was it a new kind, to the extent that my cheek, truly without my conscious participation, flushed red) — and taking a small white-bound volume from a side table, she carelessly wrote a few courteous words on the title page and signed herself:

Countess *Havapoke.*

"But Countess," I cried, pained to see her historic name distorted so — "it's Pavahoke."

"How absentminded of me!" exclaimed the countess amid the

general jollity. "How absentminded of me!" Yet I did not feel like laughing. "Tsk, tsk," I almost tutted again. The countess was laughing loudly and proudly—but at the same time her slim, well-bred leg was describing flourishes on the carpet in an exceptionally titillating and seductive manner, as if relishing the slenderness of its own fetlock—first to the left, then to the right, or in a circle; the baron was leaning forward in his armchair and looked as if he were on the point of uttering some noteworthy bon mot—but his little ear, characteristic of the Pstryczyński dukes, was even littler than usual, while his fingers slipped a single grape between his lips. The marchioness was sitting with her customary elegance—but her long, thin grande dame's neck seemed to have become even more elongated, and with its slightly withered surface seemed to be squinting in my direction. And I must add a not insignificant detail: outside, the rain was being carried by the wind and kept lashing against the window panes like tiny whips.

It may have been that I took my own rapid and undeserved downfall too much to heart—it may also have been that under its influence I yielded to the kind of persecution complex suffered by an individual of the lower spheres admitted to society; in addition, certain chance relations, certain, let us say, analogies stimulated my sensitivities—I have no wish to deny it, this may have been . . . . But suddenly something utterly extraordinary had drifted from them in my direction! And I do not deny that the refinement, subtlety, courtesy, and elegance continued to be refined, subtle, courteous, and elegant, as much as could be, without a doubt—but at the same time they were so *strangulating* I was tempted to believe that all those excellent and humanitarian qualities had become enraged, as if a bumblebee had stung them! What was more, it suddenly seemed to me (this was undeniably the effect of the slim leg, the little ear, and the neck) that in not looking, in their lordly disregard, they nevertheless saw my confusion and could not get enough of it! And at the same time I was struck by the suspicion that Havapoke . . . that Havapoke was not necessarily a mere *lapsus linguae*, that in a word, if I am expressing myself clearly, Havapoke meant have a poke! Have a poke? Have a poke in the countess? Yes, yes, the gleaming toes of her patent-leather shoes confirmed me even more in this terrifying conviction!—it seemed they were still surreptitiously splitting their sides at the fact that I had been unable to grasp the taste of the cauliflower—that for me the cauliflower had been an ordinary vegetable—they were surreptitiously splitting their sides at this, and they were preparing to do so aloud the moment I gave voice to the emotions that were agitating me. Yes, yes—they were disregarding, not noticing, and at the same time, on the side, with various aristocratic parts of the body, a slim leg, an ear, a thin neck, they were provoking and tempting one to break the seal of the secret.

I do not think I need to add how shocking it was, this quiet temptation, this concealed, unhealthy flirtation with all that was of the thinking reed within me. I referred vaguely to the "secret" of the aristocracy, the secret of taste, the mystery that none could possess who was not one of the chosen, even if, as Schopenhauer says, he should know three hundred rules of *savoir-vivre* by heart. And even if for a moment I had been dazzled by the hope that once I learned this secret I would be admitted to their circle and I would drop my *r*'s and say "fantastic" and "crazy" just like them, still, other concerns aside, the fear and anxiety of—why should I not say it openly—of being slapped in the face utterly paralyzed my burning desire for knowledge. With the aristocracy one can never be certain, with the aristocracy one needs to be more careful than with a tame leopard. A certain member of the bourgeoisie, asked once by Duchess X what his mother's maiden name was and emboldened by the apparent ease of manner prevailing in that salon and the forbearance with which his previous two jokes had been received, decided that he could permit himself anything at all and replied: "By your leave, Piędzik!"—and for that "by your leave" (which turned out to be vulgar) he was immediately ejected.

"Philip," I thought cautiously—"After all, Philip swore an oath! . . . I mean, the cook is a cook! The cook is a cook, the cauliflower a cauliflower, the countess a countess, and on this last score may no one forget it! Yes, the countess is a countess, the baron a baron, and the gusts of the gale and the wretched weather outside the windows are a gale and foul weather, and the child's little hands in the darkness and the back, bruised by a father's belt, beneath the driving waves of the downpour are a child's little hands and a bruised back, and nothing more . . . and the countess is beyond a doubt a countess. The countess is a countess, and let's just hope she doesn't give someone a telling-off!"

Observing that I had remained in a state of complete, almost paralytic passivity, they began, as if unobtrusively, to circle me ever closer, accosting me ever more openly and revealing ever more clearly a desire to taunt me. "Would you look at that terrified expression!" the countess cried all of a sudden, and they started to ridicule me, saying that I must be "feahfully shocked" and "terrahstruck," since in my spheres surely no one "blathahed" in this way or tried to prove that here there prevailed manners incomparably better and less wild than theirs, the aristocacy's. Pretending to be afraid of my strictness, they set about jokingly upbraiding and reprimanding one another, as if they cared above all what I thought of them.

"Don't talk nonsense! You're awful!" exclaimed the countess (though the baron was not awful at all; there was nothing awful about him except that little ear, which he kept touching, not without satisfaction, with the tips of his slim, bony fingers).

"Will you behave properly!" shouted the baron (the countess and the marchioness were behaving entirely properly).

"Don't blather—don't sprawl on the sofa—don't shake your leg and don't put your feet on the table!" (Heaven forfend! The countess had no intention of doing these things.) "You're hurting the feelings of this poor fellow! Countess, your nose really is too well-bred! Have mercy, ma'am!" (On whom, I ask, was the countess to have mercy on account of her nose?) The marchioness remained silent, shedding tears of amusement. But the fact that like an ostrich I stuck my head in the sand only served to excite them the more—they looked as if they had thrown the remains of their caution to the winds—as if they wanted at all costs to ensure that I understood—and, unable to contain themselves, they made ever more transparent allusions. Allusions? To what? Ah, naturally to the same thing over and again, and ever more openly, ever closer and closer they orbited, ever more brazenly . . .

"Might I smoke?" asked the baron affectedly, taking out a gold cigarette case. (Might I smoke?! It was quite as if he was unaware that outside, the damp and rain and awful freezing wind could at any moment make one stiff with cold. Might I smoke?!)

"Listen how the rain's lashing mercilessly," lisped the marchioness naively. (Lashing? Certainly it was lashing! It must have been lashing down perfectly out there.)—"Oh, listen to the tap-tap of individual raindrops, listen to that tap-tap-tap, listen, listen there if you please to those raindrops!"

"Oh, what awful weather, what a terrible wind," cried the countess. "Oh, oh—ha ha ha—what a terrible storm! It's unpleasant even to look at! The very sight of it makes me want to laugh and gives me goose flesh!"

"Ha ha ha," echoed the baron, "look how splendidly it all streams down! Look at the different arabesques the water forms! Look how that little bit of mud spreads so wonderfully, how greasily it sticks, how it's smeared, just like Cumberland sauce; and how that rain keeps thrashing and thrashing—it thrashes so wonderfully, and that little wind keeps stinging and stinging—how it browns, how it pinches, how it crumbles so wonderfully! It quite makes one's mouth water, I swear!"

"By my wohd, it's extraohdinarily tasty, extraohdinarily tasty!"

"Extremely stylish!"

"Just like *côtelette de volaille!*"

"Or *fricassée à la Heine* rathah!"

"Or lobstah in ragout!"

And in the wake of these bons mots, tossed out with the ease of manner of which only the old aristocratic families are capable, there followed movements and gestures that . . . whose meaning I would have preferred not to understand, curled up as I was in my armchair, completely motionless. It was not only that the ear, the little nose, the neck, and the slender foot were entering a fanatical state of frenzy — in addition the banker had drawn cigarette smoke deep into his lungs and was blowing small blue rings in the air. If only it were just one or two of them, dear Lord! But he kept blowing and blowing, one ring after another, forming his mouth into a little snout — and the countess and the marchioness were applauding! And every ring rose upward and dissipated slowly, in harmonious coils! The long, white, serpentine hand of the countess rested in the meantime on the patterned satin of the armchair — her nervous fetlock wiggled beneath the table, evil as a viper, black and venomous. I began to feel distinctly out of sorts. As if all this were not enough — I swear I am not exaggerating! — the baron went so far in his effrontery as to raise his upper lip, take a toothpick out of his pocket and begin to pick his teeth, yes, his teeth — rich, rotten, and densely interspersed with gold!

Dumbfounded, utterly ignorant of what to do or where to run, I turned imploringly to the marchioness, who up till this point had shown me the most kindness, and who at the dinner table had so movingly admired Pity and the children suffering from rickets — and I began to say something about pity — virtually begging for pity. "Milady," I said, "you who bestowed such devotion on the poor children! Milady! — For the love of God!" Do you know how she answered? She gazed at me in surprise with her pale pupils — she wiped away the tears produced by an excess of jollity, and then, as if recalling, she said:

"Oh, you're speaking of my little rickety ones? . . . Oh yes, it's true, when you see them moving around awkwardly on those crooked little legs of theirs, stumping about and falling over, it makes a person feel hale again! Old but hale! Long ago I used to go horse riding, in a black riding dress and gleaming boots, on English thoroughbreds, while now—*hélas, les beaux temps sont passés*—now that I no longer can, old as I am, I ride oh so merrily on those crooked little rickety children of mine!" And suddenly her hand reached down and I jumped back, for I swear she intended to show me her old but straight, healthy, still hale leg!

"For the love of Christ!" I exclaimed, barely clinging to life. "What about Love, Pity, Beauty, the prisoners, the cripples, the haggard retired schoolmistresses . . ."

"Oh, but we remember them, we do!" said the countess with a laugh that sent shivers down my spine. "Those poor dear school-mistresses."

"We do!" the old marchioness reassured me.

"We do!" Baron de Apfelbaum concurred. "We do!"—I went quite numb with fright. "Those deaah, good prisonahs!"

They were not looking at me—they were looking in the direction of the ceiling, tipping their heads back as if this alone could check the violent contractions of their cheek muscles. Ha! I was no longer in any doubt; I had finally understood where I was, and I was overcome by an uncontrollable tremor in my lower jaw. And the rain was still lashing against the windows like little whips.

"But God, God exists!" I finally stammered, with the last of my strength, desperately seeking something to hold onto; "God exists," I added more quietly, for the Lord's name had rung out so inappropriately that everyone fell silent, and their faces showed all the ominous signs of a faux pas having been committed—and I merely waited to be shown the door!

"Ah yes," replied Baron de Apfelbaum after a moment, pulverizing me with his unparalleled tact. — "Cod? — cod exists — it swims in the sea!"

Who could have come up with a retort? Who would not have been, as the expression goes, gobstruck? I fell silent—and the marchioness sat at the piano and the baron and the countess began to dance a caper—and every movement of theirs oozed such taste, style, elegance, that—ha!—I wanted to flee, but how could I possibly withdraw without taking my leave? And how could I take my leave while they were dancing? So I watched from the corner and truly—I had never ever imagined such infinite shamelessness, such brazenness! I cannot do violence to my own nature in describing what went on—no, no one can demand that of me. Suffice it to say that when the countess moved her slim leg forward, the baron pulled his back, many, many times—and this with an air that was unutterably urbane, wearing expressions that suggested the dance was just the most ordinary Milongo tango—while at the piano the marchioness was producing runs, arpeggios, and trills! But I already knew what it was—it had been forced violently on my soul—it was a dance of cannibals! A dance of cannibals!—with taste, style, and elegance—and I searched only for an idol, an African monster with a square skull, turned-out lips, round cheekbones, a flattened nose, raised eyebrows, overseeing the debauch from somewhere up above. And, looking toward the window, behind the pane I saw precisely something of this kind — a round child's face with a flattened nose, raised brows, protruding ears, emaciated and feverish, and staring so, with all the cosmic idiocy of an African idol, with such otherworldly rapture — that for the next hour (or two), like a hypnotized man I could not tear my eyes from the buttons of my vest.

And when finally at dawn I stole away, down the slippery steps of the porch, in the graying drizzle, I noticed a body lying in a bed of withered irises beneath the window. It was, of course, a corpse, the corpse of an eight-year-old boy with flaxen hair and a snub nose, barefoot, so emaciated that one could say he was thoroughly consumed — there was barely a scrap of meat left here and there under his filthy skin. Ha — so the unfortunate Bolek Cauliflower had strayed as far as this place, drawn by the bright windows visible from far off in the sodden fields. And when I ran out through the gate, from somewhere or other appeared Philip the cook, white, in a little round cap, with his ruddy beard and cross-eyed gaze, skinny and refined, with the refinement of a master of the culinary arts who first cuts the throats of chickens so as later to serve them at table in a sauce — and fawning, bowing, wagging his tail, he said obsequiously: "I hope, milord, that the meatless dinner was to your taste!"

Virginity

✦✦

There's nothing more artificial than descriptions of young girls and the fanciful comparisons that go along with them. Lips like cherries, breasts like little roses; oh, if only it were enough to buy some fruit and flowers at the store! And if lips really did have the taste of ripe cherries, who on earth would have the courage to be in love? Who on earth would be tempted by a caramel—that is, a sweet kiss?—But hush, enough, it's a secret, taboo, let's not say too much about lips.—Alice's elbow, seen through the prism of the emotions, was at times a smooth white virginal point, passing into the warmer tones of the arm; at others, when her arm dangled passively, it was a sweet round dimple, a quiet little nook, a side altar of her body. Aside from this Alice resembled any other daughter of a retired major brought up by a loving mother in a suburban cottage. Like others, she occasionally stroked her elbow, lost in thought, and like others she learned early on to poke about in the sand with her slender foot.

But never mind that . . .

The life of an adolescent girl can be compared neither with the life of an engineer or lawyer, nor with the life of a housewife and mother. Take, for instance, the longing and murmuring of the blood, perpetual as the ticking of a watch. Somewhere the idea was already once expressed that there is nothing stranger than being alluring. It's not easy to look after a being whose reason for existing is to entice; yet Alice was well-protected by her canary Fifi, by her mother, the major's wife, and by her Doberman pinscher Bibi, whom she led on a leash during their afternoon walk. These domestic animals had a curious understanding when it came to Alice's protection. "Bibi," sang the canary, "Bibi, you sweet dog, guard our young lady well. Bow and scrape to her! Bow and scrape! And drive away bad thoughts. Keep an eye on the parasol — it's so lazy; make sure it shields our beloved young lady from the sun!"

One mild August evening, at sunset, Alice was taking a walk along the garden path, amusing herself by poking little round holes in the gravel with the tip of her parasol. It was a small but agreeable garden surrounded by a wall that was covered with climbing roses; a hobo lying in the sun on top of the wall broke off a piece of brick and threw it at Alice. Struck on the shoulder, she staggered and almost fell — and she was just about to cry out when she noticed that her tormentor showed neither anger nor satisfaction, but simply dealt her another blow to the back with another small piece of brick. The brute's face expressed nothing but the idleness of an afternoon siesta, indifference, and cynicism; accordingly, Alice smiled faintly at him, her lips trembling with pain, upon which the hobo slid down from the wall and disappeared; while she returned home, repeating to herself:

"I smiled . . ."

"Alice! Alice!" called Mrs. S., her mother. "Suppertime, Alice!"

"Coming, mama," replied Alice.

"Why are you slurping like that, child? Whoever saw anyone drink tea that way?"

"It's because it's really hot, Mama," answered Alice.

"Alice, don't eat that slice of bread after it fell on the floor."

"It's so as not to waste it, Mama."

"Look at Bibi, sitting up and begging for his bread and butter. You should be ashamed to be so selfish, child — there now, why did you step on the poor creature's foot? What's gotten into you today? What's happened to you?"

"Oh, I'm so distracted," said Alice dreamily. "Mama, why is it that men wear trousers? — I mean, we have legs too, don't we? And Mama, why is it that men have short hair? Do men have their hair cut because . . . because . . . they have to, or because they want to?"

"They wouldn't look good with long hair, Alice."

"But Mama, why do they want to look good?"

As she spoke she furtively slipped into her sleeve the silver spoon with which she had been drinking her tea. "Why?" said Mrs. S. "And why do you curl your locks? So the world can be more beautiful and so Mr. Sun won't begrudge people his rays." — But Alice had already risen and walked out into the garden. She took the spoon from her sleeve and for some time looked at it undecidedly.

"I stole it," she whispered in astonishment. "I stole it! But what shall I do with it now?" And in the end she buried it beneath a tree. Oh, if Alice had not been hit by a rock she would never have stolen the spoon. Women may not like extreme measures in their outer life, but inwardly they are capable of draining the most out of every situation if they wish.

In the meantime Major S., a sturdy, corpulent man, appeared at the door of the house, calling: "Alice! Your fiancé has returned from his voyage to China and is coming tomorrow!"

Alice had become engaged four years ago, when she was still in her seventeenth spring. — "Miss Alice," mumbled the young man, "will you permit this slim hand—to be mine?" "What do you mean?" she asked. "I'm asking for your hand, Miss Alice," stuttered the young paramour. "Surely sir, you don't expect me to cut off my hand," said the naïve girl, nevertheless flushing scarlet. "Then you do not wish to be my betrothed?" "Oh yes," she replied, "but on condition that you give me your word you'll never importune me for any of my extremities; that's ridiculous!" "Wonderful!" he exclaimed. "You have no idea how enchanting you are. Intoxicating!" And he spent the entire evening roaming the streets and repeating: "She understood it literally; she thought that I . . . desired to take her hand the way a person takes a piece of cake. It makes one want to drop to one's knees!"

He was beyond question a very handsome young man; he had a pale complexion and contrasting red lips, while his spirit was in no way inferior to his physical beauty. How rich and varied is the human spirit! Some construct their morality upon rectitude, others on kindheartedness; whereas for Paul the alpha and omega, the foundation and the acme was maidenhood. It was this that formed the cornerstone of his soul and about which all his higher instincts were entwined. Chateaubriand too regarded maidenhood as something perfect and yearned for it, saying: *We see then that virginity, which rises from the lowest member of the chain of beings, stretches upward to humankind, and from humankind to the angels, and from the angels to God, where it is lost. God himself is a great recluse in the universe, the eternal youth of worlds.*

If Paul had fallen in love with Alice it was because her elbow, her slim hands and her slender feet were more virginal than one normally finds, perhaps owing to her nature, perhaps as a consequence of her parents' mindful care; and because she seemed to him maidenhood incarnate.

"A virgin," he would think. "She—she understands nothing. The stork. No, it's too beautiful even to think about—except perhaps on one's knees."

And as he passed by the municipal slaughterhouse he added: "Perhaps she also thinks that little ready-made lambs are brought by the stork? That roast lamb comes right onto the table? Oh, how sublime that is! How can one not love her?"

And how can one not worship the Creator? It's incomprehensible! How very wonderful nature is, that something like virginity is even permissible in this vale of tears. Virginity—in other words, a discrete category of beings who are closed, isolated, unaware, partitioned off by a thin screen. They tremble in fearful expectation, breathing deeply, brushing against things without penetrating them—separate from that which surrounds them, locked away from obscenity, sealed—and that is not merely an empty phrase, or rhetoric, but a genuine seal, as good as any other. A stunning combination of physics and metaphysics, abstract and concrete — from a minor bodily detail there flows an entire sea of idealism and wonders that are glaringly at odds with our sorry reality.

As she eats her roast lamb she knows nothing and suspects nothing; and it's the same with every matter from morning to evening. When was it that instead of spider she had said spidey — the spidey's eating the wee fly? A marvel! Innocent both in the drawing room and in the dining room, and also in her little young lady's room behind the white lace curtain, and on the toi- . . . Quiet! What a terrible thought! — He clenched his teeth, and his whole face twitched nervously. "No, no," he whispered. "She, she doesn't do that at all, she doesn't know that; otherwise surely God would not be in his heaven." — Yet he felt that he was lying. "In any case it happens apart from her; at such times she's absent in spirit, it's as it were — automatic . . .

"Yes, but all the same — that's a horrible thought!

"Oh! And I? I, who am thinking about this, who am capable of thinking about such a thing, who do not go deaf and blind in the face of these horrors, but look on mentally? How despicable! It's not her fault that this befell her but mine that I am rotten and dirty and that I'm not able remain silent in my mind. For my part, do I not owe her virginity a little unawareness? Yes — in order to love a virgin appropriately one should oneself be virginal and unaware; otherwise nothing will come of our idyll.

"And so I desire to be virginal, but how can I achieve this? I'm not a virgin. True, like a priest or a monk I could wrap myself in black, in fasting and a cassock, and practice sexual abstinence; but what good would it do me? Is a monk virginal, or a priest? No, not in the slightest; the secret of male virginity lies elsewhere. Above all one should shut one's eyes tight, and secondly rely on one's instinct. I sense that instinct will show me the way. Yes—the way I felt with my instinct, though I wouldn't be able to say why, that her ears are more virginal than her nose, and even more than her ears—the gentle incline of her back; her third finger more than her index finger; the way I'm able to appraise in this regard every detail of her figure—in the same way instinct will be my guide in attaining male virginity and becoming worthy of Alice."

Is it really necessary to dwell on the question of where instinct led him? After all, everyone has experienced something of this kind between the ages of thirteen and fourteen. His parents had ordained that he would become a merchant, but he was torn between two other professions—soldier and sailor. In the profession of soldier there is, to be sure, blind discipline and a hard bed, but on the other hand there is a lack of space. Whereas sailors have the advantage over others that, deprived of the company of the opposite sex, they have space, the elements, and freedom—and in addition, sea water is salty. Their ship, rocking lightly, bears them off to distant realms, amid fantastical palm trees and colorful people, to a world just as unreal as the one dreamed by Alice and her friends in their white beds. It is not without a deeper meaning that those far-off lands are called virgin—lands where the men wear plaits, where ears weighed down by metal earrings stretch to the shoulders, and where beneath the baobab tree idols devour slaves or infants, while the entire population indulges in ritual contortions. Is a kiss by rubbing noses, as practiced among the savage tribes, not something taken directly from an innocent, dreamy little head? Paul had spent long years there. He was struck by the fact that the virgins of those parts, who wore no skirts or blouses, were wholly on the surface. "Disgusting," he would think. "The annihilation of charm . . . True, the color itself settles the issue . . . When one is red, black, or yellow—it can't be helped, in a skirt or not—one cannot lay claim to the title of virgin.

"You, Moni—Buatu," he would say to one of the black women —"you bare . . . no blush . . . black, teeth bared, grotesque— you can't comprehend the divine embarrassment of innocence enwrapped in fabric, and fearfully turning away its head.

"Skirt, blouse, little parasol, prattle, holy naïveté dictated by instinct—these are delightful, but they aren't for me. As a man I can neither clasp my arms together nor sully myself innocently. Quite the opposite: honor, courage, dignity, taciturnity, these are the attributes of male virginity. But I ought to maintain in relation to the world a certain male naivety constituting an analogy to virginal naivety. I must take everything in with a clear gaze. I must eat lettuce. Lettuce is more virginal than radishes—why, can anyone guess? Perhaps because it's more bitter. But then lemon is even less virginal than radishes.

"On the male side too there exist marvelous secrets, matters that are locked up with seven seals—the flag and death beneath the flag. What further? Faith is a great mystery, blind faith. A godless person is like a public woman to whom everyone has access. I ought to raise something to the dignity of my ideal, to come to love, to believe blindly and be prepared to sacrifice my life—but what should it be? Anything, so long as I have the ideal. I, a male virgin, bunged up with my ideal!"

And here he was, after an absence of four years, walking with his betrothed along the paths of the garden. They made a handsome couple. Mrs. S. watched them gladly from the window as she embroidered a napkin, while Bibi dashed about the lawn chasing little birds, which fled chirping from his red tongue.

"You've changed," the young man was saying sadly; "you don't prattle like before, you don't wave your little hand about . . ."

"No, no, I still love you just the same," Alice replied distractedly.

"There, you see! Before, you wouldn't have said that you love me. I didn't expect this of you—that such words would pass your throat, that your lips and tongue would form that shameful phrase. You're altogether ill at ease, on edge somehow; you don't have a throat infection by any chance?"

"I love you; it's just . . ."

"Just what?"

"You won't make fun of me?"

"You know that I—I never laugh. I only smile, and only with a cheerful smile."

"Explain to me: What does love mean, and what do I mean?"

"Ah, I've been awaiting that question for a long time," he exclaimed. "Come and sit on this bench.

"When the first parents in paradise yielded to Satan's whisper and tasted the tree of awareness, as you know, everything changed for the worse. 'O Lord!'—the people begged—'grant us at least a little of that lost purity and innocence.' The Lord God looked helplessly at the motley band and had no idea where or how He could find a place for Purity and Innocence in that squalid herd. It was then He created a virgin, a vessel of innocence, locked her up tightly and set her among the people, who conceived a nostalgic longing for her."

"And what about married women?"

"Married women are nothing—humbug, a stale bottle."

"But why is it, tell me, why is it that men throw rocks at virgins?"

"What's that, Alice?"

"It's happened to me a number of times," said Alice, turning deep crimson, "that one or another man I've met on an empty street, when no one was watching—threw a rock at me."

"What did you say?" replied Paul in astonishment. "I've never heard of such a thing," he whispered. "What do you mean, threw a rock?"

"He took a rock, a big brick, and flung it at me. It hurt," Alice murmured ever so quietly.

"It's . . . it's nothing . . . They're probably bad people . . . it's for fun, or for target practice. Think no more about it."

"But why do virgins have to smile at such times?" insisted Alice.

"Why do they smile? How do you mean? What are you saying, child? Has this happened to you often, Alice?"

"Oh yes, very often, almost every day, when I've been alone, or with Bibi."

"What about your girlfriends?"

"They complain about it too. It's impossible not to smile," she went on pensively, "even though it hurts."

"This is novel," thought Paul as he returned home. "Moving,

even brutal. Throwing a rock at a virgin — I've never heard anything like it. True, such things are generally kept secret. She herself says it takes place only when no one is watching. It's brutal — yes, but at the same time enchanting; and why? Because it's instinctive. I'm touched, and curiously excited. Ah, the virginal world, the world of love, is full of such magical peculiarities. Strangers smile at one another on the street; someone strokes someone else's elbow; a smile through tears, or a kiss by rubbing noses, is not at all odder than throwing a rock. It's possible that there exists an entire code of agreed-upon signs and ways about which I, living all this time among the savages in China and Africa, know nothing.

"Maidenhood is distinguished by the fact that for it, everything takes on a different meaning than it has in reality. For a virginal man, throwing a rock is not rocking one's dignity to the same degree as even the slightest touch of the hand on a cheek. An ordinary person, a normal woman, would run away with a scream; whereas she — she smiled on account of some unfathomable depths. An ordinary person would think exclusively of fleeing the field of battle and, if only possible, saving their own skin; whereas for me, on the contrary, all is honor and the flag — the standard, that is, strictly speaking, a colored rag flapping in the wind.

"A monarchy is more virginal than a republic, since it contains more mystery than do the garrulous members of parliament. A monarch — exalted, sinless, immaculate, free of responsibility — is a virgin, while to a lesser extent a general too is a virgin.

"O sacred mystery of being, O miracle of existence: As I receive your gifts, I will not be the one to keep an eye on you. Quite the opposite — nothing but a humbly inclined head, veneration and gratitude, pantheism and contemplation, and no analyses disastrous in their consequences. Maidenhood and mystery—that alone; then let us guard against the lifting of the sacred curtain."

For her part, Alice also abandoned herself to reflection.

"How strange the world is! In it no one answers straightforwardly but always symbolically. It's never possible to find anything out. Paul was of course recounting a legend. I'm surrounded on all sides by symbols and legends, as if everyone were in cahoots against me. Paradise, God . . . who knows if that too wasn't made up especially for me—for us young ladies. I'm convinced that everyone is concealing something and pretending, and it's all a conspiracy. And Mama and Paul are in league together. It's pleasant to slurp one's tea and step on puppy-dogs' tails. . . . Yes. . . . Religion, duty and virtue, yet it seems to me that beyond this, as if it were a screen, there are certain strictly determined gestures, certain movements; that every lofty watchword like this will be brought down to a strictly determined gesture and a strictly determined point.

"Oh, I can imagine! Normally everyone is dressed and behaves politely—but when they're left one on one, the men throw rocks at the women, and the women smile because it hurts. Then—they steal . . . for did I myself not steal a silver spoon and bury it in the garden, not knowing what to do with it?—Mama sometimes reads aloud from the newspapers about thefts; now I understand what that means. They steal, slurp their tea, tread on dogs' feet and generally act out of spite, and this is love—while virgins are brought up in unawareness so that . . . things should be more agreeable. I'm all atremble."

Alice to Paul:

*Paul! Things are not quite the way you say. I feel so scattered! Yesterday
I heard Mama telling Father that the unemployed were "multiplying"
horribly—that they walk around "half-naked," eat all kinds of
disgusting offal, and that the number of thefts, brawls, and robberies
was shooting up. Tell me everything—tell me what it means, what
they need that "offal" for, why "half-naked"; Paul, I beg you, please,
I want to know finally where I am; yours forever—Alice.*

Paul to Alice:

*My darling one! What is whirling around in this noggin of mine! I
implore you by our love, never think about all that. Admittedly there
are such things, and one sees them sometimes; but by dwelling on
them, one can lose one's virginity just like that—and then what would
happen? The truth contained in purity is infinitely superior to the
sordidness of reality. Let us be unaware, let us live by innocence, by
our youthful, virginal instinct, and let us guard from mentally looking
into places we shouldn't, as once happened to me in the past, when I
met you. Awareness disfigures, unawareness adorns; yours for all time
—Paul.*

"Instinct," thought Alice—"instinct . . . yes . . . but what does
that instinct want, what do *I* want in fact? I myself don't know . . .
to die, or to eat something tart. I won't regain my calm until . . .
I'm so unaware; I have a blindfold over my eyes, as Paul says . . . at
times it's simply frightening . . . Instinct, my virginal instinct—
that will show me the way!"

The next day she spoke to her fiancé, who was gazing in rapture
at her elbow:

"Paul . . . I sometimes have the wildest notions!"

"So much the better, my darling; that's exactly what I expected of you," he responded. "After all, what would you be without whims and notions. I adore that pure unwisdom!"

"But my notions are strange, Paul . . . so strange I'm embarrassed to say what they are."

"You can't have any other kind, unaware as you are," he replied. "The wilder and the stranger the notion, the greater will be my zeal in carrying it out, my flower. Yielding to it, I'll pay homage to your virginity and mine."

"But . . . you see . . . it's—in fact, it's somehow different . . . In any case, I'm sort of scattered by it. Tell me, have . . . have you also . . . like other people . . . have you ever stolen?"

"Who do you take me for, Alice? What's the meaning of these words? Could you even for a moment be drawn to a man soiled by such an offense? I've always tried to be pure and worthy of you, naturally in my own, male domain."

"I don't know, I don't know, Paul—but tell me, only please, please be honest—tell me, have you ever, you know—deceived someone, or bit them, or walked around . . . half-naked; or have you ever slept on a wall; or have you ever beaten someone, or licked them; or have you ever eaten something revolting?"

"Child! What are you saying? Where have you gotten all this from? Alice, think for a moment . . . I, lick someone or deceive them? What about my honor? You must be mad!"

"Oh, Paul," said Alice, "what a marvelous day—there's not a single cloud, and you have to shield your eyes with your hand."

Absorbed in their conversation, they walked right around the house and found themselves by the kitchen—where on a pile of refuse lay a bone with scraps of pink meat abandoned by Bibi.

"Look, Paul—a bone," said Alice.

"Let's go from here," said Paul.—"Let's go from here; in this place there are bad smells and the shouts of the kitchen maids. No, Alice, I'm surprised that such ideas could come out of that sweet little head of yours."

"Wait, Paul, wait—let's not go away just yet—Bibi obviously didn't finish gnawing it . . . Paul . . . oh, what am I like—I myself don't know . . . Paul."

"What it is, darling—maybe you feel faint? Perhaps the sun has tired you—it's awfully hot."

"Not at all, nothing of the sort . . . See how it's looking at us—as if it wanted to bite us—to eat us up. Do you love me very much?"

They stopped in front of the bone, which Bibi sniffed and licked, refreshing her memory.

"Do I love you? I love you so much that I think you could only find another love like that in the mountains."

"I'd really like it, Paul, if you'd gnaw it—that is, if together we gnawed the bone on the trash heap. Don't look, I'm blushing"— she nestled up to him—"don't look at me now."

"The bone? What was that, Alice—what? What did you say?"

"Paul," said Alice, clinging to him—"that . . . rock, you know, stirred a particular unease in me. I don't want to know about anything, don't say anything to me—but I'm troubled by the garden and the roses, and the wall, and the white of my dress, and, oh, I don't know, perhaps I'd like my back to be bruised . . . The rock whispered to me, whispered to my back, that there's something behind that wall—and that I'll eat that something, gnaw it in this bone, that is, we'll gnaw it jointly, Paul, you with me, me with you; I must, I must"—she insisted vehemently—"without it I'll have to die young!"

Paul was dumbstruck.

"Child, what do you need a bone for? You've gone mad! If you absolutely must, then have them bring you a fresh bone from the broth."

"But the point is precisely that it has to be this one, from the trash heap!" cried Alice, stamping her foot. "And secretly, out of fear of the cook!"

And suddenly a quarrel broke out between them, as hot and dizzy as the burning July sun, which was dropping toward the west. "Really, Alice, this is disgusting, noxious—ugh—it makes me quite simply sick. I mean, it's right here that the cook throws out the slops!"—"The slops? I feel sick too, I also feel faint—I've a hankering for slops as well! Believe me, for sure, it can be gnawed, Paul, it can be eaten!—everyone does it, I feel it—when no one else is watching."

They argued for a long time. "It's disgusting!"—"It's blind, strange, mysterious, shameful and lovely!"—"Alice!" exclaimed Paul in the end, rubbing his eyes—"for the love of God . . . —though I'm beginning to have doubts. What is this? Dream or waking? I don't want to keep asking, heaven forbid, I'm not curious, but. . . . Are you perhaps joking, making fun of me, Alice? What's happened here? The rock, you say? Is it possible—that rocks should be thrown and that out of this . . . that this should result in some kind of unhealthy greed for bones? Surely that would be too wild, too—impure somehow; no, I respect your notions, but this—it's no longer virginal instinct, but—made up off the top of your head."

"My head?" replied Alice—"But Paul, is my head not virginal? After all, you yourself said that one should close one's eyes, unthinkingly and quietly, naïvely and purely and—oh, Paul, quick, look how the sun is gleaming, and that little insect is crawling so sleepily along the leaf, and I'm so scattered! I tell you, everyone does the same thing, we're the only ones who don't know about it! Oh, it seems to you that no one ever . . . at anyone . . . but I'm telling you that in the evenings the rocks whizz by like heavy rain, so much that one can't even blink; and in the shade of the trees, bones and other refuse are gnawed out of hunger, half-nakedly! That is love—love."

"Ah! You've gone mad!"

"Stop it!" she cried, tugging him by the sleeve. "Come on, let's go to the bone!"

"Not for anything! Not for anything!"

And in his despair he might have struck her! But at that moment, on the other side of the wall, they heard something like a thud and a groan. They ran across and poked their heads through the climbing roses: There, on the street, beneath a tree, a young barefoot girl was pressing her lips against her own raised knee as she doubled up in pain.

"What's this?" whispered Paul.

All at once a new rock cut through the air and hit the girl on the neck — she fell over, but leapt up right away and jumped behind the tree — and from somewhere in the distance there came a man's roar:

"I'll show you what's what! I'll give you a good hiding! You'll see! You thief!"

The air caressed and scorched; a silence descended in nature, one of those trembling, fragrant engrossments . . .

"You see?" whispered Alice.

"What's that?"

"They're throwing at girls . . . throwing rocks . . . just for enjoyment, for pleasure . . ."

"No, no . . . it's not possible . . ."

"You saw it yourself. Come on, the bone's waiting for us, let's go to that bone! We'll gnaw it together — do you want to? — together! Me with you, you with me! See, I already have it in my mouth! And now you! Now you!"

Adventures

✢✦

I

In 1930, in September, on a boat trip to Cairo, I fell into the Mediterranean Sea; I fell with a mighty splash, since at the time the sea was smooth, unruffled by any wave. Nevertheless, my fall was noticed only a minute later, after the ship had already sailed a kilometer and a half on—and when it was finally turned around and sent back in my direction, the agitated captain gave it too much speed and the immense vessel's momentum carried it past the place where I was choking on salt water. One more time they turned and set course toward me—but this time too the ship sped past me like a freight train and stopped much too far away. This maneuver was repeated perhaps ten times, with uncommon persistence. In the meantime a private steam yacht sailed up and took me on board; on seeing this, my ship, the *Orient*, sailed away.

The owner and captain of the yacht had me bound and thrown

into a compartment below deck; this was because when he was changing his shoes in my presence I foolishly betrayed my surprise at the sight of his white foot. Though his face was white, I would have wagered good money that his foot would be black as pitch — and yet it was absolutely white! As a result of which he conceived an undying hatred for me. He realized that I had seen through his physiological secret, which no one in the entire world besides me had guessed — that is, that he was a white black man. (In fact, if the truth be told, that whole affair was merely a pretext.) For the following eight months he sailed without a break, always forward, ahead, across numerous seas, stopping only to take on fuel — and all the while he reveled in the boundless freedom of his will with regard to me, locked up as I was in the windowless compartment — and always at his disposition.

Of course, all hatred soon had to vanish in the vastness of that freedom; and if despite this fact he condemned me to a cruel death, it was not so much for my suffering as for his own gratification. He thought for a long time about how, with me as an intermediary, he could enjoy experiences that he would never have dared to try on his own — just like the Englishwoman who placed a bug in a matchbox and threw it over Niagara Falls. And when I was finally brought up on deck, besides fear I also experienced the emotions of nostalgia, sorrow, and gratitude — for I had to confess the kind of death he had contrived for me was almost the same kind that I had once imagined, or dreamed about, once before, in my early childhood. — With the aid of specially procured devices which I shall refrain from describing, an extraordinarily difficult task was accomplished — as a result of which I found myself inside a glass bubble in the shape of a large egg, large enough that I could move my arms and legs freely, and too small for me to shift from a lying position.

The glass was about three centimeters thick. On its entire surface there was not a single blemish or seam — in one place only a small opening had been drilled to let in air. Take a huge egg and prick it with a pin — that was the egg in which I found myself, and I had as much room as a chicken embryo has.

Then the black man showed me a chart of the Atlantic Ocean and indicated the position of our boat; we were more or less in the middle of the ocean, between Spain and northern Mexico. In this place there flows the powerful Gulf Stream from America toward the English Channel and the northern shores of Britain and Scandinavia. Yet the map clearly indicated how at a distance of a thousand miles from Europe the Gulf Stream splits, and its southern branch turns south, to the right, and becomes the Canary Current. After which, somewhere around Senegambia the Canary Current turns right once again (or rather, left on the map) as the Equatorial Current; and the Equatorial Current then swings right — or upward — to become the Antilles Channel, named for the islands — and the Antilles Channel, once more turning right, joins with the Gulf Stream to begin everything all over again. In this manner the currents form a closed circle with a diameter of between fifteen hundred and two thousand kilometers. If you had thrown a piece of wood from the deck of our boat into the ocean — you could be sure that in half a year or one year, or perhaps three years, the frothing waters would bring it from the west back to the same place whence it had floated eastward.

"We'll throw you into the water in the glass bubble"—the black man's words could be summarized thus. "No storm will drown you—you have with you a packet of three thousand bouillon cubes, in other words, if you suck one cube a day, you have provisions for ten years; you also have a small but reliable device for filtering water . . . Besides, you'll never run short of water; you'll have quite enough of it as you bob constantly on the waves and below the waves, involuntarily, round and round, for a decade; and later, when you die from the lack of bouillon cubes, your corpse will continue to circulate on its designated route, around and around and around."

They threw me into the ocean. At first the egg sank down deep —after which it floated up. . . . An approaching wave (and the day was windy and sunless, the surface of the water deeply furrowed, in constant, intense movement) seized me on its olive-colored crest and for a moment bore me heavily along—then, having lifted me before it, with a roar and a splash it cast me down into the swirling waters. Below the surface things were calm and green. But I had barely managed to notice once again the murky and blurred sky when, like the finger of God above me, a vertical column of water thrust me into a whirling chasm, this time for at least a minute. A third wave bore the bubble along gently for some time—it ran before me, I slipped down its retreating slope and found some peace in a dip. Then there came a fourth, a fifth, and a sixth wave. And what happened during a storm was something else again! Stooping giants, hunchbacked monsters lifted me up to raging heights, only to hurl me down to the very bottom of the precipice!—while naturally, there could be no question that they might drown me. The black man's boat followed behind me for two weeks or so — in the end, apparently tired and sated, he sailed away.

In accordance with the instructions I had received, I sucked on one bouillon cube a day, washing it down with filtered water which I drew in through a rubber pipe. In this way I had the privilege of satisfying the longing felt by all those who have looked upon the sea from the several-storied heights of steamships, unable to participate in it. And I was never able to determine any sequence whatsoever in my perpetual motion; I was never able to predict whether the water would carry me, or thrust me down, or merely jostle me and toss me aside, whether it would turn me face up or face down to the sky; nor could I ever discern any forward movement — though I knew I was going in an easterly direction. Nothing else was there but peaks and valleys, roaring and plashing, little geysers, chance gurglings, rushing, billowing, vertical walls, inclined slopes, masses that disappeared — goodness knows how — beneath me, great swells, sudden drops, retreating crests that loomed up, the view from the top and the view from below, peaks and valleys, peaks and valleys, the work of the Ocean. And in the end I gave up. Only once did I observe a solitary log, which for many days had accompanied me at a distance of a few kilometers, gradually moving farther away and vanishing in the murky space steeped in salt and mist. At that time I wanted to shout out in my egg, because I realized that the log was being carried toward the shores of Europe, while I was turning with the southern branch of the current toward the Canary Islands, in order to remain forever in a closed circuit — around and around and around — the black man had calculated it well! But instead of shouting I began to sing, because the element of the sea disposed me to singing.

A ship of the French Chargeurs Réunis Society collided with me, breaking the glass, and fished me out of the water. In such a way these wanderings of mine came to an end. But this happened only after a few years. Set down in the port of Valparaiso, I immediately began to flee from the black man, because I knew he would pursue me.

2

That the black man would pursue me was as obvious as the stars in the sky, for this reason: that anyone who has once experienced someone the way he had experienced me—or to put it even more plainly: anyone who has once experienced the fun that he experienced with me—can never let go again, like a tiger who has had a taste of human flesh. In human flesh there is without a doubt an element that you cannot find anywhere else. And so I fled across the entire continent of America and farther to the west—and of all the places on earth it seemed to me that the safest would be Iceland. But as bad luck would have it, I lacked the strength to withstand the stare of the customs officer in Reykjavík, and I confessed. I have never smuggled anything in my life, and I have always looked customs officers right in the eye and opened my suitcases of my own accord. Every time I would walk away having earned their praise. Consequently, this time my unclean conscience did not endure the mute reproach in the official gaze and I confessed —that though my luggage contained nothing in contravention of the regulations, nevertheless not all was in order with me, for I was smuggling myself. The officer did not make any difficulties—but he must have informed the appropriate person, for less than two days later the black man appeared and imprisoned me on his boat.

And once again I found myself in the compartment below deck, appeasing through my captivity the black man's domineering unboundedness; he steered the ship forward at full speed, sparing neither coal nor steam, while he himself was constantly scheming and debating with himself—which fate of the infinite number of fates, and which point of the infinite number of points on the map, he should make mine. As for me, I accepted this completely naturally, as if I had been destined for precisely this since birth. Besides, I knew how it would end—certainly not with something that was entirely new and unknown to me, but with something I was familiar with, something I knew, for which perhaps I had long been yearning. When finally, after months of stifling confinement, I felt the refreshing sea air, I saw that the deck in the stern was sagging under the weight of a steel sphere (or rather, a steel cone) whose shape was somewhat reminiscent of an artillery shell.

For this pleasure he must have laid out a good few million. I realized at once that the sphere must be hollow inside, for otherwise—where was I supposed to go? And indeed, when a hatch on the side was unscrewed and I looked inside, I saw a little room the size of an ordinary little room. This steel room without ornaments or additions I greeted as *my* room. Yet—despite the fact that the walls of the sphere were extraordinarily thick—I still did not entirely understand the black man's intentions, and it was only when he told me that we were located on the Pacific Ocean at the point where the deepest trench in the world is found, dropping to a depth of seventeen thousand meters, that I got it . . . and though I felt terror in my neck and in my fingertips, I still gave an enigmatic smile with the corners of my mouth, greeting what was long known, long familiar, long *mine*.

And so I was to be the only living creature who would experience the gentle thud of the sphere against the ocean bed beneath us, the only being who would squirm in the place where there are not even any crustaceans. The only one who would know absolute darkness, deadness, and despair. In a word, it was a thoroughly unique fate. And as for the black man, it was clear he was burning with curiosity (nor was he alone in this) to know what was down there — and he was tormented by the thought that that realm was forever inaccessible to him, that the cold, rocky region was foreign to his embraces, and while he sailed on the surface, it was there in the depths — thoroughly there. So it was not at all surprising that he wanted to *find out*, and that tomorrow at this time . . . tomorrow he really would *know*, through seventeen kilometers of water, that I was squirming on the ocean bed, and without showing it outwardly, he would possess the secret of the depths — having lowered me as a probe to the very bottom.

And yet, just as I was about to enter my tomb, it emerged that an error had been committed in the calculations and that despite the thickness of the walls the specific gravity of the sphere was insufficient — it would not sink beneath the water. In light of this the black man gave the order to fasten a huge hook to the sphere, to attach a chain to the hook, and on the chain to hang ballast that was to pull me after itself — ballast so calculated as not to unduly shorten the time of the descent.

For the last time the black man showed me the map—it was very important to him that, as I perished, I should have before my eyes the point with which I was to be united for all time. I was screwed into the sphere. The final darkness came; I felt a rough jolt—I had been thrown into the sea and had begun to drop down. But I must say that what I experienced then was quite different from what I had expected. Namely, I had expected a certain relation to reality at this moment—yet in fact the darkness and the thickness of the sphere's walls meant that I lost all mental sense of what was happening, and I knew only that I was descending, that I was falling, being submerged, that I was moving downward. Curled up on the steel floor, I breathed shallowly. On the other hand, there was only a slight bump at the conclusion of my two-hour journey! A bump that announced I had already come to rest! I saw with my penetrating brain how first the ballast touched down on the ocean floor, and then the sphere's impetus caused it to knock against the ballast and then how in turn it rose upward slightly, stretching the chain. And so here I was finally—I was at the very bottom, in the most secret place of the Atlantic—I was here—and I was alive!—leg touching leg! And up above, directly over me, at a distance of seventeen kilometers was the black man, the black man reveling in the thought that he now knew what happens down on that unattainable ocean floor, that he had imposed his will on it, that he had sent down a probe, that he had warmed and possessed that cold and alien floor by means of my torture.

But the torture gradually intensified to the point that I began to worry it might render suffering and possession impossible, turning everything, including myself, into nothing but a dance of madmen. I began to fear that the torture would end up becoming something insufficiently human for the black man to draw any benefit from it. I will spare you the details. I will mention only that immediately after the sphere settled for good, the darkness, which, as I already indicated, was from the very beginning at its greatest, increased even more, to the point that I had to hide my face in my hands and, having done so, was quite unable to tear them away again even for a second—they stuck to my face. Furthermore, my consciousness could not tolerate the terrible pressure, the fearful crushing and pushing, and I began to choke—since the air was still relatively good, I was choking imaginarily—I was choking prematurely, as I was still breathing, which is possibly the most dreadful form of asphyxiation. And what was worse, my convulsive movements, the movements of an insect, seemed to me here, in seclusion, to be so monstrous in their subjectlessness that I was overcome by fear of myself and could not stand the fact that I was moving. My individuality peeped out from that awful underwater abyss so differently from what it had been like in the light of day, or even (I may use this term here) by the light of night up there, above —how monstrous it had become! My pallor, which the perfect darkness seemed to have deprived of hue and expression—my pallor, crammed inside, blinded, mute, gagged—was something that in its essence was different from any pallor, even the most ghostly, but which could be seen—and also my hair standing on end, here, in the steel, under the water, was almost as terrible as a terrible cry would have been in this situation—a cry from which I forcibly restrained myself, since immediately after it I would have had to go mad—and that was something I did not wish.

Oh, I simply cannot convey how terrifying our Self becomes when it is displaced to a domain in which it is alien—nor how inhuman a person can become when he is used as a probe, nor the extent to which inhumanity surpasses any evil a person may encounter. Yet this was not what I meant to speak about, in fact—rather I wish to describe the manner in which I managed to escape from my plight. Well then: All of a sudden, unable to stand it any longer, I began to thrash and toss myself about, to jump up as high as I could and knock against the walls with all my strength (and this certainly figured into the plans of the black man, who was waiting patiently up above)—I began with all my power to push, to smash, to attack the steel, crashing into it, to clench my fists, strain, and thrust until I produced some result. This futile frenzy evidently produced some movement, some friction outside. I don't know if the chain broke, perhaps rusted through, or if the loop of the chain slipped off the hook, or if the ballast had been poorly constructed and had fallen apart at the slightest jolt; suffice it to say that suddenly there came liberation, deliverance, relief . . . The sphere moved upward with increasing speed and a few minutes later, driven by massive pressure, I shot into space like a cork, to a height of one kilometer or more.

I was soon unscrewed by the crew of the merchant ship *Halifax*. I do not know what became of the black man. Perhaps the sphere smashed his yacht as it fell; or perhaps, entirely satisfied with what had happened, he had sailed away to reminisce. In any case, for the longest time I lost sight of him. The *Halifax* put into Pernambuco, from where I returned to Poland to take a rest.

At this same time a gigantic flaming meteor fell into the

Caspian Sea, which evaporated in its entirety in a single moment. Bulging, swollen layers of cloud encircled the earth and hovered just above it, threatening a second great flood; and sometimes the sun burst out from between them with a cluster of hot rays. A great despondency reigned. No one knew how to drag the huge sluggish bodies safely back to the seabed they had come from. Finally someone began to tickle one of the clouds — just as it happened to be approaching the empty sea — at the darkest purple place on its drooping, distended torso. It opened its sluices. Then, when it was completely emptied, into the blue vacuum created by its disappearance there began to float other clouds and one after another, mechanically and automatically now, they poured out their waters and formed the lake once again.

3

Returning to my home in the country, in Sandomierz province, I rested, hunted a little, played some bridge, rode out to visit the neighbors . . . and on one of these visits there was a young person whom I would gladly have clothed in a veil and wedding gown. Everything had quieted down. The black man, as I said, had vanished somewhere, or perhaps he did not exist at all; moreover, fall was coming, leaves were falling, and the air, crisper every day, inclined a person to exhortations, speed, longing, and playfulness. Just for fun I started thinking about constructing an excursion balloon of the Montgolfier type. And soon this balloon of mine was ready. It was covered with a special impermeable canvas that was extremely light yet strong, and its lifting power was heated air. That is to say, at the bottom the canvas was pulled tight around an iron band in such a way as to leave a sizable opening—into the opening was put an ordinary kerosene lamp fixed on two iron prongs attached to the band. One had only to light the lamp and turn the wick up a little for the balloon to inflate and stretch the cords linking it to the basket. I was easily able to store the rolled-up material of the balloon in a barn—and when I filled it with air (which always took about an hour) its diameter was between thirty and forty meters.

Such a simple solution to something of the greatest difficulty—that is, the use of a tiny lamp with a balloon of such dimensions—I attribute less to my own technical abilities than to a certain sluggish unrestrainedness which at that time had swept over nature. But I do not deny that the first time I sat in the basket, I took fright at the sight of the immensity that was becoming reality above me—but it was an immensity that was light and empty inside, and gentle as a child.

The very process of heating the balloon, of the swelling of that huge sphere, the tautening of the ropes, the growing elasticity, the hissing of the lamp—this alone provided great satisfaction. I had to wait a considerable time for the air to expand sufficiently. At last the balloon unexpectedly and quickly began to rise. I hurriedly turned down the wick; nevertheless, it stopped ascending only above the highest trees in my garden. A mild breeze carried it over the fields in the direction of that familiar neighbor's house. I floated across the woods and the river, then the village, from which the delighted populace sent me shouts and greetings—and I found myself at a height of fifty meters over the familiar court-yard, before the columned entranceway familiar and so dear to me. I turned down the wick, and the balloon landed softly on the lawn; next to it the house looked like a child's toy. What astonishment there was! How much laughter and applause, how many compliments for me and for the balloon! Nothing like it had ever been seen! Supper was interrupted to come and marvel—then I was invited to have coffee with cheese and preserves, after which I took one single passenger into the basket and turned up the wick.

The physical delight of this ride above all came from the fact that the balloon was *huge and inflated*, and also from the following: 1) that one could float right over people's heads, yet out of reach of their outstretched hands; 2) that on encountering a house or a tree, one could rise up higher and then return to just above the earth; 3) that the balloon, though immense, was extraordinarily sensitive, quiet, and responsive to the slightest caprice of the air, while we in the basket were exactly the same as the balloon, and took on its mild, childlike soul; 4) that a gust of air, which would do no more than graze the cheeks of other people, would in our case lift us up, and it was never possible to predict our movements in space; 5) that there was no machinery at all except for a single kerosene lamp, not even any gas, but only canvas, ropes, a basket, and us in the air, canvas, ropes, a basket, and us in the air; 6) and lastly—the magnificent spherical *shadow* passing over the lawn. But to me personally the balloon's passenger brought more joy than the balloon itself. Over the meadows, fields, and groves I grew acquainted for the first time in my life, I grew acquainted without a break and ever more closely, and she listened to me so willingly that I would have kissed her small, attentive, comprehending ear a thousand times over. But despite the fact that women are supposed to love romanticism, I said nothing to her about the black man or about my other adventures—on account of a puzzling yet burning sense of shame that warned me not to say too much.

The day came for us to exchange rings—then the wedding day began to approach. During all this time I had not once had any bad thoughts; I had driven away all my memories, and lived only for her and the balloon; I lived from today, from yesterday—unless I hastened into the future, on a calm, level road of happiness—and even bad dreams forsook me. Never . . . not one deviation . . . not one glance toward what had after all once truly existed . . . but had vanished . . . —and a birch tree was a birch tree, a pine—a pine, a willow—a willow. —And here is what happened. —One day, a week before our wedding ceremony in the local church, when a mysterious, joyful prenuptial shiver was running through me, and everyone was congratulating and sending good wishes, I suddenly got the urge to try a balloon ride on a stormy night. I just wanted to experience swinging in a violent gale—I swear I had no other intentions, no bad desires. However, the gale swept me away with furious force (and in fact it was probably not the gale, but the black man himself), and when after many hours the curtain of dawn rose with alarming rapidity, I could not believe my eyes—beneath me lay the Yellow Sea.

I realized at once that the other matter was over, and once again . . . it had started . . . and . . . and . . . some fearful Oriental things awaited me—I bid farewell forever to the birches, pines, and willows, and the familiar countenance and eyes, and I opened myself submissively to the crooked pagodas, bonzes, idols, mandarins, and dragons. As the last drop of kerosene was burning down in the lamp, the basket dropped into the water off the shore of a small islet. From a nearby thicket a Chinaman emerged—he shouted when he noticed me and ran up, but I began to wave at him to stop, because (of course) he was a leper. He stood undecided, looked at me watchfully, gave a nondescript grunt, as if in surprise, touched his hideous, lumpy exterior—and led me to a dozen or so wretched reed shacks that could be seen in the distance. He went on staring at me attentively, and I could not figure out what that stare meant. I already sensed something . . . yet despite this, I continued to follow him.

When, however, we reached the settlement, my skin began to cry for help—it contracted, it crawled, it tightened, it went mad from terror! The entire village without exception was composed of lepers: the old folk, and the men, and the women, and the young girls, and the young boys, apart from a few small children who were set glaringly apart by their smoothness. This particular form of the illness was called, to the best of my knowledge, *lepra anaesthetica*, or perhaps *lepra elephantiasis*; everything was rough, lumpy, carbuncular, tumid, and excrescent, in dull white, brown, or dirty red blotches, in pustules, scales, calluses, hardenings, in chronic ulcers. But they were not humble or modest like their brothers in the cities of Asia who warn of their revolting presence from far off with a cry. Oh no, not at all; it must be acknowledged at once that they had nothing in common with modesty or humility! Quite the reverse—they formed a circle around me and crowded in on me so inquisitively and shamelessly, and they reached toward me so with horny and twisted fingernails, that I threw myself at them, screaming and waving my fists. They instantly disappeared into their shacks. I left the village at once—but when I turned my head a few hundred paces on, I saw that the mob had come back out and was following me at a distance. I stamped my foot. They disappeared, but a moment later they reemerged.

The island was no more than fifteen square kilometers in area, and it could be said that it was entirely uninhabited; the greater part of its surface was covered by a dense forest. I walked along not particularly quickly and yet without a pause, not particularly nervously and yet stiffly, not particularly fearfully, and yet with a slightly quickened pace—for the whole time I could sense the blotchy monsters behind my back. I didn't want to turn around; I wanted to pretend that I knew nothing, that I could see nothing, and that only my back warned me of their slow approach. I walked and walked . . . I walked in various directions like a traveler, like a tourist, like a searcher, first here, then there, more and more hurriedly, like a person with urgent business, but in the end I ran out of space and, having exhausted all the unwooded places, I started down a path into the tangled depths of the forest. They drew significantly nearer—they were already right behind, and I could hear their whispers and the rustle of the branches. Spotting someone's lumpy skin creeping along behind a bush, I turned sharply to the left, jumped to the side as I caught sight amid the lianas of something like a hand in an advanced state of elephantiasis—and came out onto a little clearing. They followed me. Again I stamped my foot—they retreated into the jungle. I walked on; they thronged forward again, persistent as rats, and their whispers, prods, and nudges were becoming ever bolder. Every hair of mine was stiff as a wire—what had these carbuncle-people seen in me? What were they after? Women know this—when all at once they're accosted from behind with filthy jokes by an unruly band of good-for-nothings, while they scurry along with lowered head—and that is just how it was with me, exactly the same, point for point . . .

What did they want? I did not yet understand, I did not immediately grasp the new idea, but I already mentioned the resemblance point for point . . . and if one went deeper into the essence of the situation from which I had been torn and suddenly transported onto this island—into that premarital anxiety, the church and the veil—then things could not have been any different . . . In a word—it had become clear that I excited them, that I excited them in a particular way—and though I could not fathom the source of this excitement, nor the meaning of their exclamations, their laughs, their revolting jokes, nevertheless the filthiness, the licentiousness, the lasciviousness were palpable—and in the voices of the men-monsters I sensed the lustful brutality, and in the voices of the women-monsters the spiteful amusement, which tended without exception to be brought out in human beings of all races and latitudes in only two cases—innocence or immaturity . . . Oh, I would have accepted the leprosy alone; but not leprosy and eroticism together, oh no, for the love of God, erotic leprosy? I took flight like a madman. Seeing this, they rushed after me with a shout. But their plodding elephantine shanks were no match for my mad panic! I hid in the spreading crown of a tree, armed myself with a stout cudgel and swore to myself I'd crack the skull of the first one who came near.

And there gradually was revealed to me the infernal combination—the infernal substance of this torture . . . I discovered the entire complex mechanism of probabilities that made this fantasy real. No ship had visited the island for two or three centuries; it had been forgotten, as sometimes happens with such small and infertile little islands. Its inhabitants had never seen a stranger here either in their own lifetime or that of their parents.

Very well—but how should one understand the bawdiness, the lascivious jibes, the fearful pursuit, and the desire to accost? Oh, it was easy! It was easy—one had only to enter into the psychology of the black man's Spirit, which had arranged all this (and in this respect I had already notched up certain experiences). Since time immemorial, perhaps several generations, perhaps four, leprosy had afflicted them—and over the years they had assimilated it, accepted it as a natural quality of humankind. . . . Blotchiness was, in their eyes, as natural to human beings as colorfulness is to butterflies; lumps were as natural as a rooster's comb; and it would have been no easier for them to comprehend a person without carbuncles and pustules than it would have been for us to comprehend a person without a single hair on his skin. And since they had not renounced love—since their children were born healthy, smooth, and pure—since it was only after a few years that they yielded to the pestilence, and the time when the skin began to thicken and form scales coincided with puberty . . . coming at the time of the first kiss . . . the first charms of love . . . accordingly, seeing me ridiculously smooth, utterly uncarbuncled, amusingly thin, just some hopping creature with a little pink face (oh yes, for them carbuncles, blotches, calluses, star-shaped and spindle-shaped pustules were what colors are for a butterfly, and what for us is the hair that turns a child into a man)—they had to think what they thought. They had to nudge one another, taunt, mock, and torment, and when they realized that I was afraid of them, that, embarrassed and disgraced, I was running away—they had to send their monstrous maturity in delighted pursuit of my timid innocence, by the same infernal law that governs boys in school!

On that island I survived two months of a monkey's existence, hiding in the hollows of trees, in dense bushes and the tops of palms. The monsters organized formal hunts for me. Nothing could have amused them better than the embarrassment with which I rushed from their touch—they hid in the undergrowth, jumped out unexpectedly, ran along with a merry and lascivious roar—and had it not been for the characteristic *odor hircinus*, had it not been for the decrepitude of their degenerated limbs, and the desperate fear that augmented my strength, I would have fallen into their clutches a hundred times over. And above all, if it had not been for my skin—my skin, contracting without a moment's rest, susceptible, chapped, terrified, exhausted, in eternal perturbation. I ceased to be anything else but skin—with it I would fall asleep and wake up, it was my only, it was my all.

In the end I discovered by chance a few bottles of kerosene that had probably come from a shipwreck. I managed to patch up the balloon—and I sailed away. . . . But when I saw once again the beeches and pines, et cetera, and the familiar eyes, what on earth was I to do? What was I to do, I, who was after all smooth, without lumps, without blotches, without calluses, without scales or ulcers, thoroughly uncarbuncled? . . . What was I to do; could I now, pink and childlike, look into those eyes?

But since I could not—then I could not—and I parted from that which parted from me. . . . Besides, soon afterward I was swept up by other adventures; oh yes, I never lacked for adventures. I remember that in 1918 it was I and no one else who broke through the German line. As was common knowledge, the trenches reached all the way to the seashore—it was a true system of deep, dry channels that stretched unbroken for five hundred kilometers or so. And I was the only one who conceived the idea of irrigating those channels. In the night I crept up, dug a ditch, and linked the trenches with the sea. The water, surging uncontrollably, flooded them along the entire front, and the astonished Coalition armies saw the Germans soaked to the skin and jumping up in panic in the faint light of a misty morning.

The Events on the *Banbury*

⊁⊰

I

In the spring of 1930, I decided to undertake a trip by sea—for personal reasons—to do with health and relaxation. It was mainly that my situation on the European continent was becoming more disagreeable and indistinct with every day. So I wrote to a shipping magnate of my acquaintance, Mr. Cecil Burnett of Birmingham, to request that he find a berth for me on one of his numerous ships —and in no time at all I received a short reply by telegraph: "*Berenice* Brighton 17 April 09.00 sharp." But at Brighton, at the docks, there were so many sailing ships and steamships at anchor, and my baggage hindered my movements so, that I was a little less than fifteen minutes late, and the sailors and stevedores starting calling out urgently, as they always do—"Over there, over there, hurry up, sir, you can still make it!—hurry, hurry—get a move on, sir! You'll get there in time!" I caught up with the *Berenice* by motor launch, though without my luggage. A rope ladder was lowered, up which I climbed onto the deck, in my haste not reading the name painted in large letters on the port side of the hull.

It was a large three-masted brig with a capacity of at least four thousand tons—and, as I inferred from the arrangement of the sails and the design of the bowspit, was sailing to Valparaiso with a cargo of sprats and herring. Captain Clarke, an old sea dog with cheeks reddened by the wind, said straightforwardly:

"Welcome aboard the *Banbury*, sir."

The first officer agreed for a small sum to let me have his cabin. But soon the seas began to swell, and I was beset by seasickness with an intensity I had never experienced before. I rendered to the sea all that I had to render, and I groaned, void as an empty bottle and unable to meet the demands of the element, which was insisting on more, more . . . In a state of physical and moral torment, because of my unbearably empty stomach, I devoured my blanket, pillow, and window blind—but none of these objects remained inside me for longer than a second. I further devoured the bed-sheets and the first officer's underwear, which he kept in a trunk marked with the letters BBS—but that too stayed only temporarily in my innards. My groans passed through the cabin wall to the captain, who took pity on me and had a barrel of herring and a barrel of sprats rolled in. It was only toward the evening of the third day, after consuming three-quarters of the barrel of herring and half the sprats, that I more or less came to, and the movement of the pumps that cleaned out the ship came to a halt.

We were passing the northwest coast of Portugal. The *Banbury* was drifting at an average rate of eleven knots with a favorable headwind. The sailors were scrubbing the deck. I gazed at the rocky land of Europe as it receded. Farewell, Europe! I felt hollow, aseptic and light; only my throat hurt hellishly. Farewell, Europe! I took a handkerchief from my pocket and waved it a couple of times—at which a little man standing in a mountain ravine responded also with a wave. The ship moved briskly; water splashed at the bow and astern, and foaming billows rose as far as the eye could see.

The deckhands, who up till this point had been scrubbing the fore-gangway, now began scrubbing the aft-gangway—their bent backs came close to me and I had to move out of the way. The captain appeared for a moment on the bridge and raised a moistened finger to gauge the speed of the wind. That same day, toward evening, a curious, as it were cautionary incident occurred that was related in some unspecified manner to my recent sickness: one of the sailors, a certain Dick Harties of central Caledonia, accidentally swallowed the end of a thin rope hanging from the mizzenmast. As a consequence, I believe, of the peristaltic action of his digestive tract he began abruptly to draw the rope into himself—and before anyone had noticed, he had risen up it to the very top like a cable car in the mountains, his mouth gaping terrifyingly wide. The peristaltic character of his digestive tract proved so powerful that it was impossible to pull him down; in vain did two sailors cling to each of his legs. It was only after long deliberations that the first officer, whose name was Smith, had the idea of applying an emetic—but here another question arose: how could the emetic be introduced into the digestive tract since the latter was completely blocked by the rope? At last, after even longer deliberations, it was decided to act solely on the imagination through the eyes and nose. At the officer's order one of the deckhands shimmied up onto the mast and showed the patient a handful of severed rats' tails on a plate. The poor fellow looked at them with bulging eyes—but when a small fork was added to the tails, he suddenly remembered spaghetti from his childhood years—and he slid back down to the deck so fast he almost broke his legs. This incident ought to have made me think, as, I repeat, it bore a certain analogy to my indisposition—it was not exactly the same, yet both cases involved feelings of sickness, with the difference that his case was of an absorptive, inward character, whereas mine was quite the opposite—outward in direction. There was a certain erroneous resemblance here, much as in a mirror—the right ear appears on the left side, though the face is the same. Aside from this, the rats' tails also inclined one to reflection. Nevertheless, for the time being I did not pay sufficient heed to all this—nor to the fact that the ship and the backs of the sailors were not so foreign to me as they should have been, given the short time I had been on board.

The next day, over lunch, I asked Captain Clarke and Lieutenant Smith about the ship and about prospects for the remainder of the voyage.

"The ship is a good one," replied the captain, puffing away at his pipe.

"First rate!" confirmed Smith sarcastically.

"And even if it weren't first rate!" said the captain, surveying the expanse of waters with a proud and imperious gaze. "Even if it weren't first rate! Let's say there may be a crack here and there!"

"Exactly," said the first officer, looking at me antagonistically. "Even if it weren't first-rate. Anyone who's afraid of getting wet— is free to leave the ship whenever they wish. By all means!"—he gestured at the waves. —"The landlubber! God darn, that is, the . . . godda . . ."

"Mr. Smith," said the captain, jiggling his finger in his ear, "order the crew to shout three times: Long live Captain Clarke, hip hip hurrah!" We sailed on. The weather was favorable. The *Banbury* was plying an even course, its jib fully unfurled, amid steady waves. A sea cow appeared on the horizon. The sailors were now scrubbing the brass railings. They were being supervised by the second officer, while the captain gazed out of the window of his cabin, a toothpick in his mouth.

In this manner several days passed, in the course of which I explored the ship. It was an old vessel, seriously gnawed by rats, huge numbers of which had bred below—in places the hull was completely eaten away, while the stern, as if out of spite, was filled with rat droppings. All in all it was reminiscent of the old Spanish frigates. The excess of rats I found far from delightful—these rodents have disagreeable habits; their fat tails are so long, the pointed tips so far away, that they lose their sense of the tail's being connected with the rest of their body, as a consequence of which they are continuously prey to the ghastly illusion that they are dragging behind them a tasty piece of meat which is quite foreign to them and just right for devouring. This makes them very nervous. Sometimes they sink their teeth into their own tail, writhing with a squeal, as if mad with craving and in terrible pain. The arrangement of the rigging and the disposition of the tackle, like the design of the port side of the ship, entirely failed to meet with my approval—and when I saw the shape, dimensions, and hue of the ventilation pipes, I returned to my cabin with signs of great dissatisfaction and remained there till evening.

The crew intrigued me. I shall pass over the stoicism with which the sailors would scrub clean a designated part of the ship, utterly unconcerned by the fact that they were tossing dirty water over the part they had previously cleaned. But each time I tore my gaze from the sea and turned it toward the ship, I was struck by some unexpected sight. Thus, for example, I would see four sailors sitting cross-legged on the deck and staring at their own feet. On another occasion I saw a couple of seamen staring at their own hands. In the evenings, I would overhear phrases chanted for hours on end:

"Fish and sea birds feed behind the ship."

A great *cleanliness* prevailed on the vessel; soap and water were applied almost constantly. As I passed the sailors they would not raise their eyes—on the contrary, they would stoop all the more energetically over their work, such that I only ever saw backs bent like hoops. Yet I had the obscure impression that whenever I was engrossed in contemplation of the horizon, the deckhands would begin conversing, of course only if no officer was in the vicinity— on land I have seen street sweepers who in similar fashion would set aside their broom and sprinkler when no one was watching. The captain and the lieutenant mostly played dominos or, sitting opposite one another at the table, sang old music-hall songs from 1897—for navigation in a steady and favorable wind did not present any difficulties. Nevertheless, not everything on the ship ran like clockwork. The sailors' backs were bent too low when I passed by; their spines seemed fearful, and their big coarse hands, which they moved sluggishly beneath them, too easily became swollen and suffused with blood. Encountering Smith as he strolled about the deck, I expressed my profound trust and faith that the crew of the *Banbury* was composed exclusively of good and brave fellows.

"I keep them in line with this, sir," replied the lieutenant, displaying a small gimlet in his sinewy hand and swallowing the profanities that multiplied on his tongue. "I keep them by the throat . . . The hardest thing is not to give one of them a kick on the backside—you see how they stick them out. G . . . d . . .—and if I were to kick one of them, for equality's sake I'd have to kick them all without exception, and that would be foolish, foolish by Chr . . . I mean, the . . ."—He shrugged, indicating he was at a loss. The astonishing feeling of his own helplessness in the face of extraordinary idiocy struck him like a blow to the head. The ship was moving forward, but monotonously, wave chasing after wave. On the bridge I spotted the faint little glow of a small pipe—the captain was striding to and fro in his mackintosh.

"Sir," he said, "do you know what it means to be the master of life and death? Hello there—Mr. Smith, come here a moment and take a look—ha ha . . ."

"Ha ha," laughed Smith, looking at me with small bloodshot eyes—"Papa and mama . . By J . . . , I mean, the . . ."

"Papa and mama," the captain repeated, his shoulders shaking with suppressed laughter, "while here in fact there is no papa and mama! This is a ship, sir—a ship on the ocean! Far away from any consulates!"

"By my granny's granny," Smith swore with relish. —"There's

no gingerbread or cakes here, nor any da . . . I mean, the . . . nothing but discipline. An iron fist and that's the end of it—by . . . keep them by the thro . . ."

"All right, all right, that's enough now, that's enough, Mr. Smith. After all, Mr. Zantman is a passenger . . . But by the by, it wouldn't do any harm to show him what a captain at sea really is, what the meaning is of that huge word composed only of fancies. Hee hee, Mr. Zantman probably imagines a captain in a braided cap and spotless pressed white pantaloons, like one sees on picture postcards. Think up something good, Mr. Smith."

He reflected for a moment, taking a few puffs at his pipe.

"I could give orders, eh? If I order them to jump, they'll jump," he said. "Tomorrow and the day after."

"We already did that," murmured Smith.

"I'll give orders—eh, Mr. Smith? I'll order them to cut something off—to cut off an ear . . ."

"Perhaps," said Smith, "but it's a devilish tricky operation . . . that is . . . um . . . Afterward. It's problematic."

"Then I'll give orders, eh? I can order anything! By three hundred devils—I'm the captain! Those devils will feel it . . . call one of the sailors here, Mr. Smith."

"The sailors all feel it already," said Smith after a moment, in no hurry—he spat his gum onto the palm of his hand, looked at it closely and slipped it back into his mouth.

"Choose the one who feels it the least," Captain Clarke replied, growing impatient. "Quick—I want to show Mr. Zantman. Think something up, Mr. Smith. You're rather unimaginative. Remember Baffin Island and the seal."

"I'm out of ideas," said Smith, looking dully with the glazed pupils of a gin-lover. "Everything's been used. They're all used up, crumpled, covered in sh . . . that is, I mean the . . ."

"You're a fool, Smith," said the captain, bridling. "Quickly— quickly—I need someone to feel me. Sometimes I have doubts. Sometimes I'm beset by doubts."

At this moment I made the mistake of moving—but my heel had begun to itch, and with me it is innate that a heel always itches when it shouldn't.

"Maybe Mr. Zantman could be used," murmured Smith, eyeing me with undisguised malice.

"You know, that's not a bad idea," exclaimed the captain. "We'll use Mr. Zantman. He's still fresh. He hasn't felt me yet—he'll be the best one to feel me on his own skin . . . That's right—that'll be the simplest."

"If those are your orders, captain," said Smith, and he took my hand warmly and squeezed it as if in a pair of pincers (I once had my hand shaken in just this way by a certain sergeant on land— first warmly, then very strongly)—"in that case we'll knock together a big fishing pole, we'll stick Mr. Zantman on a hook and with this bait we'll catch a great deep-water fish. The fish will swallow Mr. Zantman, and we'll slit open its belly and pull him out still alive, like Jonah. It'll be a capital lark. You remember, captain, we got up to worse tricks in the Caribbean Bay—now that was the real thing—ho, ho . . ."

"You're a fool, Mr. Smith," repeated the captain. "That's all hogwash. What will he feel in this manner? He won't feel a thing. Besides, he's a passenger . . . hmm . . . But no violence, Smith, no violence. You're a fool," he roared; "be silent now, sir! I've had it up to here with your pranks and your jokes; to be honest, they make me puke! They don't make an ounce of sense. I need him to feel, to feel Captain Clarke, to feel without a figleaf or any other extras, as the Lord God created him. I spit on pressed white pants and a captain's braided cap! I want to take my clothes off, I want to be naked —you understand!—naked and hairy! But after all your idiotic Jonahs will Mr. Zantman recognize me, me, Clarke, when I take my clothes off?"

"We've no need to stand on ceremony," said Smith indistinctly through a mouthful of gum. "There aren't any boarding-school girls here. Or any consulates!"

"He won't recognize me," said the captain thoughtfully, "but what if I don't allow him to fasten his garter? What if I don't allow him to fasten his garter, Smith, and he goes around with his sock hanging down? What then? By hell! Then he'll recognize me, then he'll know who I am, because the calf is hairy! Dammit! These landlubbers with their white pants and their blue-and-white postcards forget that a captain's calf is hairy. Quickly now, Mr. Zantman, did you hear? Quickly! Look lively, sir!"

"Quickly, sir!" repeated Smith and clasped my hand.

"That I like," said the captain more calmly after a moment. "I see that with you one can come to terms, Mr. Zantman, even though you don't sway as you walk. We had one landlubber here two years ago—he was a hopeless dunderhead. He had to be thrown off the ship and straight into the water, because when I ordered him—a trivial thing—to lift up the collar of his jacket, he squealed like a stuck pig, and we sailors, you know, are not fond of squealers."

"I think that's enough now," I said when Clarke had gone, leaving me alone with the lieutenant. "I think that it's all right now to fasten the sock," I added confidentially, hoping to resolve the matter amicably, in an approving and understanding tone of discreet tolerance for the captain's unrefined eccentricities. "What?" responded Smith, stepping back at arm's length from me. "What? What do you imagine? I'd advise you not to — I'd advise you not to, even when you're alone in your cabin. What is this!" he thundered, so ominously it gave me gooseflesh — "Don't you try to be funny! Godda... Sh..." I grew embarrassed and, flushing deep crimson, I stammered only: "Oh no, no, no... I was merely... that, that... Not in the slightest! Far from it!" — just like on the tram once, and once at that picnic...

We sailed on; the weather was marvelous, the sky clear. Here and there amid the silver and emerald waves a ray or a swordfish appeared; a school of sharks sped along behind the stern, and tiny little fish flew above the water; but the ship was also moving ever more slowly, as if wondering whether it shouldn't stop for good — while the crew, under the supervision of the tireless second officer, after washing the leeward side of the brig would carry their cleaning rags over to the windward side. The second officer was a flaxen-haired young man in his twenties, vigilant, expressionless and not given to familiarity. In essence he existed only pro forma, so that the first officer should be able to exist too. The captain and Smith spent whole days almost entirely in their cabin, since the sea was tranquil. Walking on deck I could see them through the porthole, sitting at the table and throwing small balls made of some substance — probably bread — at something or other. It seemed boredom was making itself felt rather strongly—at times they quarreled bitterly and poured invective on one another, and they themselves probably did not know what it was about. They also mixed cocktails with Bols liqueur and flavored their whisky with ginger root. From time to time, at a given signal the crew would begin to chant: "Fish and sea birds feed behind the ship." Recently I had noticed that the sailors were performing bizarre movements with their torsos; specifically, as they bent over their rags they would suddenly lean on their hands, stiffen their legs and arch their backs, just like certain earthworms do.

I did not, however, ask anyone for an explanation. I put it down as a "novel way to pass the time." Truth be told, I generally avoided conversation, since I considered that the line of the mainspar twisted needlessly into a letter S. The letter S began one word that I had thought up myself and that I would have preferred not to know. In fact, it was not the mainspar alone—there were also other disagreeable shapes and outlines on the ship; it was cracked all over from the heat. And so it was not I who entered into conversation with Smith—but Smith who came up to me as I was leaning on the rail, and asked flat out if I did not know any good card games, or dicing games, or others—or if I didn't have any puzzles to solve.

First is father, second mother,
While the third is yet another.

"Earlier on we used to play dominos, old maid, snap, and jackstraws, and we would take turns at singing old songs from operettas. Then we'd look through the horse breeder's calendar. For

the last few days," he said frankly, swallowing a variety of imprecations, "we've been throwing balls of bread at a deuced tiny little
bug that we pulled out from under the cupboard. But we're sick of
it. Then (since we always sit opposite each other at the table) we
started to fix one another, you know, sir? — stare at one another —
to see who could hold out longer. And as we started to stare at each
other, we also started to prick one another with pins — to see who
could hold out longer. Now it's hard for us to stop, and we're
pricking each other harder and harder. The captain strikes, then I
strike, back and forth. Perhaps you could think something up —
perhaps you know something good, Mr. Zantman. I'm pricked all
over already."

I forgot myself and said improvidently: "It's because you've
formed a kind of vicious circle and there's no side release. Pins need
pincushions — take a pincushion and put it on the table between
you." Smith's mouth dropped open, and he looked at me with
respect. "I'll be sc . . . Mr. Zantman! We had you for a greenhorn,
sir, but it's clear you're a seasoned mariner. You have experience!"

"God forbid! I assure you . . . . It's quite by chance . . . . What are
you saying, Mr. Smith? I'll be angry with you. I give you my
word of honor, this is my first time at sea!" I spluttered, deeply
embarrassed.

"You're a devilish seasoned mariner!" repeated the lieutenant,
bowing to me. "Come along now, sir! Don't play the fool! You
must have sailed to your heart's content on all those damn ponds,
the Red and the Yellow, and the Okhotsk, and the Sargasso, and
the China, and the Arabian. — You've never sailed? Come now, sir,
you have the flair of an old sea wolf; you go directly, as they say, to

the root of the matter. A pincushion—yes indeed! That's the best remedy! If we put a pincushion down we'll stop jabbing one another at once."

"Excuse me, sir, but I've just remembered I left a spirit stove burning in my cabin; the coffee may boil over.—Excuse me, Mr. Smith."

Around four in the afternoon I saw pelicans playing with deep-water fish. Two of them glided in from the southwest and began wheeling over the ship. Pelicans are big snow-white birds with large crops and extraordinarily sharp bills a meter long. Of course they cannot dream of managing to swallow a shark or whale, but they are tempted by their absolute superiority over those marine monsters, arising from the fact that neither sharks nor whales can fly. This tempts them and gives them no peace. For that reason they fly quietly up and—plop—they plunge their razor-sharp bills into the back of a deep-water fish that is fleeing into the depths or thrashing about, trying to leap out and chase after the pelican into the forbidden element of the air. The deckhands interrupted their work in order to stand and stare, which brought down on them an awful series of curses from Smith.

"Scoundrels," he bellowed at the compact, silent group— "worthy gentlemen! Thompson!—you're the worst of them, I've got my eye on you, you swine, Thompson! I'll have a word with you this evening! You and I—Thompson—we'll have a word— this evening—you'll see."

Then he began to confess to me that as far as the crew were concerned, they were old stagers, old hands, rovers gathered from every port, who needed to be kept tightly by the throat.—"All they think about is how to wheedle their way out of work and lie there on their backs. For instance there's one of them, by the name of Thompson; he's the worst of them."

"The worst?"

"Thompson? He's a leech. Take a look at his mouth—it always forms itself into a little snout, as if poised for sucking. He hides it, working like everyone else, but I told myself I'd show him at the first opportunity, and I'll show him this evening. He'll be so frightened he won't be able to stand when I show him."

"The mouth," I said in a conciliatory manner, "is probably because he's a mammal, and they suckle. Everyone is a mammal. We belong to the family of mammals."

I delicately expressed some doubt concerning the torso movements, the foot-staring and the recitations of "Fish and sea birds feed behind the ship."—I spoke cautiously, with a certain moderation, and indicated as if in passing that it was possible to have too much of a good thing. To this Smith replied that he thought I, a seasoned sailor, was making fun of him. After all, worse things happened in the waters of the Far East with the Chinese. Or on the Aden-Pernambuco line, where they were constantly using melted stearin. The torso movements were intended to develop flexibility of the spine, while staring at one's feet was a punishment for inadequate cleanliness—whoever had dirty feet had to stare at them for almost an hour. And as for the line: "Fish and sea birds feed behind the ship"—it sounded like a handwriting exercise and in fact the point was to inscribe it in the sailors' brains in a pearly roundhand.

"A brig like this moves of its own accord, unless there's a storm.

I mean, the sailors can't keep endlessly scrubbing this grr . . . frr . . . deck, or they'd scrub it into oblivion. And discipline must be maintained, these scoundrels have to be kept in line; and so the captain chose that rather than anything else."

"Oh, rather than anything else."

"Yes, the captain's a seasoned, experienced sailor too, a genuine sea wolf. You ought to get to know him better, Mr. Zantman; I'm sure you gentlemen would find a great deal to talk about.

"The old man has often said to me," continued Smith, "'Mr. Smith, what are the duties of the captain of a ship: He has to think things up, because otherwise everything would go mad from boredom. You, Mr. Smith, should think things up with your mug, and I should think things up with my head, and that's all the difference between us. And now, what am I to think up, Mr. Smith? After all, darn it, we can't play ball, Mr. Smith. After all, confound it, we're not children, Mr. Smith, in short pants.'"

"Ahem — so playing ball is childish, and those, ahem . . . legs . . . aren't," I said with a cough.

"Certainly," he replied swaggeringly, "the legs — aren't, because which of us doesn't have corns? — and at the same time they maintain discipline among the crew. They have to perform everything without a murmur. The same with the pin — by God! — it was utterly mad — insane — brainless. How do you like that, Mr. Zantman? Come now! You, with your experience, cannot fail to admit that's right. That's how things always are, everywhere. Without that we'd drop dead from boredom."

He licked his finger and raised it to the wind.

"All the more so because the wind is dropping and it seems

there's a danger of a sea-calm. Sh . . . godda . . . ff . . . pl. . . . That's always the way. You know the saying—water and boredom are the sailor's elements."

Toward evening I saw some large flounders and I discerned the head of a hammerhead shark three or four inches below the surface.

Captain Clarke appeared on the bridge and beckoned to me. Smith must have been gossiping with him about the pincushion and about how I was a seasoned mariner—since the captain now treated me entirely differently than before, even giving the impression that he wanted to sound me out. He evidently thought that I knew something he didn't, or that I was somehow able to set myself up so I was less distressed. When I climbed up to the bridge, Clarke said:

"Boredom, sir. Sea boredom."

"Hm," I replied.

"Not a pleasant thing, boredom. Eh? Not pleasant. Things are boring. It's not clear what."

"It's bearable," I said. "It's not so boring as all that. There's the water, the fish . . ."

"Come now, sir, Mr. Smith has told me," said the captain amicably, nudging me. "You must have your own ways of dealing with boredom, so you're not bored. If I only knew. That pincushion, ho ho. It's just that you don't want to share them, you're being miserly . . . hm . . . hm . . . you're saving it all for yourself."

"Nothing of the sort. Really, I'll be angry with you, captain. Smith's been talking poppycock."

"Now then, let's not get offensive! I just meant to indicate that you're the kind of man a person can talk to, Mr. Zantman, you're not like any old landlubber—and you don't need to conceal it from us—I don't understand why it matters so much to you. . . . Well, but you're free to do what you want."

I was in a very disagreeable and difficult position and I cautiously plucked at a button on my jacket, since Clarke had a vein in his temple that stood out clearly against the receding corners of his forehead. He suddenly grew morose and began to scratch himself behind the ear.

"Boredom," he said, returning to his old topic, kicking something with his feet—"boredom. I signed a contract with the company and now I have to travel the Birmingham-Valparaiso run, to and fro. What the hell is it? It's boring on land—the trams, the bars—land boredom drives you to sea. And what happens at sea? You've already set off—you've already left under full sail—the coast is disappearing—you're already being rocked—the trail astern is already churning—and all at once boredom, eh? Sea boredom."

"Nature is standing in the way," I murmured, clearing my throat. "Such is nature."

"What do you mean?" said Clarke.

"Nature doesn't like it," I murmured. "It doesn't like it."

"The best thing for boredom is your companion the pipe," he said mawkishly. "Whiskey's good too—biting your fingernails—taking snuff . . . if someone has a cavity in their tooth, then poking the tongue in it. If there's an itch it can be scratched—you know, in

Mukden I once went into a club; there were four captains having lunch, and they were all scratched till they bled, all scratched up as if they had a rash. And what about you, Mr. Zantman?"

"Me? — I sometimes . . ."

"I was just thinking that you look so fresh and ruddy," the captain said with interest. "I swear — it's as if you'd never let go of your mommy's skirts. How do you do it?"

"But, captain, I really . . . I assure you."

"Ha ha ha ha ha," he laughed at length. "Ho ho ho, you're quite the slyboots, Mr. Zantman. But I'm not going to force you, since you don't want to; in the end, let's agree that this is your first time — ha ha ha . . . We could use a bit of a storm, eh?" he added, nudging me once again. "Then we'd have a decent ride, eh? And here a fellow's dragging along — and in addition the wind's dropping. I'm all twisted up — it's so boring — dammit — I can't stan . . ."

"That's unhealthy," I said. "Very unhealthy. Bad thoughts. Bad thoughts come."

"Blast it," muttered the captain. "Just look at those masts. They're so foolish standing there. It's foolish. And I'm also standing foolishly. I'm standing, and this glass is standing too. Tell me, what can be done with a glass — it can only be smashed, eh? And that's what I did yesterday evening. On this sh . . . brig nothing happens from morning to evening. When I look at this rail" — he struck it with his hand — "and I see that it's still gleaming so foolishly — I look at it and I feel like leaping out of my own skin." He started complaining painfully, in a low voice, that everything was foolish — foolish. "Everything has to be cleaned, everything in its place, the sailors don't do anything but scrub and clean for days on end. On ships, as you know, an inordinate, simply excessive cleanliness is in force. What the hell for? Or those flying fish . . . Just tell me, why do they jump so foolishly out of the water—there, take a look"—he showed me one that flew over the deck in a high arc—"That's foolish too, foolish as anything. Tell me, why do they do that, eh? I mean, they don't have wings."

I replied after some thought that this phenomenon should be ascribed to certain specific properties of these gill-bearing creatures, which are capable of swelling themselves up to such a degree that at a given moment the water cannot take it any longer and expels them, out of fear that they might burst. In the same way some land toads often swell up with cigarettes to terrifying proportions, but the land, which is worse in this respect than the water, does not let them go and for this reason they burst.

"By my word!" cried the captain with unaccountable excitement.—"Ha ha ha! That's right! That's it! You're a one, sir! Of course—the little rascals! Swell up, get frightened, and that lily-livered f . . . water is afraid and expels them—ha ha! It's afraid, dammit—it's filled with fear, it's in a funk, in a funk! In the throat! In the throat and by the throat!" he shouted in delight. It seemed that my words had aroused some kind of terrorist streak in him. —"Bravo, splendid! How could I not have thought of that. You're a real expert. You're a naturalist," he added, swelling slightly and looking at me with admiration. "And you say you've not traveled?"

"I know a little about nature," I said, "but only theoretically." I started coughing, said it was growing cold, and returned to my cabin, which I did not leave for the whole of the following day.

That day (the following one) there once again occurred a curious incident, which I, however, did not see (since I was in my cabin). It is common knowledge that sharks are extraordinarily voracious, hence the expression "sharklike appetite." Well then, the galley boy accidentally dropped a large copper saucepan in the water, and the saucepan—snap—instantly vanished into a greedy maw. This fact brought him such pleasure and such bizarre delight that he could not resist, and also threw overboard a few forks, which were caught in midair; and then he began to throw out everything he could get his hands on, which meant plates, kitchen knives and table knives, teacups, his own pocket watch, a compass, a barometer, his three-month salary, and a full set of the sailing encyclopedia. Smith caught him as he was tearing the shelves from his completely stripped cabin. It can be imagined what happened next. The lad came down with malaria that same evening and, it seemed, would not appear again till the end of the voyage. Either way, we were deprived of necessities and we had to eat our omelette straight from the frying pan. Learning of this occurrence, I frowned and said to myself, though rather loudly and wisely, as if it mattered to me that someone should overhear: "Aha, right—that's very wise. Very well thought out. This is an illness well-known in medicine, involving a certain obduracy—it is, to speak scientifically, a particular kind of *tumulus,* the result of a certain lack of control—it's a certain kind of delight derived from imperfections of the senses and from errors of instinct blinded by undue voracity, a certain, one might say, fascination with automatism, in a word an illness that is as it happens automatic, arising from the application of great universal forces of gravitation, projection, and hunger to a game of blindman's buff. And on top of this—how will the objects ache in the belly?"—Yet a moment later the muscles of my face relaxed; on it there appeared an awful, hopeless foolishness, and I said more quietly: "Oh Lord! Very well, but why so foolishly? Why so foolishly, emptily, incessantly, without a break, without a single moment of respite, why so foolishly-wisely and wisely-foolishly somehow? Someone's being wise here and someone's being foolish; oh Lord, grant at least five minutes' respite." And I even allowed myself to add: "It's as if I'm in a dark forest, where the bizarre shapes of the trees, the plumage and calls of the birds entice and amuse with a curious masquerade, but from the depths of the woods there comes the distant roar of a lion, the thunder of the buffalo and the creeping step of the jaguar."

2

The *Banbury* was advancing ever more slowly. The sun was burning ever hotter; melted tar dripped from the sides of the vessel into the sea, the sea was sapphire blue, and the water used to scrub the deck evaporated into the equally sapphire-blue sky. Captain Clarke appeared on the bridge, licked his finger, and said:

"I knew it—the breeze is dying down. And it's quite possible that we'll have an adverse wind. Mr. Smith—have them put up the side foresail. On this run it's always the same way—always, whether we're going to Valparaiso or coming from Valparaiso, there's an adverse wind. And this is called sailing? *This* is sailing! *This* is supposed to be sailing!" he shouted furiously.

A school of dolphins remained by the stern. They were not after meat—their only wish was to scratch themselves a little against the ship's rudder, since they were suffering terribly from water lice. It was not often that they had such a golden opportunity—a solid object in the boundless waters against which they could rub themselves. They would swim about the ocean for weeks on end in search of such an object. Yet they did not see that the ship, though very slowly, was nevertheless moving forward, and they were continually missing the edge of the rudder by a couple of inches. The wretched fish, failing to understand the reason, kept repeating the maneuver unsuccessfully.

On a sheet of paper I noted the following: "I feel there's too much of all this. Dolphins missing the edge of the rudder, rats biting their own tails, sailors who stare at their own feet and straighten their bent backs, pelicans jabbing the backs of whales, the captain and the lieutenant jabbing each other with pins, whales incapable of rising in flight above the water, flying fish that on the contrary swell up so much that the water cannot stand the pressure and expels them into the air—this is all decidedly too monotonous. I imagine that from time to time something different could be shown. If I'd known it would be like this I never would have set off on a voyage. A little tact wouldn't go amiss. Repeating the same thing over and over is dotting the *i*, utterly unnecessary—and furthermore, someone might suspect something.

"Besides, sights are one thing, but on the part of the captain and Smith there's now a glaring lack of tact; those feet and those pins are impossible, and the conversations are even worse. What's supposed to be the meaning—pardon me—of these confidences? 'We mariners'—what does 'we mariners' mean? Who wishes to 'rock' here; what's the meaning of 'drive' and 'devouration,' what's the meaning of 'boredom' and 'getting carried away'? I have no desire to know. It was clearly a tip of the head in my direction—they're all tipplers. They're tipplers and people with disastrous tendencies, cocaine or morphine addicts I'll wager, thoroughly corrupted in some Pernambuco somewhere. I'm not going to talk to them any more. I'm not a mariner and I want nothing to do with the captain's nautical 'imagination' and his nautical 'boldness.' I'll try cautiously (since the sock is after all still lowered) to loosen our relations. I'll put Smith in his place too, with his ideas and his gimlet. It's not true that I spoke about the pincushion or the flying fish (something's bound to pop out from time to time, since they're always on at me) so they would immediately declare me a 'seasoned mariner' and initiate me into everything, whether I want it or not.

"I confess that I imagined life on board to be completely different. But it's a quagmire. There's no breeze. I was hoping for the salty smell of the sea and of the open spaces and so on, so much healthier than the stifling smells of land; whereas I see that things are cramped here—cramped, intrusive, and in addition there's some kind of apery. Above all there's not an ounce of tact. The day before yesterday, not wishing to continue a conversation with Clarke, I returned to my cabin; but some large insect, I believe a scorpion, crawled out of a crack in the floor, stared at me for a while, wiggling its feelers, and then out of the blue it rolled into a ball and injected into itself all the venom in its abdomen—in this way committing suicide. I've heard that this is a common occurrence among such hymenoptera. But why did he come to my cabin to do it? Could he not have managed in the crack? I pretended not to see. On land, too, one sometimes sees dogs or horses, but there's more discretion, and no one will crawl out specially to someone else just to show them.

"I wish we would just arrive in Valparaiso as quickly as possible. Will we ever arrive in Valparaiso, though? I don't know; though perhaps this is normal and anticipated in our travel schedule — I know nothing about the constellations and I don't know how to use a sextant or compass, but if the stars (as it would seem) are unfavorable, and even apishly malicious in some way, and we've entered the undesirable sign of Aries or Capricorn, then in my opinion the captain and Smith are too forward and are taking too many liberties. I was always afraid of that officer's nautical imagination — paying no attention to anything, only holding things by the throat in bachelor fashion — a bachelor's imagination and a bachelor's way of traveling. At times one needs to quiet down and wait it out. One needs to know when and what. It's cramped here, just like in a box, and some scandal could result; I don't like the look of the sailors' faces, though I only see their backs."

Having written this I burned the paper as quickly as I could over the candle. Then I took a sheet of paper and added:

"Yes, I don't like the look of the sailors' faces, though I only see their backs. Their backs, naturally, are meek and timorous, as backs usually are, but in the evenings, through the floor of my cabin, I hear beneath the deck a flat, persistent buzzing, akin to the hum of a nest of insects. This buzzing comes from the sailors. And so Smith keeps them by the throat by day, but not at night. Are they snoring? Are they talking? And if they're talking, what could they be talking about, and are they not by any chance gossiping overmuch, as can happen on long sea voyages? For it's possible that out of boredom they're spinning one another some endless tall tales that don't contain a word of truth. After all, as Smith reminded me—they're globetrotters, old stagers of the quayside; and they're bound to have heard a thing or two in their lives. I knew a fellow like that—he used to recount with great glee that he once heard from a barber in Tokyo about a gentleman who was 'very well dressed, and must have been from the upper crust,' who cautioned his manicurist 'not to cut my fingernails too short, or I won't be able to pick my nose.' There's an example of their attitude to intelligence. It's only things like that they can grasp—nothing more. And they're prepared to talk about it for hours on end, always with the same repulsive, sarcastic sneer."

I burned this paper too—yet that did not mean I didn't put into action my resolution concerning Clarke and Smith. I kept my distance from them, and when I saw them on one side of the brig I moved to the other. It was worse, I will not deny it, when one of them was on one side of the ship and the other on the other side. In the meantime a sea wind had blown up, but instead of coming from the side or from behind, it began to blow softly right from the bow. The *Banbury* did not move backward, but it was all unspeakably irritating—low waves were slapping against its nose.

To make matters worse, it turned out that Thompson really did have a mouth like a snout—seeing this, I couldn't hold back (I blame myself for this rashness) and asked: "Thompson, why do you do it? Surely that's not the right way, Thompson." He was a strapping fellow, tall, broad-shouldered, with a weather-beaten face, a hairy chest, earrings in his ears and short bangs on his forehead — they were too short in relation to the rest of his figure. He looked around to check that no one else was nearby, came up very close to me, and said, sticking out his lips: "Me, I like it, sir."

"Now then, Thompson," I said hurriedly. "Here's five shillings for tobacco, Thompson." Thompson closed the paw into which I had slipped the money and said:

"That won't be of any use."

"I expect it's boring for you on board, Thompson," I said benevolently.

"I'll say it's boring," groaned Thompson. "It's hard to stand it, sir. I have to go to bed at nine like a good little babby, sir, and in the daytime I have to sing songs. The captain and the lieutenant are too strict, sir. I can't enjoy myself — I can't have fun — I'm dying, sir. Once I was ruddy, I was red as fire, sir, I was in good shape, and now I'm pale and exhausted — I'm going to hell, sir, I'm going to waste, sir."

I brought him out some milk in a bowl, which he lapped up.

"That will do you good, Thompson. Milk is white, and that's the best thing for redness — I'll leave you a bowl like this outside my cabin door every day. Milk and lots of fruit. But for the love of God, don't make a scandal, Thompson. Try to hold out till Valparaiso. The ship is slowing down, but the captain told me that soon a favorable wind will be blowing. Please, please though — no funny business, Thompson; here's five shillings more."

We were still at 76 degrees latitude, a good 450 miles southwest of the Canary Islands — though no canaries were to be seen. Those small, golden-feathered birds were obviously afraid of excessive distances; they preferred to hop from branch to branch in a dappled grove of tropical trees, where their chatter rang out much more loudly than at sea. These are not sea birds but land birds. The wind was blowing lightly yet constantly, right into the bow of the ship; small waves were making small flicks over and again, and little mild white clouds were passing in single file across the violet sky.

Thompson must have spread the word that I had given him a few shillings—for in the afternoon, I was approached amidships by the mate—a large, fat, asthmatic man with drooping, puddingy cheeks and a bug-eyed, pale, exhausted gaze. He complained of boredom and said that he had dirty feet—that this tormented him, and he asked for a few shillings. When I upbraided him sternly, he declared more quietly:

"All right, all right. Life's like that. I know. I'm forty-seven, and I've never had clean feet—never, it just wasn't possible. Other people can have clean feet, but not me—never—it's a dog's life for me. One thing or another always gets in the way and it's not possible—and when it's possible you don't feel like it. In fact, I feel I want to—but I don't feel like it and"—he added dully—"I've found other ways, here"—he tapped his forehead with a shrewd expression, staring at me. I quickly gave him five shillings for beer and advised him to at least powder his feet—it's practical and takes less time. I asked him not to tell anyone that I had given money. But he obviously couldn't help himself. One of the sailors, whose name I did not know, whispered supposedly to himself as he passed by, looking around to check that no one was listening:

"Nasturtiums."

I gave him a few shillings too. Hmm . . . I was beginning to be seriously worried, for in my view the crew was becoming too importunate. Not two days had passed since my conversation with Thompson, yet the notebook in which I recorded my daily expenditures was black with a series of new entries. It looked almost as if the crew had found some poems of mine under my pillow, but I had no poems, for after all I had clambered onto the *Banbury* from a motor launch, without any luggage.

Thompson for "I like it" and snout: 10 s.

Mate for feet: 5 s.

X for nasturtiums: 2 s.

Stevens for certain tomatoes and buds: 5 s.

Buster for bashfulness: 5 s.

Dick for small vegetable patch tended with trowel amid tall reed stems: 1 s. 6 d.

O'Brien for huge milk cows grazing on meadow full of round pebbles: 3 s. (Meant to give less, but he knew about "Primrose" too.)

O'Brien again for ladle, with recommendation that he refrain until Valparaiso. (NB he refuses; says he ran with blood again yesterday. For this another 6 d. extra.)

To carry forward: 31 s. 6 d.

To the above reckoning I appended the following note: "I pay because it's mine. If it weren't mine, I would not pay. I shouldn't have rubbed shoulders with that character (Thompson)—now they all keep approaching me, one after another. There's nothing worse than entering into contact with riff-raff who prattle without thinking and fawn idiotically, solely in order to extract money. I'm sure that among themselves they make fun of the fact they managed to tap the passenger, and that they repeat the same words in a vulgar manner—roaring with laughter and holding their bellies. I'm curious, though, where they got those words from. It has to be admitted there's a blatant lack of discretion on board; in this respect I could hold it against not just the seamen but also the ship's pipes, which enact some sort of bizarre flourishes, including my own. The men ape and twist, and turn everything instantly into such filth or foolishness that one has to blush.

"The situation requires immense tact. The captain possesses too much nautical imagination, and Smith knows how to give a warm handshake—so much so it's even pleasant. At any moment they could throw me overboard. When I set off I was forgetting the absolute power of a captain, and that's an important point that should not be forgotten. I also forgot that at sea there are only men (I'm not referring to the large passenger steamers). They're all men, and the sock came at the right time. As for the crew, it's composed of old stagers, older than I thought even, and one needs to temporize with them, because for them nothing is sacred— they're like fraternity boys or soldiers in their barracks. You can see it by looking at them. It's just as well that Smith has them by the throat. Today, as I stood in the bows I saw an unfamiliar animal the size and shape of an anteater, which slipped out a long tongue narrow as a tape and tried to use it to lick a piece of wood that was floating a few meters away—and so I went to the stern, but there in turn there was a host of oysters—and these snails are swallowed live and perish torn from their shells in the dark cavity of the stomach. No one can be more consumed alive than they are, and they are afraid of nothing so much as of lemon. (To be afraid of lemon!) At that point I turned from the sea and looked in the direction of the deck, but here one of the deckhands put down his brush, raised his leg, and scratched himself on the heel, exactly like a little doggie relieving itself behind a bush. In the end I locked myself in my cabin once again for several hours, ostensibly because of the damp. There is a need for immense tact; one should not be surprised at anything, one should show no surprise, surprise would be entirely out of place, since everything is this way—everything is this way, and I have no grounds for surprise, and if they throw me overboard I'll go without surprise—surprise in such circumstances would without a doubt be a huge impropriety, a glaring lack of tact. In any case one must be circumspect and avoid disputes and move very cautiously, since boredom is pressing down and the sun is burning. I wish, I wish we would arrive in Valparaiso—alas, the wind is blowing against us.

"The order, discipline, and cleanliness on this ship are a thin membrane that could burst at any second and is ever more likely to do so."

After writing this I burned the paper. Before long it transpired that my concerns were well founded—and I had been wrong to hand out money to the sailors, since this had a provocative and emboldening effect on them. One takes money and then—ever onward, now with money in one's pocket! (Once, a long time ago now, I gave out caramels in the same way, and with no better consequences.)—One day, strolling astern, on the boards of the deck I noticed a human eye. No one was around except for a sailor standing by the helm and chewing gum; the whole deck was bathed in subtropical sunshine and criss-crossed by a bluish network of shadows from the rigging of the foremast. I asked the helmsman:

"Whose eye is that?"

He shrugged.

"I don't know, sir."

"Did it fall out, or was it removed?"

"I didn't see, sir. It's been lying there since this morning. I'd have picked it up and put it in a box, but I'm not allowed to leave the helm."

"Over there by the rail," I said, "there's another eye. But a different one. Belonging to a different person. Have Barnes pick them up when he leaves the helm."

"Yes, sir."

I continued my interrupted walk, debating whether to tell the captain and Smith—the latter had appeared on the steps of the forward hatch.

"There's a human eye on the deck over there."

He pricked up his ears. "I'll be f . . . sp. . . . Where? Is it one of a pair?"

"Do you think, lieutenant, that it fell out, or that it was removed from someone?"

We heard the captain's voice from the upper gangway:

"Has something happened, Mr. Smith? Why did you curse?"

"Those . . . dr . . . da . . ." Smith replied angrily, "Those . . . ba . . . pr . . . they're starting to play the eye game."

"Do you mean to tell me," I asked, "that out of boredom the sailors have invented a game that involves one of them catching a second unawares and trying to poke the other man's eye out with his thumb — more or less the way schoolboys trip one another up?"

The captain's voice rang out from above:

"Don't forget, Mr. Smith, that independent of the punishment the guilty party should eat the eye that was poked out. Nautical customs require it."

"Damnation," swore the lieutenant. "Once they've begun there'll be no peace. One time, in the waters of the southern Pacific, while we were becalmed we lost three-quarters of the eyes of the entire crew in this way. They're scared to death of it, but once they begin they can't stop themselves. I'll show them — now then, good gentlemen — they'll remember me, they'll remember me, those good gen . . . en . . . gen . . ."

"It's more along the lines of tickling," I said. "A schoolboy is terrified of tickling and for that reason he can't refrain from tickling his chum; then the chum starts tickling and an all-around tickling commences."

"I'll tickle them," muttered Smith, seething and roughly patting his pockets. I merely added sadly and almost painfully: "I'm sorry. It's a flimsily attached organ, a sphere inserted into a socket in a person, nothing more."

I went to my cabin, lay on my bunk, and wrote with my finger on the wall: "A fine business. — Now Smith will tickle them, and they'll tickle Smith in return. It's much worse than I suspected. It seems to be dreary and foolish, but it's growing ever more pressing and more cramped — these are already personal provocations — things are dangerous. I'm like a sheep among wolves, like an ass in the lions' den. It'll be necessary after all to have a serious talk with Clarke."

An opportunity to talk arose that very evening on the bridge. Clarke was leaning on the rail and conferring with the lieutenant; both wore extremely concerned and disgruntled expressions. They were evidently discussing the situation, since I heard Clarke saying: "Yes, but if things go on like this, there may be a shortage of eyes. Something must have stirred them up—someone must have roused them—they'd never have started of their own accord. Now there'll be no peace.

"Who stirred them up?" he roared, waxing angry.

The sea was pellucid—the setting sun had not yet managed to sink below the horizon, yet darkness was already enveloping the waters with great rapidity. Storks appeared in the sky, on their annual journey from northern Scotland to the eastern shores of Brazil. These familiar birds are in the greatest trouble when, at the time of their departure, their young are not sufficiently practiced in the art of flying—on the one hand a powerful migratory instinct drives them to sea, whereas on the other hand an equally powerful maternal instinct binds them to the poor juvenile fledglings—at such times they emit terrifying cries.

"The eye is almost the most sensitive organ of the body," I mentioned after a short pause. "It's very easy to remove an eye." I added further that on the subject of the eye I was particularly sensitive. "Personally I can't stand it even when someone shoots a straw at my eye. It seems that the crew is a little restless. It seems that things are a little cramped or uncomfortable for them, that they're lacking something—could they not be calmed down a little?"

"Now this one!" shouted Clarke rudely, in the unexpected voice of a man with more important problems. "Dammit. Have you lost your spine? At times you give the impression of being a bold mariner, and at others you look like a weepy woman."

He was most irate.

"The crew has gone mad, and you're wasting our time. What are you—a woman?"

"No, I'm not," I replied resentfully. "But if women get involved in all this, things will be even worse. I only want to mention that I know a conspiracy is being hatched on board."

"A conspiracy?" he exclaimed in astonishment.

"A general conspiracy is being hatched," I said reluctantly. "There is without doubt a conspiracy, though it appears there is not; everything is scheming and plotting behind our backs. I know in advance how it will end. It will end very badly."

"What? What?" cried Clarke inquiringly. "A conspiracy? On the *Banbury*? You know something. What do you know, Mr. Zantman? A conspiracy?"

I looked him in the eye.

"You know as well as I do," I replied. "There's a problem of cleanliness and modesty—my cleanliness and modesty."

"What do you mean?" he asked.

"I know," I replied. "It's because I am clean and modest. If I weren't modest, there wouldn't be so much immodesty. I know you all," I added, "you're all thinking about the same thing. You have a yen for goodness knows what, and I'm in the way—I'm a hindrance, isn't that the case? — my modesty is a hindrance. That's why everything around here either fawns or threatens, peeps or mocks; that's the reason for the constant importunings and the fact that there's only one unchanging thought — oh, one unchanging thought!"

"What?" said the captain, his mug agape. "Indecent, you say? Immodest? My, you're a. . . . Come on, let's have a drink; I have a first-rate drop of brandy," he shouted in his excitement. I was most disgusted by the captain's behavior, for he had turned red, and his beady little mariner's eyes shone like lighted cigars; I realized that in my fervor I had said too much and, embarrassed, I quickly walked away.

3

The wind was blowing hard; thin, tattered little clouds were racing overhead — the masts and the parts of the rigging made of steel were moaning, gulls were struggling against the air current, which carried them windward, and on board there could be heard plaintive, doleful exhortations and songs . . . . I had said, had I not, that I knew how things would end — and for that reason I was not surprised to see something like the beginning of the end. I had even said, it seemed, that if women were to become involved things would get even worse. And if you please: the sailors scrubbing the boom-pulleys were crooning:

"I'll be true, so love me do!"

And from the stern they were answered by a wild and passionate cry from those who had remained by the buckets and brushes:

"Kiss me! — Kiss me!"

I shouldn't have mentioned women. That subject should never have been raised. Walls have ears.

The bow of the ship was plunging in large, fleecy combers; it rose and fell, but did not retreat an inch, despite the fact that the sea wind was blowing directly from the front to the back. The songs of the crew did not cease. True, Smith had warned them that if they didn't stop he would make sure they were forced to eat their words and they would swallow them — but the old stagers, the old hands, knew how to handle this. Instead of singing obvious love songs, they put their entire souls into their ordinary nautical callings, and the result was the same. It was embarrassing. Passing the rope they called into the wind: "Loop it, loop it!" Bending over their bucket and brush: "Wash, scrub — clean, rinse!" — unrestrainedly, with heartfelt yearning. Smith could not forbid them this, since maritime law permits sailors to utter nautical cries. A male whale was circling the ship furiously, spouting fountains of water higher than the mainmast; the sharks were cowering in fear, and a sea dog brought its offspring out onto a wave, and the whole family stared at the vessel.

What a spectacle we were making of ourselves — how much abasement and ridiculousness — though at least none of our acquaintances was present. In fact, it was all the fault of Smith's recklessness; it was all because the previous day, out of boredom, Smith had ordered a hunk of salted meat to be put on the anchor, and with this bait a huge female whale had been caught. The crew had gathered to pull out the gigantic fish and watch its dying dance on the deck. Smith ran up too — and instantly burst out with the filthiest words: "Jump to it, get rid of this carcass, this carrion, this mound of blubber that looks like nothing on earth—I can't look at this bloated torso!" But it was too late. The sailors were watching rather tenderly, and Thompson said as he stretched:

"I'll be true . . ."

The whale, as everyone knows, is a mammal; for this reason a female mammal had excited them—had it been some cold-blooded fish, it would have had no effect whatsoever. Thompson, who was also a mammal, reacted particularly strongly. Smith burst out with more derision and imprecations. "Good God, it stinks! Disgusting! That rancid stench is unbearable. It must be old—I know what I'm talking about—it must be at least seventeen years old." How incautious! seventeen years! For a female whale this was indeed old age, but—seventeen years! He shouldn't have mentioned seventeen years. The deckhands wordlessly pushed the monster into the water, and half an hour later there had already begun nostalgic, passionate moanings, an inconsolability strangely unsettling to the nerves.

Around midday the captain appeared on the bridge, looked around at the foaming seas, nodded, and said:

"The ship is holding up in the wind with the stubbornness of a mule. Very good. Mr. Smith! Issue the sailors a tablespoon of cod-liver oil each."

The sailors tried to worm their way out of the cod-liver oil as best they could—they had no wish to spoil their own dreams—but Smith gave each one of them a full spoonful. After the cod-liver oil things calmed down a little. But these were old stagers who had roamed every corner of the globe; one had only to look at them— they stuffed themselves with wholemeal bread and salt to cover the taste of the cod-liver oil and they began again, da capo, even more boisterously. The heart of the matter was that since their departure they had not seen a woman. "We"—this was how they presented the case—"we haven't seen a woman since our departure, and so this yearning arose in all of us at once, with elemental power." Of course they suffered from yearning—but this didn't prevent them from stirring it up inside themselves any way they could; one provoked another to yearning, the latter returned the favor with a double dose and thus it continued. The sufferings of the male whale, which did not cease from circling insanely and spouting like a geyser, acted on them merely as an encouragement and a stimulus.

"He can yearn," they thought to themselves, "and we can't?"

What sons of bitches! What slyboots, what schemers; it hurt even to watch, and I tried to spend as much time as possible in my cabin. True, I already knew that they were a band of schemers, but I hadn't realized it was to such a degree. Since Smith did not let them out of his sight, and the gimlet poked out of his side pocket, they could neither sing nor call things by name—if one of them had tried, Smith would have immediately summoned him to the hold for a word. —But one had to see how they were able to induce yearning in anything that came to hand. They picked up a brush caressingly and looked steadfastly into one another's eyes. Or, as they were pulling the rope, they bent deliberately like hazel branches—as if they were ever-so-young boys. I was in no state to watch all this. I would have liked to give milk to the entire crew, but I knew it would not be drunk. Thompson's bowl lay untouched, though I had put under it not one but two shillings. I ran to the back of the ship and wrote with my finger on the port-side wall:

"Now then! Mother of God! These men are unbelievable scoundrels. But what will become of me?"

The captain said sternly:

"Mr. Smith — make sure all gaps are tightly stopped up for the night. Give each of them an extra spoonful of cod-liver oil and forbid them to whisper."

The captain and Smith seemed seriously concerned; I even know that the captain gave Smith a sharp dressing-down for his recklessness. Yet despite the prohibitions, despite the roar of the sea and the creaking of the brig, the usual nighttime buzzing and dreaming sounded through the cabin floor with redoubled strength, and much more clearly than on previous nights. I couldn't restrain myself. Incapable of resisting my inadvisable and ill-starred curiosity about what they were saying and how among themselves, and also convinced that 80 percent of it must be about me — I dug out an opening between the floorboards and pressed my ear to it. Sounds immediately burst out, along with the stale smell of tobacco and cod-liver oil, but to begin with I couldn't make anything out. They were tossing and turning, groaning, moaning, cursing Smith and the cod-liver oil, which tormented them and got in their way — some were singing in subdued voices, while others were spinning confused, anguished yarns. It was only after a while that I heard:

"The girls of Singapore."

And then:

"The girls of Madras . . ."

"The girls of Mindoro . . ."

"Of San Paolo de Loamin . . ."

More moans, and painful writhings in the greasy embrace of the cod-liver oil. Then one voice rose above the others.

"So long as they don't have the mange."

"They can't have the mange! Everyone knows!"

Then once more—the same thing over and again:

"A sweet little hand . . ."

"A sweet little foot . . ."

(How the imagination was at play!)

The hubbub intensified; then after a moment a single voice rang out once again:

"I was loved. I didn't give a single shilling. I was loved for free. She didn't take one peseta."

There was an uproar:

"Come off it! You probably gave earrings instead, or a neck-lace!"

"Who couldn't be loved?" growled the mate in a deep, ponderous voice. "But not everyone feels like it. To love, you have to wash your feet. Right now, when I have to wash my feet, I don't have a woman, and when I have a woman then I don't need to wash my feet, and so on around and around. On the other hand the passenger gave me five shillings."

"That's not it," said someone else. "It's obvious that anyone could be loved. But there's no time. There's no time, my friends, I tell you—because when you have time then you also have money, and when you have money you go to a brothel, where you take care of things without love. And when you don't have money you have to climb on board and earn some. It's a shabby trick."

(How very true this was!)

And once again, even more heatedly:

"Sweet little teeth . . ."

"Sweet little eyes . . ."

(So much passion! So much fervor!)

"That's not it, my friends," said Thompson gloomily, turning over—"that's not it, my friends, it's that damned travel bug. You see me here—there's more than one woman has come running after me; in San Francisco, or in Aden one Sunday, I'm walking down the road, undergarments, my friends, are drying on the clotheslines, and the women are ogling me . . ."

"Who wouldn't ogle you," said the ship's boy ingratiatingly. (What? Such insolence! It's true, I took a dislike to that ship's boy the moment I set eyes on him—he inveigled twenty shillings out of me for "flirtation," as I recorded in my notebook.)

"Accursed is our lot, I say," mumbled the mate—"Accursed. Scrubbing and scrubbing! I'm fifty years old already—an accursed lot, I say."

"My friends," repeated Thompson gloomily, "I tell you—it's all because of that travel bug. It's that accursed itch, tempting, sending you in every direction—you know—it moves through your bones and won't let you sleep, my friends! How many times have I been on a woman! And each time, I thought I'd get transported, like on a ship—I'll take a trip, I thought, but not a bit of it—she stayed in one place. All this had me bursting, running around, I tell you! Goddammit! I hurried down to the docks to hop on the first ship I could find and go to sea—it was all the same which ship—so I could rock as one should, so I could gad about a little! That's the main cause. Women, you see, give us the travel bug."

"You've traveled far," someone laughed. "In two weeks we've done maybe thirty knots."

"We've not moved an inch," someone cursed from the corner. "The sea wind has turned about."

"And even if we did move, what of it?" snorted another. "In Valparaiso there's the same wh . . . as in Bombay, only under a different streetlight."

"I don't know," said the mate uncertainly through his nose, "all day just cleaning, scrubbing, washing our feet. Why do they make us wash our feet when they won't allow us even one woman? Is it on purpose? Is it always this way?"

He began cursing in a repulsive fashion, slowly and deliberately, choosing his words with care.

"A person goes to waste," the ship's boy said in his high-pitched voice. "Isn't that so, Tommy? What are you thinking about, Tommy?"

"And the passenger's feeding us with milk, like puppies!" Thompson burst out vulgarly. "If we were to change our course by half a point—and turn side on to the wind—then we'd be sailing, my friends! Then we'd be on our way. There in the south they say there are completely unknown waters, and they say there are sea cows as big as mountains, overgrown with trees, and in those trees—ho ho . . ."

(Aha! What are they dreaming about! Some sorts of walks! They mustn't be allowed!)

"There are marvels there," said the boy.

"And it's warmer," muttered the mate. "The sun gives more heat."

" 'Neath Argentina's bright blue skies, a lovely girl delights the eyes. Let's sing, my friends! For yearning, song is the best medicine; and everyone suffers from yearning!"—There came a soft, subdued song, like a moan. 'Neath Argentina's bright blue skies.... I stopped up the crack, went to bed, and tried to get to sleep, but after a moment I jumped up and ran onto the deck, for my cabin had filled with the stench of cod-liver oil and it was stifling.

The seamen were undoubtedly giving themselves over with all their souls to those never-ending fairy tales, to nautical fantasies about unknown waters, marvels, tropical wonders, and the adventures of Sinbad the Sailor. They had undoubtedly begun to tell those tales, heard a thousand times over, of mountains, groves, and cliffs, in the style of the biblical Solomon—breasts like a herd of lambs, hair like a roaring waterfall, eyes like a pair of young fawns. Imagination, like a vicious dog let off the leash, was baring its teeth, growling low and lurking in recesses. The deck was completely deserted. The sea was swirling in an impressive manner; the wind blew with twofold strength and in the murky waters the furious trunk of the whale loomed up, relentless in its circling motion. Hmm . . . to my right I had Africa, to my left America; in between, in the depths swam some little fish of the gudgeon family. Those tiny fish are so terrified of solitude that they never set out to sea except in schools of ten thousand or more, and if you catch one of them and dangle it over the water, the others poke their snouts pathetically out of the waves and perish—just like sheep!

"It's just as well," I whispered, "that there are no women, because if even one were to be found on the ship . . . ugh . . . who could protect me? But luckily we're far away and there is no woman, nor could there be—whatever else were to happen there couldn't be, for there is none and the men cannot. Thank you, Lord!"

At that moment I heard, behind me and somewhat to the left, the distinct sound of a juicy kiss. I looked around, thinking it was a sail flapping—no one was there—but a moment later the same sound reached me with even greater clarity. A kiss? A kiss on the ship? How on earth could that be, since there were no women? I cleared my throat and walked slowly windward, that is, toward the bows. Here I once again heard the same most unseemly sound, distinctly, as if it were just by my left ear. I decided to return to my cabin right away. Since there were no women, there could also be no kisses—and therefore I ought not to have heard something that did not exist. If, on the other hand, there really was a conspiracy, retreat was the appropriate course of action. —"I don't want to get mixed up in anything. Let them be by themselves and . . ."

Nevertheless, right by the cabin door I stopped, hearing behind the foremast, no more than three paces away, the tender, high-pitched voice of the ship's boy.

"Tommy, Tommy—give me a scarf and I'll go to the circus with you."

"Thompson," I called, "Thompson! What are you up to? Dear God, Thompson, think what you're doing!"

"What?" barked Thompson, not letting go of the ship's boy, who was clinging to him.

"Thompson, he's not a woman! Here's a pound sterling, Thompson, a pound sterling! I beg you!"

"But I resemble a woman," squeaked the ship's boy. "I have a high-pitched voice like a woman"—and all of a sudden Thompson insolently poked his thumb directly at my eyes—and they stopped paying any attention to me. I pretended I'd forgotten my handkerchief and I quickly left. But by the forward hatch, in the dark of night I suddenly caught sight of two other sailors walking along arm in arm. So I turned around—and again I saw two other sailors, near the galley, whispering to one another.—"It's not nice," I murmured, "that from now on I won't be able to look without embarrassment at two sailors, or even at one sailor. I'll have to turn my head away. In any case it would be a good idea to wake the captain. They're whispering and conniving together."

But Clarke was not asleep. I was surprised to spot the will-o'-the-wisp of his little pipe on the bridge. He had evidently decided to watch over the brig in the night. He stood staring intently at the tip of his bent finger. A good captain, I thought beseechingly, a noble captain, somewhat eccentric on the surface, but conscientious and experienced, a stalwart captain. He won't let it happen! He won't allow it! I went up and mentioned briefly in passing— that kisses had appeared on the ship, and that the crew was swarming about the deck and tossing and turning on the hard bedding of the fo'c'sle. In addition, the sailors were walking together—and saying things to one another—leaning toward each other and embracing.

"What? The crew is mutinying?" cried the captain, awaking from his revery. "Mr. Smith, have them bring my storm helmet! A mutiny needs to be punished by all the maritime and nautical statutes. The culprits will be sewn into sacks, then I'll read them the prescribed passage from the New Testament, after which they'll be thrown into the sea with stones around their necks. The only difficult part is catching them in the sacks. You have to put bait at the bottom of the sack."

(What foolishness! At such a moment! Why was it that foolishness wouldn't leave me alone for even a second? A terrible weariness flowed over me like olive oil.)

"If the ship is sailing to Valparaiso then I, as captain of the ship, should see to it that it reaches Valparaiso. I have to maintain cleanliness and order. Is that not so? Mr. Zantman — is that a misguided line of reasoning?"

He looked at me with unutterable pride and puffed himself up till his eyes bulged, and he turned so horribly crimson and scarlet that I took a step back and involuntarily covered my ears out of fear that he would burst — and suddenly he rose up from the ground, flew a few feet through the air and dropped back down. What was that? For all the world like a flying fish. Why on earth had I mentioned it to him then? It's clear that speaking is a bad idea, since the reach of words is unpredictable, and the borders of dreams become blurred.... "It's afraid!" he wheezed triumphantly as he descended. "It's afraid! — f . . . ing nature! In the throat! In the throat! Forward! Onward! Hurrah!" — he seemed to have lost his mind. — "Look here, Mr. Zantman" — he showed me the middle finger and index finger of his right hand — "What do you see? A tiny little spider.

"Just imagine," he went on, swelling up again automatically

and shouting into my ear, since the wind was growing stronger, heavy clouds were gathering to the north, and his pipe had gone out. "I found him a moment ago here on the bridge. I saw a huge she-spider that this tiny little spider was crawling toward. Blast it! Two steps away from me. You had to see how black and motionless she was, sitting there astraddle and waiting hypnotically. Like Mene, Tekel, Peres; and how he begged her not to devour him. He whimpered, I tell you! What do you say to that? I swear to God — you were right that hereabouts everything is having fun any way it wishes, and it's only foolish me . . . Foolish me! What do you say to that? — what do you say to the spider?"

"What's worse," I whispered, looking to the side and trembling, "is that snakes behave in exactly the same way with tiny little birds. My mind is weak. My mind is weak. Because of this there's a blurring of the difference between things, and also between good and evil."

The captain stared open-mouthed. "What? Mr. Zantman! That's right! Little birds — snakes — it never occurred to me. It really gives me gooseflesh. A fine bunch of scoundrels! Everything's scheming, everything's pairing off with one another, spiders, birds with snakes, sailors, everything's having fun — while I . . . Even here on the ship, under my nose, while I . . . Bah, after all there are fish in the sea, there are damn fish — there are hermaphrodites!" — he roared — "I never thought of that! By all the sulfurous fires of hell! Have you ever considered the fact that a hermaphrodite fish, having everything it needs — that it *really* must have fun?! And I alone have to stand here — I have to stick out like a peg?"

"It's a marriage," I said cautiously, since all the hairs on my head were standing on end and I was afraid of offending one of them. "It must be a marriage—in each fish there's a man and a woman, and a tiny priest."—Why wake sleeping dogs? Why so loud all of a sudden? "Now then, captain," I added, leaning on the rail, "there on the deck there are not a few but a great number of sailors—it seems even that all the sailors are together; they're whispering, embracing one another and heading this way—excuse me, I think I'll go back to my cabin."

"Aha," said the captain, rubbing his hands, "Aha! They're heading this way? Very good. Mr. Smith, come here on the double. Summon the second officer. Hurry now. They're heading this way? Right, now we'll have a dance."—And before I could shout out, with a gesture profoundly offensive to public decency he pulled a noiseless bluish Browning out of his pocket.

With a hurried step I returned to my cabin, where I lay on my bunk and fell asleep at once. But my dreams were troubled—I dreamed that everyone had gathered on deck very close together, that there arose a mingling, embraces, vulgar rolling about, subdued whispers, groans, hideous curses and imprecations. Something began squeezing together in the vicinity of the bridge, after which it surged to the rear of the ship, but I wasn't certain if this was a mutiny, since I heard no shots. It also seemed to me that in my sleep I heard my own name being spoken several times, to the accompaniment of raucous laughter, screams, derision, and hand-rubbing—"Zantman, Zantman"—as if I had funded it. As if all this were paid for out of my money.

The ship swayed and was hoisted slowly upward and I heard

someone explaining loathsomely that this was happening because the momentum of the ship had encountered an adverse wind—owing to which both the momentum and the wind were escalating, and the ship was being hoisted into the air to a great height. I tried to cry out but I couldn't make a sound, since I was asleep, and in the meantime someone touched the wheel with his finger, a turn was made, and the *Banbury* suddenly moved side on to the wind so abruptly that I fell from my bunk onto the floor.

4

Around midnight the sea wind turned into a storm. The brig pitched like a child's swing, creaking as it hurtled forward; and in a short time the momentum had increased so much that I could not tear myself away from the back wall of the cabin. The *Banbury* held out valiantly, meeting the wind with a sharp starboard tack. After twenty-six hours the pitching ceased, but I preferred not to go out on deck. For there most certainly had been a mutiny, and if not a mutiny then in any case something like it—so I thought I was better advised to stay on my own till I knew for certain what I would find outside. I locked my door and blocked it with a cupboard; in the corner I had a packet of sponge biscuits and eleven bottles of beer.

In the morning I peered warily out of the window, but I withdrew my head at once and pulled down the blind, and even covered the window with my overcoat. What I had seen confirmed me even more in my decision not to leave the cabin until they came themselves and broke down the door. My position was extremely disadvantageous, since I could run out of sponge biscuits. What was more, despite the fact that I put a blanket on top of the overcoat, light was seeping in through the chinks—a most unseemly light, replete somehow and dazzling—and the walls of the cabin had split and warped because of the storm, forming numerous fissures and cracks, all of which were contorted. These fissures were quite needlessly of a know-it-all, cerebral character and quite needlessly all of them were contorted and ended spikily. This too inclined me toward caution.

However, I do not know whether they had forgotten about me, whether they thought a wave had swept me overboard during the storm, or whether they perhaps had other things to do—in any case, in the course of three days no one gave any signs of life. It was becoming swelteringly hot. I looked out the window once again, but I retreated quickly to the far corner of the cabin; for I had seen some very garish willow-green colors, and it appeared at first glance that the garish willow-green colors could be worse than dark and gloomy nights. Furthermore, a tiny, overly garish hummingbird had come and perched on the railing, and the horizon shimmered with the splendor of all the colors of the rainbow, something I am not fond of; quite the reverse, a satiety of light, richness of decoration, and sumptuousness of colors disposes me unfavorably—I prefer a drab autumn dusk, or just as well a misty dawn—I dislike ostentation—I would rather have a quiet, modest spot where I always know how things will end.

And now this is the fourth day I've not moved from the corner, despite the fact that the biscuits are almost gone. The ship, it appears, is sailing ever more rapidly, but without the slightest rocking, evenly, like a boat on a pond—and the light that creeps through the chinks is constantly growing in clarity. There must already be great painful condors—and strange, raucous parrots—and goldfish as in an aquarium—and perhaps in the distance baobabs, palm trees, and waterfalls. . . . Yes, yes. . . . For there is no question that the mutineers, taking advantage of the force of the wind, have steered the *Banbury* toward unknown tropical waters—but I would rather not guess which willow-green colors the ship is passing through and what fantastical archipelagoes it is headed for as it moves along, borne by an underwater current. And I would rather not hear the savage, licentious cries with which the crew greet these hummingbirds, parrots and other signs on earth and in the heavens, proclaiming (to speak plainly) some rapid and magnificent merrymaking.

No, I do not wish to know. I do not wish to know and I have no desire whatsoever for hot weather or glamour and luxury. And I would prefer not to go out on deck for fear of seeing something . . . something that previously had been obscure, hidden, and unspoken, now parading in all its brazenness amid peacock feathers and the hot glare. Because from the beginning everything was mine, and I, I was just like everything—the exterior is a mirror in which the inside can be observed!

Philidor's Child Within

※

The prince of the most gloriously famous synthesists of all time was without a doubt the senior synthesist Philidor, professor of Synthetology at the University of Leyden, who hailed from the southern regions of Annam. He operated in the lofty spirit of Higher Synthesis, using the addition of +infinity, and in cases of emergency also using multiplication by +infinity. He was a man of respectable height and impressive rotundity, with an unkempt beard and the face of a prophet in eyeglasses. But a mental phenomenon of such magnitude could not fail to evoke in nature its counter-phenomenon, along the lines of the Newtonian principle of action and reaction; for this very reason an equally outstanding Analyst was soon born in Colombo and, completing his doctorate at Columbia University and receiving a professorship there, quickly rose to the highest ranks of an academic career. He was a lean, diminutive, clean-shaven man with the face of a skeptic in eyeglasses, whose sole inner mission was to hound and confound the eminent Philidor.

He operated by breakdown, and his speciality was breaking down a person with the aid of calculations, especially with the aid of flicks. And with the aid of flicks to the nose he stimulated the nose to independent existence, causing it to move spontaneously in every direction, to the consternation of its owner. He often performed this trick in the tram during moments of tedium. Following the voice of his most deep-rooted calling, he set off in pursuit of Philidor, and in a small town in Spain he even managed to acquire the aristocratic appellation of Anti-Philidor, of which he was extraordinarily proud. Philidor, having learned that the other man was after him, naturally also set off in pursuit, and for a considerable time both scholars pursued one another to no avail, for pride prevented either of them from accepting that he was not only the pursuer but also the pursued. And accordingly when, for instance, Philidor was in Bremen, Anti-Philidor would rush to Bremen from the Hague, unable or unwilling to take into consideration the fact that at the same time and with the same purpose Philidor was leaving Bremen for the Hague on an express train. The collision of the two speeding scholars — a disaster on the order of the greatest railway disasters — took place entirely by chance on the premises of the first-rate restaurant at the Hotel Bristol in Warsaw. Philidor, accompanied by Mrs. Philidor, was holding the railway timetable in his hand and was just working out the best connections when Anti-Philidor burst in breathlessly straight from the train with his analytical traveling companion, Flora Gente of Messina, on his arm. We, that is, the assistant professors present, Doctors Theophile Poklewski, Theodore Roklewski and myself, realizing the gravity of the situation, immediately set about taking notes.

Anti-Philidor walked up to the table and in silence, using only his gaze attacked the professor, who stood up. Each attempted to impose his will mentally upon the other. The Analyst drove coldly from beneath; the Synthesist responded from above, with a look full of hardy dignity. When the duel of stares produced no definitive results, the two mental foes began a duel of words. The doctor and master of Analysis said:

"Noodles!"

The synthetologist responded:

"Noodle!"

Anti-Philidor roared:

"Noodles, noodles: that is, the combination of flour, eggs and water!"

While Philidor parried at once with:

"Noodle, that is, the higher essence of the Noodle, the supreme Noodle itself!"

His eyes flashed thunderbolts and his beard waved; it was clear that he was the victor. The Professor of Higher Analysis took several steps back in helpless rage, but immediately afterward he hit upon a terrible cerebral notion, namely, the sickly weakling, in the presence of Philidor himself, attacked his wife, whom the worthy old professor loved above all else. Here is the further course of the encounter according to the Minutes:

1. Mrs. Philidor, the Professor's wife, is extremely plump, podgy, rather stately; she sits, says nothing, concentrates.

2. Professor Anti-Philidor took up a position opposite the pro-

fessor's wife with his cerebral lens and began to stare at her with a gaze that undressed her completely. Mrs. Philidor shuddered from cold and shame. Professor Philidor silently wrapped a traveling rug around her and cast a withering glance filled with boundless contempt at his arrogant opponent. Yet at the same time he betrayed signs of unease.

3. Then Anti-Philidor declared quietly: "The ear, the ear!" and burst out in derisive laughter. Under the influence of these words the ear was brought to light and became indecent. Philidor instructed his wife to pull her hat over her ears, but this did little good, for Anti-Philidor muttered as if to himself: "Two nostrils," in this way laying bare the nostrils of the venerable Professor's wife in a manner that was as shameless as it was analytical. The situation was becoming perilous, especially because covering the nostrils was out of the question.

4. The Professor of Leyden threatened to call the police. The scales of victory had visibly begun to tip toward the side of Colombo. The Master of Analysis said cerebrally: "Fingers, fingers of the hand, five fingers."

Alas, the largeness of the Professor's wife was not large enough to conceal the fact that suddenly revealed itself to those present in all its unheard-of luridness: the fact of the fingers of the hand. The fingers were there, five on each side. Mrs. Philidor, utterly defiled, attempted with what strength she still had to pull on her gloves, but—a quite incredible thing—the Doctor of Colombo hastily performed an analysis of her urine and exclaimed with a victorious roar:

"H_2OC_4, TPS, a few leucocytes, and some proteins!"

Everyone stood up. Professor Anti-Philidor moved away with his lover, who snorted with vulgar laughter, while Professor Philidor, aided by the undersigned, took his wife without delay to the hospital. Signed: T. Poklewski, T. Roklewski, and Anthony Świstak, assistant professors.

The next day we gathered, Roklewski, Poklewski, the Professor, and I, at the sick bed of Mrs. Philidor. Her breakdown was steadily progressing. Touched by Anti-Philidor's analytic hand, she was slowly losing her inner cohesion. From time to time she merely groaned softly: "I leg, I ear, leg, my ear, finger, head, leg"—as if bidding farewell to parts of her body that were already starting to move of their own accord. Her personhood was in its death throes. We all racked our brains in search of some means of immediate succour. There were no such means. After conferring among ourselves and also with Associate Professor S. Lopatkin, who flew in from Moscow at 7:40, we once again acknowledged the unavoidable necessity of the most extreme synthetic, scientific methods. There were no such methods. But then Philidor concentrated all his powers of thought, to such an extent that the rest of us took a step back, and said:

"The cheek! A slap on the cheek, and a sound one at that—this alone of all the parts of the body is capable of restoring my wife's good name and synthesizing the scattered elements into some higher honorable meaning of clap and slap. To work then!"

But the world-renowned Analyst was not so easily found in the city. It was only in the evening that he let himself be caught in a first-rate bar. In a state of sober inebriation he was emptying one bottle after another; and the more he drank, the soberer he became, and his analytic lover too. In fact, they were getting drunker on sobriety than on alcohol. When we walked in the waiters, pale as ghosts, were cowering behind the counter, while the two of them, in silence, were devoting themselves to some otherwise undefined orgies of cold blood. We formed a plan of action. The professor was to begin by making a feint with his right hand to the left cheek, then was to strike the right with his left hand, while we — that is, Assistant Professors of Warsaw University Poklewski, Roklewski, and I, along with Associate Professor Lopatkin — were to begin at once keeping the minutes. The plan was simple and the action uncomplicated. But the Professor's raised hand dropped back down. And we, the witnesses, were dumbstruck. There was no cheek! I repeat, there was no cheek; there were only two rosebuds and something like a vignette involving doves!

Anti-Philidor had predicted and anticipated Philidor's plans with devilish cunning. This sober Bacchus had tattooed on his cheeks two rosebuds on each side and something like a vignette involving doves! As a consequence the cheeks, and along with them the slap on the cheek intended by Philidor, lost all meaning, let alone a higher one. In essence a slap on the cheek administered to rosebuds and doves was not a slap on the cheek — it was more like striking wallpaper. Not wishing to allow the widely respected pedagogue and educator of youth to make a fool of himself by hitting wallpaper because his wife was sick, we firmly discouraged him from actions he would later regret.

"You cur!" roared the old man. "You despicable, oh, despicable, despicable cur!"

"You pile!" retorted the Analyst with fearful analytic pride. "I'm a pile too. If you like, kick me in the stomach. You won't kick *me* in the stomach; you'll just kick in the stomach—and nothing more. You meant to accost a cheek with a slap on the cheek? You can accost a cheek, but not mine—not mine! I don't exist at all! I don't exist!"

"I'll accost one day! God willing, I shall!"

"For the moment they're impregnated!" laughed Anti-Philidor. Flora Gente, who was sitting nearby, burst into laughter; the cosmic doctor of the two analyses cast her an sensuous look and left. Flora Gente, however, remained. She was sitting on a high stool and gazing at us with the creeping eyes of an utterly analyzed parrot and cow. Right away, at 8:40, we—Professor Philidor, the two medics, Associate Professor Lopatkin and I—began a conference together. As usual, Associate Professor Lopatkin held the pen. The conference took the following course.

ALL THREE DOCTORS OF LAW

In light of the preceding, we see no possibility of resolving the dispute by an affair of honor and we advise the Esteemed Professor to ignore the insult as coming from a person incapable of satisfying his honor.

PROF. PHILIDOR

Even if I ignore it, my wife is dying over there.

ASSOC. PROF. S. LOPATKIN

Your wife cannot be saved.

DR. PHILIDOR

Don't say that, don't say that! Yes, a slap on the cheek is the only medicine. But there is no cheek. There are no cheeks. There is no means for divine synthesis. There is no honor! There is no God! Yes, but there are cheeks! There is the cheek! God! Honor! Synthesis!

I

I see that logical thinking fails you, Professor. Either cheeks exist or they do not.

PHILIDOR

You are forgetting, gentlemen, that there remain my two cheeks. His cheeks do not exist, but mine still do. We can still stake my two untouched cheeks. Gentlemen, if you care to grasp my idea — I cannot give him a slap on the cheek, but he can give me one — and whether I slap him or he slaps me, it makes no difference — there will still be a Cheek and there will be Synthesis!

"Of course! But how on earth can he be made to — to slap you on the cheek, Professor?! How can he be made to slap you on the cheek?! How can he be made to slap you on the cheek?!!"

"Gentlemen," replied the brilliant thinker intently, "he has cheeks, but I have cheeks too. The principle here is a certain analogy and for that reason I will act less logically than analogically. *Per analogiam* is much more certain, for nature is governed by a certain analogy. If he is the king of Analysis, then I am the king of Synthesis, am I not? If he has cheeks, then I too have cheeks. If I have a wife, then he has a lover. If he has analyzed my wife, then I shall synthesize his lover, and in this manner I'll force him to administer the slap on the cheek that he recoils from administering. In this way I will force him and provoke him into slapping me on the cheek — since I cannot slap him on the cheek." — And without further ado he beckoned to Flora Gente.

We fell silent. She came up, moving every part of her body: with one eye she squinted at me, with the other at the Professor; she bared her teeth at Stefan Lopatkin, thrust out her front toward Roklewski, while wiggling her rear in Poklewski's direction. The impact was such that the associate professor said quietly:

"Professor, are you really going to apply your higher synthesis to these fifty separate parts? To this soulless, mercenary combination of cube roots (bs + sb) raised to some power?"

But the universal Synthetologist was such that he never lost hope. He invited her to sit down at his table, poured her a glass of Cinzano, and to begin with, to test the waters, he said synthetically:

"Soul, soul."

She responded with something similar, but not the same; she responded with something that was a part.

"I myself," said the Professor searchingly and insistently, trying to awake in her her ruined self. "I myself!"

She answered:

"Oh, you, all right, five zlotys."

"Oneness!" cried Philidor vehemently. "Higher oneness! Oneness!"

"It's all oneness to me," she said indifferently, "old man or child."

We gazed breathlessly at this infernal analyst of the night, whom Anti-Philidor had trained perfectly in his own way and may even have raised since childhood.

Nevertheless the Creator of Synthetic Studies persisted. There began a session of gruelling struggles and exertions. He read her the first two songs of *King Spirit*; for this she demanded ten zlotys. He had a long and inspired conversation with her about higher Love, the Love that gathers and unifies all, for which she took eleven zlotys. He read her two cliché-ridden novels by the best-known women writers on the topic of rebirth through Love, for which she charged a hundred and fifty zlotys and not a penny less. And when he tried to rouse a sense of dignity in her, she demanded no less than fifty-two zlotys.

"Eccentricities cost, my little gingerbread man," she said. "For that there are no fixed rates."

And, setting her blank owlish eyes in motion, she continued not to react as the prices rose and Anti-Philidor laughed up his sleeve about town at the hopelessness of these efforts and maneuvers ...

At a conference with Dr. Lopatkin and the three associate professors the eminent researcher reported his failure in the following words:

"It's cost me several hundred zlotys in all, and I really do not see any possibility of synthesis; in vain I ventured the highest Unities, such as Humanity; she turns everything into money and gives one back the change. Humanity valued at forty-two ceases to be a Unity. It's truly hard to know what should be done. And meanwhile my wife is losing what remains of her inner cohesion. Her leg is already setting off on walks around the room, and during naps — my wife's, of course, not her leg's — she has to hold onto it with her hands; but her hands refuse too; it's a terrible anarchy, a terrible unruliness."

T. POKLEWSKI, M.D.

Anti-Philidor is spreading rumors that you are a disagreeable maniac, Professor.

ASSOCIATE PROFESSOR LOPATKIN

Would it not be possible to get through to her precisely by means of money? If she changes *everything* into money, then perhaps she could be approached precisely from the point of view of money? I'm sorry, I don't have a clear picture of what I mean, but there is something of this kind in nature — for instance, I had a patient who suffered from bashfulness; I couldn't treat her with boldness because she could not absorb boldness, but I gave her such a dose of bashfulness that she couldn't stand it, and because she couldn't she had to be bold, and she immediately became as bold as anything. The best method is *per se*, to turn the sleeve inside out, that is, within itself. Within itself. She should be synthetized with money, though I confess I don't see how . . .

PHILIDOR

Money, money . . . But money is always a figure, a sum; it has nothing in common with Unity. In fact, only a penny is indivisible, but a penny in turn doesn't make any kind of an impression. Unless . . . unless . . . gentlemen, what if she were given such a huge sum that she were dumbfounded? — dumbfounded? Gentlemen . . . what if she were dumbfounded?

We fell silent; Philidor leaped up, and his black beard shook. He sank into one of those hypomaniacal states that geniuses enter every seven years. He liquidated two apartment buildings and a suburban villa, and converted the resulting 850,000 zlotys into one-zloty coins. Poklewski looked on in amazement; a shallow country doctor, he was never able to fully understand genius; he could never fully understand and for this reason he really did not understand at all. And in the meantime the philosopher, already sure of what he was doing, sent an ironic invitation to Anti-Philidor, who, answering irony with irony, appeared punctually at nine-thirty in a private room at the Alkazar restaurant, where the deciding experiment was to take place. The scholars did not shake hands; the master of Analysis merely laughed drily and maliciously:

"Do your worst, sir, do your worst! My girl isn't as eager to be put together as your wife was to be taken apart; in this regard I have no worries."

And he too sank gradually into a hypomaniacal state. Dr. Poklewski held the pen, Lopatkin held the paper.

Professor Philidor set about things in such a way that he first put down on the table a single one-zloty coin. Gente did not react. He put down a second coin—nothing; a third—nothing too; but at four zlotys she said:

"Aha, four zlotys."

At five she yawned; at six she said indifferently:

"What's this, old man, more sublimity?"

But it was only at ninety-seven that we noted the first manifestations of surprise, and at a hundred and fifteen her gaze, which till that point had been flitting between Dr. Poklewski, the Associate Professor and me, began to synthesize somewhat upon the money.

At one hundred thousand Philidor was wheezing, Anti-Philidor had become somewhat anxious, and the previously heterogeneous courtesan had acquired a certain concentration. As if riveted, she stared at the growing pile, which in fact was ceasing to be a pile; she tried to calculate it, but the calculation no longer came out. The sum was ceasing to be a sum and was becoming something unencompassable, something incomprehensible, something higher than a sum; it burst open the brain with its immensity, equal to the immensity of the Heavens. The patient was moaning dully. The Analyst leaped to the rescue, but the two doctors held him back with all their strength—it was to no avail that he advised her in a whisper to divide the whole into hundreds or five hundreds—for the whole could not be divided. When the triumphant archpriest of integrating knowledge had put down everything he had, and had sealed the pile, or rather the immensity, the mountain, the financial Mount Sinai, with one single indivisible penny, it was as if some god entered into the courtesan; she stood up and exhibited all the symptoms of synthesis—sobs, sighs, laughter, and pensiveness—and she said:

"I am the state. I myself. Something greater."

Philidor gave a cry of triumph, and then Anti-Philidor with a cry of horror broke free from the doctors' grip and struck Philidor in the face.

This blow was a thunderbolt—it was a lightning shaft of synthesis torn from analytical innards; darkness was loosed. The associate professor and the medics offered heartfelt congratulations to the profoundly dishonored Professor, while his bitter enemy writhed in the corner and howled in torment. But once set in motion, the course of honor could not be stopped by any howling, for the matter, until now not one of honor, had entered on the customary honorable course.

Full Professor G. L. Philidor of Leyden appointed two seconds in the persons of Associate Professor Lopatkin and myself; Full Professor P. T. Momsen, who bore the noble appellation of Anti-Philidor, appointed two seconds in the persons of the two assistant professors; Philidor's seconds symbolically accosted Anti-Philidor's seconds, who in turn symbolically accosted Philidor's seconds. And with each of these honorable steps there was an increase of synthesis. The Colomban twisted as if on burning coals, while the man of Leyden smiled and stroked his long beard in silence. Meanwhile, in the city hospital, the professor's sick wife had begun to unify her parts; in a barely audible voice she asked for milk and the doctors took heart. Honor peeped out from behind the clouds and smiled sweetly at the people. The final combat was to take place on Tuesday, at seven sharp.

Dr. Roklewski was to hold the pen, Associate Professor Lopatkin the pistols. Poklewski was to hold the paper, and I the overcoats. The steadfast warrior under the sign of Synthesis entertained no doubts at all. I remember his words the morning before:

"Son," he said, "he could just as easily perish as I, but whoever perishes, my spirit will always be victorious, for it is not a matter of death itself, but of the quality of death, and the quality of death will be synthetic. If he should fall, with his death he will pay homage to

Synthesis; if he kills me, he will kill me in a synthetic manner. And thus victory will be mine beyond the grave."

And in his elation, wishing to celebrate the moment of glory the more appropriately, he invited both the ladies, that is, his wife and Flora, to watch from the sidelines in the capacity of ordinary spectators. But I was oppressed by forebodings. I was afraid—what was it I was afraid of? I myself did not know; all night long I was tormented by my not knowing and it was only at the appointed place that I understood what I was afraid of. The daybreak was dry and bright, like a picture. The mental adversaries stood opposite one another. Philidor bowed to Anti-Philidor, and Anti-Philidor bowed to Philidor. And it was then I realized what I was afraid of. It was the symmetry—the situation was symmetrical, and in this lay its strength but also its weakness.

For the situation was such that every movement of Philidor's had to be matched by an analogous movement of Anti-Philidor's, and Philidor had the initiative. If Philidor bowed then Anti-Philidor had to bow too. If Philidor fired, then Anti-Philidor also had to fire. And everything, let me emphasize again, had to take place on an axis drawn between the two opponents, an axis that was the axis of the situation. All very well! But what would happen if the other man were to break away to the side? If he were to jump aside? If he were to play a trick and somehow manage to evade the iron laws of symmetry and analogy? Who knew what excesses and acts of treachery could be concealed in Anti-Philidor's cerebral head? My thoughts were in disarray when suddenly Professor Philidor raised his arm, took aim convergently straight at his opponent's heart, and fired. He fired and missed. He missed. And then the Analyst raised his arm in turn and aimed at his opponent's heart. We were already on the point of uttering a cry of victory. It already seemed that if the other man had fired synthetically at the heart, then this man too must fire at the heart. It seemed that there was simply no other way out, that there was no intellectual back door. But suddenly, in the blink of an eye, with a supreme effort, the Analyst let out a quiet squeak, yelped, dodged slightly, departed from the axis with the barrel of his pistol, and all at once shot to the side, and at what? — at the pinkie finger of Mrs. Philidor, who was standing nearby with Flora Gente. The shot was the height of mastery! The finger fell off. Mrs. Philidor raised her hand to her mouth in astonishment. And we, the seconds, for a moment lost control of ourselves and gave a cry of admiration.

And then a terrible thing happened. The Senior Professor of Synthesis could not withstand. Spellbound at the accuracy, the mastery, the symmetry, and stunned by our cry of admiration, he also dodged and also shot at Flora Gente's pinkie finger and emitted a short, dry, guttural laugh. Gente raised her hand to her mouth; we gave a cry of admiration.

Then the Analyst fired again, taking off the other pinkie finger of the Professor's wife, who raised her other hand to her mouth — we gave a cry of admiration — and a split second later a shot of Synthesis, delivered with unerring conviction from a distance of seventeen meters, took off Flora Gente's analogous finger. Gente raised her hand to her mouth, and we gave a cry of admiration. And so it went on. The shooting match continued unremittingly, furious, brutal, and splendid as splendor itself, while fingers, ears, noses, and teeth fell like leaves from a tree shaken by a storm, and we seconds could barely keep up with the cries that the lightning marksmanship wrested from our mouths. Both the ladies were already divested of all natural appendages and protrusions and had not dropped dead for the simple reason that they too could not keep up, and besides, I think they also took their own pleasure in all this. But in the end the ammunition ran out. With his last shot the master of Colombo pierced the very top of Mrs. Philidor's right lung, and the Master of Leyden in an instantaneous reply pierced Flora Gente's right lung; we gave one more cry of admiration, and silence descended. Both torsos died and slumped to the ground; both sharpshooters looked at one another.

And what now? They looked at each other and neither really knew—what? What, in fact? There was no more ammunition. Besides, the corpses already lay on the ground. In fact there was nothing to do. It was nearly ten o'clock. In fact Analysis had won, but what of it? Nothing whatsoever. Synthesis could just as well have won and nothing would have come of it either. Philidor picked up a rock and threw it at a sparrow, but he missed and the sparrow flew away. The sun was beginning to swelter; Anti-Philidor picked up a clod of earth and threw it at a tree trunk—it hit. In the meantime a chicken had presented itself to Philidor; he threw and hit, and the chicken ran away and hid in the bushes. The scholars stepped down from their stations and moved off—each in his own direction.

By evening Anti-Philidor was in Jeziorno, and Philidor in Wawer. The one was hunting crows by a haystack, the other had spotted an out-of-the-way lantern and was aiming at it from a distance of fifty paces.

And in this way they wandered around the world, taking aim at whatever they could with whatever they could. They sang songs and enjoyed breaking windows; they also liked to stand on balconies and spit on the hats of passersby, and things really got interesting when they managed to hit some fat gentlemen from the eastern provinces riding in a dorozhka. Philidor honed his talent until he could spit from the street on someone standing on a balcony. Anti-Philidor on the other hand could put out a candle by throwing a box of matches at the flame. Most of all they enjoyed hunting for frogs with a fowling piece or sparrows with a bow, or throwing scraps of paper and blades of grass into the water from a bridge. And their greatest pleasure was to buy a child's balloon and chase after it through the fields and woods — tally ho! — waiting for it to burst with a pop as if struck by an invisible bullet.

And when someone from the scientific world mentioned their former eminent past, their mental battles, Analysis, Synthesis, and all their irrevocably lost glory, they would only reply dreamily:

"Yes, yes, I remember that duel . . . the shooting was good!"

"But, Professor," I cried — and with me Roklewski, who in the meantime had married and started a family on Krucza Street — "but Professor, you're talking like a child!"

To which the old man in his second childhood replied:

"Everything has a child within."

Philibert's Child Within

➔←

A peasant of Paris had a child toward the end of the eighteenth century; that child had a child in turn, that child in turn had another child, and again there was another child; and the last child, as tennis champion of the world, was playing a match on the center court of the Parisian Racing-Club, in an atmosphere of nail-biting tension and with endless spontaneous rounds of thunderous applause. And yet (how terribly perfidious life can be!) a certain colonel of the zouaves in the crowd sitting in the side stands suddenly grew envious of the faultless and captivating play by both champions and, wanting to show the six thousand spectators gathered there what he too was capable of (the more so because his fiancée was sitting at his side), all at once he fired his revolver at the ball in flight. The ball burst and fell to the ground, while the champions, unexpectedly deprived of their target, for a short time went on waving their rackets in a vacuum; but, seeing the absurdity of their movements without the ball, they leaped at each other's throats. Thunderous applause rang out from the spectators.

And that would probably have been the end of it. But an additional circumstance occurred: the colonel, in his excitement, had forgotten or had failed to take into consideration (how important it is to consider things!) the spectators sitting on the opposite side of the court in the so-called sunlight stand. It had seemed to him —it was unclear why—that once the bullet punctured the ball it ought to stop; whereas unfortunately, it continued its course and struck a certain industrialist and shipping magnate in the neck. Blood spurted from the severed artery. The injured man's wife's first reaction was to throw herself at the colonel and wrest the revolver from his grip, but since she could not (as she was hemmed in by the crowd) she simply smacked her right-hand neighbor in the chops. And she did so because she was unable to vent her outrage in any other way and because in the deepest recesses of her being, driven by a purely feminine logic, she thought that as a woman she was entitled to, for who could do anything to her in return? It turned out, however, that this was not the case (how everything must constantly be taken into consideration in one's calculations!), since her neighbor was a latent epileptic who, as a result of the psychological shock brought on by the slap, had an attack and erupted like a geyser in twitches and convulsions. The poor woman found herself between two men, one of whom was bleeding at the neck, the other foaming at the mouth. Thunderous applause rang out from the spectators.

And then a gentleman who was sitting nearby, in a terrible panic jumped on top of a lady sitting below him; the latter picked him up and leaped onto the court, bearing him along at full tilt. Thunderous applause rang out from the spectators. And this would probably have been the end of it. But another circumstance arose (how everything always needs to be anticipated!): not far away there sat a certain modest, latent retired dreamer emeritus from Toulouse who for a very long time at all public events had dreamed of jumping on top of those sitting below him, and up till now had only by force restrained himself from doing so. Carried away by the example, he instantly leaped onto the lady sitting below him, who (a junior clerk newly arrived from Tangiers in Africa), believing that this was the appropriate thing to do, that it was the necessary thing, that this was how things were done in the big city—also picked him up, trying as she did so not to betray any awkwardness in her movements.

And then the more well-mannered segments of the crowd began to clap tactfully in order to cover up the scandal in the presence of representatives of foreign legations and embassies who had come in large numbers to the match. But here too there arose a misunderstanding, for the less well-mannered segments took the clapping as a mark of approval—and they too climbed onto their ladies. The foreigners manifested ever greater astonishment. In such a case, what else could the more well-mannered segments do? So as not to attract attention, they also climbed onto their ladies.

And this would almost certainly have been the end of it. But then a certain Marquis de Philibert, who was sitting in a courtside box with his wife and his wife's family, suddenly remembered that he was a gentleman and went out onto the court in a light summer suit, pale but determined—and asked coolly if someone was try-

ing to insult the Marquise de Philibert, his wife, and if so, who?
And he tossed into the crowd a handful of visiting cards bearing
the inscription: Philippe Hertal de Philibert. (How terribly careful
we must be! How hard and treacherous life is, how unpredictable!)
A deathly silence ensued.

And all at once, at a walk, bareback, on slender-fetlocked, elegant, fashionably dressed women, no fewer than thirty-six men
began to ride up to the Marquise de Philibert so as to insult her
and remember that they were gentlemen, since her husband, the
Marquis, had remembered he was a gentleman. She in turn, out of
fright, gave birth prematurely — and the whimpering of a child was
heard at the Marquis's feet beneath the heels of the trampling
women. The Marquis, so unexpectedly finding a child within, provided with and complemented by a child just as he had stepped out
alone as a grown and self-sufficient gentleman — became embarrassed and went home — while thunderous applause rang out
from the spectators.

On the Kitchen Steps

✈✦

At the gray hour, at the time when the first street lamps are lit, I liked to go into town and accost maids, maids of all work. This imperceptibly became a habit, and as is commonly known, *"consuetudo altera natura."* Other employees of the Ministry of Foreign Affairs, and all the attachés of the embassies (those who were not married, of course), also used to go out on the streets and accost one thing or another, according to taste, whim, or temperament; but I would always accost fleshy, beshawled maids, maids of all work. To such a degree that when I was assigned to Paris as second secretary—a considerable honor for a man of my years—after a certain time a powerful nostalgia obliged me to return home. I was too distressed by the foreignness of the calves, those slender, tense calves sheathed in stockings, shown by the maidservants of that country. The murderous nimbleness, the hideous nimbleness, unbearably Parisian, was just too fine, and clicked its slim little heels too much, and on the Place de l'Etoile or even in the neighborhoods on the left bank of the Seine one would look in vain for an ordinary frowze with a basket over her arm, leaving a household goods store or a corner grocery. Weyssenhoff writes: "The thrilling rhythm of the Parisienne's dainty feet." It was precisely this rhythm that was the death of me; I sought a different rhythm and a different melody . . .

It would take place in the following way: spotting a maid of all work in the distance as she plodded sluggishly along on podgy legs, I would quicken my pace and follow till she turned into the gateway of an apartment building. I would catch up with her on the kitchen steps and would start by asking: "Does Mrs. Kowalska live here?" and then: "Perhaps we could get acquainted." There was nothing concrete in this, for instance, no kissing, though in the course of some five years I must have approached well over a thousand maids; no, they were too timid, no doubt because their mistresses were too strict. I had no substantive gain from all this, other than the fact that perhaps it made it easier for me to live . . .

But one time I was indiscreet and was seen by one of my friends who, as was to be expected, told our mutual acquaintances:

"Guess what: yesterday I saw Filip on Hoża Street; I'm telling you, he was eyeing some revolting slattern!"

It went the rounds; the tenth or twentieth gossip started poking fun at me and congratulating me on my taste, saying that apparently I was fond of fresh turnip, while others made snide remarks along the lines of: "I know something, but I won't say a word." You can imagine how alarmed I was. It was of course true that all sorts of things happened in the Ministry; as is always the case, different people were fond of different things. But after all, a fashionable stocking is one thing; quite another was this embarrassing object, a vulgar, barefoot maid of all work. If they had at least been comely and firm—then I could have said something about fresh turnip, that I prefer a fresh turnip to the unhealthy delicacies of the city. But basket-laden maids, maids of all work have nothing in common with turnip—rather with lard, frying grease, or coconut butter. Often, in their rancid ugliness I bitterly perceived my own personal ill luck, some malign star; why was it, I wondered, that in any class or sphere one could find a maiden, or a girl, or a lass, in a word—poetry, while it was only the maids of all work who were doomed to be devoid of beauty and grace? It was only later that I discovered the rule of unnatural selection: It was the mistresses who unnaturally selected the most unsightly drudges, misshapen, bloodshot, or overweight, with horrendous backsides, broken noses, smashed right in the face by some unknown fist—for a housemaid has to look like this so that none of the gentlemen of the house should feel drawn to her by the will of God.

In fact, I too felt no passion, at least of that sort—no passion, but a great bashfulness, sweet as can be, from somewhere deep within me. It remained in me from my childhood years, when with bated breath and pounding heart I would stare at our maid of all work. As she was serving dinner, scrubbing the floor, bringing breakfast . . . or during spring cleaning while she was washing the windows . . . I would stare fervently, bashfully, through half-closed eyes. Today I wouldn't be crazy enough to suggest that such a revolting, common maid meets needs of an aesthetic or any other character; but at that time, I recall, if she had a gumboil, for me in my bashfulness that gumboil was more wonderful than all the potted geraniums of the window-washing, and, I recall, it was all in all a miracle before which one lowered one's gaze. Later, of course, there came lessons both pedagogical and non-pedagogical; there came "good manners," patent-leather shoes, neckties, the brushing of teeth and the cleaning of fingernails, there came success, awards and five-o'clock teas, there came Paris and London; but the bashfulness that was suppressed by refinement had already conceived an enduring affection for kitchen frowzes crowding around corner grocery stores, and found consolation in them. And not despite the fact, but precisely because of the fact that I was one of the most elegant employees of the Ministry of Foreign Affairs, I liked to love beshawled maids and, beneath my bowler hat and my English overcoat, to revive my former giddiness, the former pounding of my heart. It seemed that in this lay my homeland.

But it was bashfulness. If only it had been boldness. If only it had been boldness—as they say, a young girl, or a night on the town, or a private room at a restaurant and then to a hotel, something merry, something flashy, I'd pay no heed to the tittle-tattle and would simply say that I was a wolf. But since it was bashfulness, what could I do, how could I defend myself, how could I explain myself?

"Just imagine, Filip once eyed a beshawled maid of all work."

I took fright—to such an extent that soon afterward I married a person who constituted the absolute antidote to a maid. I was afraid of ridicule. There is tyranny! I renounced maids, wiped them from my memory, released them all from the first of the month and slammed the door of my inner being upon them. Did fleshy calves planted on shuffling feet still flash by on Krucza or Hoża Street? Perhaps—but for me that was terra incognita. My wife was immensely soothing and calming. Her legs were supple as lianas, long, slender at the fetlock; she constituted the best possible evidence of my taste; and her figure too was slender and elegant—in every respect this union made an excellent impression. Furthermore, we engaged a nimble girl who did not in the slightest resemble a basket-carrying maid; she bustled sprucely about the table in a white lace cap.

My wife set our home on its feet; those feet were refined, pure-bred, with a high arch, a hundred miles from those other fallen, sunken, irreparably flat feet. In actuality hardly anything changed; only two parenthetic twilight hours disappeared, and otherwise from one morning to the next everything remained the same, since even in her moments of ardor my wife was able to remember that I worked for the Ministry of Foreign Affairs. As for me, I moved around the apartment and kept repeating to myself: *"Ah, quelle beauté, quelle grâce!"* I did so with all the more self-denial because somewhere deep down lurked the nagging suspicion that my wife and my friends, and even the girl in the nimble cap, had guessed at certain things, and that I was undergoing treatment and being observed. For how else could it be explained? . . . such curious acts of cruelty . . . that they perhaps too often, too thoroughly brushed their teeth, scrubbed those teeth too severely, that the pumps they wore seemed too pointed, their patent-leather shoes too shiny. My wife, for instance, bathed every day, and did so I believe not without certain tyrannical intentions. There was too much cruelty in this, and too little heart; too much of a kind of cold hydrotherapy. It appeared as if they meant to stifle even the shadow of a longing, the very fancy of a fancy, the memory of a memory...

For my part, I obediently appreciated and admired my wife, just as I had once admired the Arc de Triomphe in Paris; but the Arc had lacked a certain characteristic straddling quality, a certain grotesquery, and that was why I had returned home. Why did I not have the strength to act in the same way with my wife, who equally lacked grotesquery; why, instead of roaming indubitably marvelous yet foreign lands and seas, had I not settled permanently at home—is that not a prime duty, that a person should live in his own country?

Instead, like a traitor, a turncoat, with a false admiration I gazed at the hostile, icy realm of my wife, at her smooth white panoramas, at details that for me were extinguished and dead, like moonlight. "A charming hillock," I thought, watching her as she slept; "it's round, small, snow-white. The slim outline, the supple waist —how sinuous they are, how fashionable, how aesthetic! A delightful leg—how harmonious it is as it streams in serpentine white down the snowy bed sheets." It was an abominable lie. It was the moon, while mother earth had gone to ruin somewhere. Yet my wife was able even in her sleep to prevent the very thought of rebellion or resistance—and there was something despotic in the way her leg narrowed downward, as if only this were permissible.

Oh, that delicate, pure, high-arched little foot, its arch equally Parisian, equally triumphal—I've already spoken of setting our home on its feet—my wife was capable of maneuvering that little foot with absolute authority, slipping it out from under the quilt like a once-and-for-all established truism. I kissed it with cold lips and went into raptures about it being so small, every toe as pink as could be; see, everything was correct, finished, fashioned. Across the entire expanse of her skin, nowhere, nowhere was there a single blemish—only infinite whiteness and smoothness. Only cold, statuesque moons, only aesthetic views, only trimmed hedges, Chinese and Japanese lanterns! It was a fantastical sight. And it bore alien names, in foreign languages, beginning with "manicure," through "coiffure" all the way to *"savoir vivre"* and "bon ton." And I too was European, I was washed clean, I was purified. And in the outside world too everything was purified and treated, everything was a glistening pump, a patent-leather shoe, a walking cane, a fashionable peignoir.

And how easy it all was, how accessible; it required only agreed-upon signals. With the help of a small number of these I won my wife's heart, and in the Ministry too everything took place with the aid of agreed-upon signals. The manicurists, secretaries, and chorus-girls who constituted the usual quarry of the employees of the Ministry of Foreign Affairs also required only agreed-upon signals, a handful of operations—movie, dinner, dance club, and sofa—like slot machines they gave out caresses when the right switches were pressed. True, everywhere there gleamed English snap fasteners; but these gave way so long as one knew their abra-cadabra and turned the appropriate key. In this way, the most thoroughly armored women (and I'm convinced that this included my wife) opened like oysters when one uttered the right, time-honored words and performed the ritual gestures. Everything was as smooth, facile, fluid as my wife's conventional leg, and likewise everything narrowed downward into a teensy little foot, and everything depended on the following few words: "Did you invite the Piotrowskis to tea?"

But the other thing with the maids was different, a little harder; let's recall, incidentally, how it was with that thing. There, on all sides appeared stubborn resistance, and in addition a sort of dreadful arousability; my eyes, nose, touch did not want it, only I wanted it. I'm walking along, staring intently from a distance, and I see—she's walking along, waggling her rump, plodding sluggishly on her short, fleshy calves, bare in summer and in winter wrapped in thick white cotton stockings. I quicken my pace; but here already my overcoat and bowler hat make themselves felt, already the difficulty and the torment are beginning. Because of course I want to see her face, to see what she's like; yet how can I look at her, she's an object of embarrassment. What will the ladies say, what will the elegant hats think of my bowler? And so I pass the maid, walking at a smart pace; then I turn around on some pretext (and now it's already harder to walk, I can already feel my movements being hindered beneath my English overcoat), I cast a fleeting glance, and at last I know what she's like. Is she one of the red-faced and saucy ones, or one of the pallid and puddingy ones, or one of the browbeaten and timid ones, or a shrill one, or a giggling one? And when, after numerous household goods stores and numerous idle chats with her friends, she turns into a gateway, then I rush forward, catch her on the kitchen steps, and ask breathlessly:

"Does Mrs. Kowalska live here?"

The maid doesn't yet suspect anything; she diligently heaves her shapeless legs onto the steps and says she doesn't know. In the meantime my ear listens for a rustle, ascertaining that no one is coming down from upstairs nor up from downstairs, that no mistress is about; then quietly, bashfully (with my heart pounding) I suggest:

"Maybe we could get acquainted."

The maid stops, looks — and something along the lines of a smile begins to appear, and some kind of fumbling begins underneath the wretched shawl, and with an embarrassed smile there emerges happiness — a soiled little hand, a mastodon's little hand, not very far, just as much as decency permits. I take it, stroke it, and whisper:

"I've taken a great fancy to you, Miss Marysia. I've been following you all the way from Marszałkowska Street."

The maid smiles, flattered:

"Come off it . . . What could of took your fancy?"

My eyes lowered and my heart thumping, I reply:

"Everything, Miss Marysia, everything!"— and I strive to speak as steadily, as naturally as possible, so as above all not to provoke her as yet thoroughly unaccustomed arousability.

The maid laughs:

"Mucky tricks!" she laughs. "Mucky tricks!" And immediately sets about poking at a rotten tooth with her finger.

And she forgets about me, completely absorbed by the tooth, while I stand there waiting — and waiting. All at once she removes her finger, studies it, and then suddenly — something changes in her!

"I don't appreciate getting to know someone on the steps!"

Some primitive pride has awakened in her. Then suddenly, sharply:

"See him there; he's took a fancy; who does he think he's dealing with!"

I bow my head and hunch my shoulders; I sense timidity, shyness, arousability stirring—once again, like so many times before, it will come to nothing! (And other maids have already noticed, they're already peeping at us through half-open kitchen doors, and one after another they are leaning out onto the steps—there's giggling everywhere and a crowd is forming.) All of a sudden my maid creases up in an attack of good humor—has something made her shake with laughter, does she wish to romp? She plonks her rear on the steps, stretches her pudgy legs in front of her and roars:

"Hee hee hee, hey diddle diddle, hey diddle diddle!"

"Quiet, quiet," I whisper, afraid of the maids' mistresses.

For at any moment one of them might come outside. But the other maids, the ones loitering higher up on the steps, repeat in piercing voices:

"Hee hee hee, hey diddle diddle, hey diddle diddle!"

Hey diddle diddle? I wonder where this arousability comes from. There must be something in me that provokes, that acts like a red rag upon their organ of laughter. I must excite their comic sense in more or less the same way that they excite my sense of smell. Could my stylish overcoat act in this way? Or my cleanliness, the gleaming mirrors of my fingernails, just as dirt in turn is amusing to my wife? But above all it's probably my fear of the mis-

tresses — they sensed this fear and that was what made them laugh
—yet now that the laughter has begun, I already know that everything is lost! And if, in an attempt to calm her and dispel the arousability, I should try to take her by the hand — God forfend! That
just fans the flames! She'll recoil, wrap herself in her shawl, and
issue a scream heard up and down the steps:

"What's with the pinching!"

I run quickly down the steps, my head bowed, an entire inferno
released behind me.

"See that bastard!"

"Chuck him down the stairs, Mańka!"

"What a sonofabitch!"

"He needs his hide tanned!"

"Pinching young ladies!"

"Pinching young ladies," "Tan his hide!" Yes, yes — yes, yes — it
was all a little different than with the manicurists and the chorus
girls — here everything was enormous, untamed, shameful, and
terrible, like a kitchen jungle! Everything was this way! And of
course it never came to anything improper. Ah, those forbidden,
outdated memories — what an unreasonable creature is man; that
is, how his feelings always get the better of his reason! Today,
calmly surveying the irretrievable past, I know, just as I knew then,
that it could never come to anything between me and the maids,
and that this was because of the gaping natural chasm between us;
but now too, just as then, I absolutely refuse to believe in that
chasm, and my anger turns on the mistresses! Who knows? If it
were not for them, if it were not for their hats, their gloves, their
sour-tempered, sharp, dissatisfied expressions, if it were not for

that paralyzing fear and shame that one of them might appear at any moment on the steps — and if they hadn't deliberately inculcated that fear in their maids, disseminating various stuff and nonsense about thieves, rapists, and murderers. . . . Yes, those mistresses produced a terrible timidity and arousability with the help of those hats of theirs. Oh, how I hated those shrewish dames, dames of the courtyard, dames with one maid of all work; I ascribed the entire blame to them — and perhaps not without reason, for who knows if without them the maids would not by nature be more kindly disposed toward me.

I was beginning to grow old. Gray hairs had appeared at my temples; I occupied a high-ranking position as undersecretary of state, and I was even more scrupulous about washing than my wife.

"Spruceness," I would say to her. "Spruceness is essential, spruceness first and foremost. Spruceness is boldness!"

"Boldness?" my wife asked, raising her eyebrows indifferently. "What do you understand by boldness?"

"Well, untidiness is a kind of bashfulness!"

"I don't really follow you, Filip."

"Cleanliness creates smoothness! Spruceness is refinement! Spruceness is the model! I can't abide all these aberrations, these individualisms — they're like a virgin forest, a primeval woods 'where the boar and the hare roam free.' I hate the naked primitive, recoiling with a squeal, a shriek. . . . It's awful. . . . Oh, it's awful!"

"I don't understand," my wife said reservedly. "But that reminds me . . . à propos of cleanliness. . . . Tell me, Filip, what do you get up to in the bathroom? When you bathe, the racket from in there can be heard throughout the apartment—splashes and noises, the occasional snort, gurgling sounds, coughs. Yesterday the postman overheard and asked what it was. I must confess that one should wash quietly; I see no reason to raise a racket."

"That's true. You may well be right. But when I think of what goes on in the world—when I think about all the dirt that's inundating us, that would inundate us if we didn't wash. Oh, how I despise it! How I hate it! It's disgusting! Listen! You despise it too, just as I do; say you despise it."

"I'm surprised you take it to heart so," my wife said dispassionately. "I don't despise it. I disregard it."

She looked at me.

"Filip, in general I disregard a great deal."

I replied with alacrity:

"So do I, my treasure."

Disregard? Very well, since she had said it, I had nothing against it; I too for years had been plunged in dull-witted disregard. But one night it transpired that my wife's disregard had its limits after all, and there was very nearly a marital scene. I was woken by a rough tug on the shoulder. She was standing over me, having hurriedly thrown on her dressing gown; she was altered beyond recognition, shaking with anger and disgust:

"Filip, wake up; stop it! You're shouting something in your sleep! I can't listen to it!"

"Me, in my sleep? Really? What was I saying?"

"*Does Mrs. Kowalska live here?*" she said with a shudder. "*Does Mrs. Kowalska live here?* And then you shouted—it was awful—about some sort of *hey diddle diddle*"—she barely touched these words with the tip of her tongue. "And then you groaned and began muttering something to the effect that you would strangle some sort of pale, cold, strangling moon, and you started repeating over and over, *I hate*. Filip! What are these moons?"

"It's nothing, my sweet. I have no idea what nonsense a person spouts when he's asleep. Moons? Perhaps it was something to do with sleepwalking..."

"But you said that you'd strangle . . . strangle . . . and on top of that, there was a stream of coarse language!"

"Perhaps it was some recollections from my youth. You know, I'm already growing old, and as one ages one recalls one's youth, like soup one had once, thirty years ago."

She looked askance at me—quivered—and all at once, to my astonishment, after so many years of married life I realized that she was afraid. Oh, she was afraid, like a mouse afraid of a cat!

"Filip," she said anxiously, "the moons . . ." (that was what frightened her the most) . . . "the moons..."

"You've no reason to be alarmed, my sweet—I mean, you're not lunar yourself."

"Lunar? What do you mean? Of course I'm not. What does 'lunar' mean anyway? Of course I'm not lunar. Filip!" she exclaimed suddenly. "I've not had a single peaceful night with you! You don't know it, but you snore! I've never told you before, out of discretion, but for heaven's sake get a grip, try to enter into yourself somehow and explain it all to yourself, because nothing good will come of it, you'll see!"

She moaned.

"Not one night! How you toot, how you whistle, how you

trumpet in the night! It's just as if you were going out hunting. Oh, why did I marry you? I could have married Leon. And now, since you've started to age, it's worse and worse — and in addition spring is on the way. Filip, explain those moons to yourself somehow or other."

"But I can't explain them to myself if I don't understand them, my sweet."

"Filip, you don't want to understand them." And she added further, drumming her fingers on the bedside table: "Filip, let me emphasize that I don't know the meaning of these moons, this cursing and so on, but whatever should happen, remember that I've always been a good wife. I've always been well disposed toward you, Filip."

I was surprised to hear that I snore — and what did she mean? — and why was she taking this tone of voice with me? After all, I was a passionless, that's it, a harmless, graying gentleman, rather jaded by life, regular at work and in the quiet of my home — it was only that, out of all this, I gradually began to ogle our nimble chambermaid. My wife noticed, dismissed her immediately and engaged another. I set about ogling her too. My wife gave her her notice also, but I began making sheep's eyes at the new girl, till my wife had to discharge her in turn.

"Filip!" she said. *"C'est plus fort que moi."*

"That's too bad, my dear! I'm growing old, as you can see, and before I'm put out to grass I'd like to gambol a little. Besides, these nimble young things, so refined in their little caps — as you know, this is a dish of ambassadors, consumed at the very best tables!"

Then my wife employed an older girl. But the same thing was repeated with her—ah!—and then my wife, thinking that it was just a passing whim of mine, some momentary obfuscation, finally took on a beshawled frowze by whom, she imagined, no one could be tempted.

And I did in fact calm down. The indispensable trunk was carried into the servant's quarters, and I didn't so much as raise my eyes; and it was only during dinner that I saw an awful, fleshy finger; I saw the rough blackened skin of her forearm; I heard her steps, shaking the house; I breathed in the ghastly aroma of vinegar and onion; and, reading my newspaper, I discerned the shrillness, the clumsiness, the gawkishness of all the movements of her immense body. I heard her voice—that slightly hoarse voice, not quite either of the country or the city; at times a piercing giggle reached me from the kitchen. I heard without listening, I saw without looking, and my heart pounded, and once again I was bashful, apprehensive, like long ago on the kitchen steps—I ambled about the apartment, and at the same time I was calculating and planning. No—my wife's anxieties were preposterous; what kind of insidious betrayal could threaten her from a quiet man whose days were coming to an end . . . and who at most, before he departed, wished to draw into his breast a little of the former air, and watch a little, and listen a little . . .

And I closely observed the play of elements, the tragicomedy of life—how my wife acted upon the maid, and how the maid acted upon my wife, and how in this encounter both wife and maid manifested themselves to the full. To begin with my wife would say nothing more than: "Oh!" And I could see that at the thudding of the maid's footsteps she quaked like a leaf; but on my account she was prepared to put up with a great deal. Along with her trunk the maid brought into our apartment her own affairs, in other words vermin, toothache, chills, picking her fingers, lots of crying, lots of laughing, lots of laundry; it all started to spread around the apartment, and my wife compressed her lips ever more, leaving only the tiniest crack. Of course, the process of instructing the maid commenced at once; to the side, I noticed out of the corner of my eye that this took on ever crueler forms and eventually became a kind of leveling of the terrain. The maid writhed as if burned by red-hot iron; she couldn't take a single step that was in accordance with her own nature. And my wife was unremitting—deep within her grew the spirit of strangulation, of hatred, the more so because I too was slightly hateful off to the side, though I could not have explained why or to what purpose. And I watched with narrow-eyed amazement as before my wife there arose primitive powers, truly different than Majola soap, and a vicious and prehistoric battle raged.

It turned out that among other things the maid had a rumbling stomach. My wife gave her medicine, but nothing helped: from her stomach a mysterious, chasmic growling emanated continuously; the dark chasm still called out. My wife ordered a restricted diet, forbidding her anything that could provoke such a din; in the end she shouted:

"I'll throw you out, Czesia, if you don't stop this once and for all!"

The maid took fright and from that moment rumbled twice as loud from fear—while my wife, pallid and exasperated, and seeing that nothing could be done, pretended that she couldn't hear. She was given away only by a slight trembling of her eyelids.

"Czesia," my wife declared, "I demand that you bathe once a week, on Saturdays; and Czesia, you need to scrub well with brush and soap!"

A few weeks later my wife crept up on tiptoe and peeped quietly through the keyhole. Czesia was standing fully clothed by the bathtub, splashing the water about with a thermometer, while the soap and brush lay to one side, untouched and dry. And once again there was shouting. And the constant vexation imperceptibly turned my wife into one of those sour, implacable mistresses from the courtyards—it was enough to scare me—she shouted like a furious magpie at the boyfriend who came to see the maid in the evenings, and asked:

"What are you after? Be off with you! You're not needed here! I won't allow anyone to sit here! Off you go! This minute! And don't come back!" She was exactly, exactly like one of those strict mistresses from the courtyards!

I watched everything, all these bizarre transformations, in what was in fact a cataleptic state, drawing patterns with my fork on the tablecloth for hours on end. What could be done—there was no turning back now; I could only sum things up, settle accounts—and perhaps listen one last time to the sweet, sinful whisper of youth. Ancient, long-forgotten stories, ancient shame and ancient hatred tapped at me the way a woodpecker hammers at frozen, leafless trees in wintertime; they beckoned to me from around the corner with a fleshy, unsightly finger. Oh, how impoverished I was at present, how washed into gravel by constant streams of water; what on earth had become of the fear, the apprehension, the shame and the embarrassment? Just a moment — I broke off these painful questions — could it be that I had wasted my life? Was only sin, only dirt profound? Did profundity lie beneath a dirty fingernail? And I wrote absently with my finger on the window pane: "Woe betide those who abandon their own dirt for the cleanliness of others; dirt is always one's own, cleanliness always another's."

And I thought perfunctorily of hazy matters: that a maid of all work is made up of a certain amount of ugliness and dirt; that if this dirt and ugliness were taken away, she would no longer be a maid of all work. But every maid has a boyfriend, and if that boyfriend loves her, then he passionately loves the whole, including the beauty and the ugliness, and so it's possible to say of the ugliness that it too is loved. And if it's loved, then why should it be combated? And I thought further that if someone loves only beauty and cleanliness, then they love only half of a being. And then I began to daydream unconnectedly — it mustn't be forgotten that my mind was deteriorating — I dreamed of little birds, lace, nuts, and a huge derisive moon rising over the earth. Boldness pokes fun at abject bashfulness — a fine, beautiful, triumphant leg ridicules a lugubrious, antediluvian leg. Someone once said that life is boldness. No: Boldness is slow death, whereas life is apprehensive bashfulness. Whoever loves a monstrous maid is alive; whereas he who favors a traditional beauty will gradually wither away.

"Czesia," I said one day to the maid, "the mistress says that you're awfully shrill. The mistress says it gives her a migraine."

The maid groaned:

"The mistress doesn't think a maid is a human being!"

Then I asked:

"Czesia, is it true what the mistress says, that when you cross a room the Dresden china on the shelves rattles as if it were about to shatter?"

Czesia said gloomily:

"Everything bothers the mistress."

I replied:

"The mistress is opposed to maids! She's against you, Czesia, and also against the others in our courtyard. The mistress thinks they're too loud, that their chattering and prattling is too vulgar—it makes her ears ache—and on top of that they spread all kinds of diseases. And another thing the mistress doesn't like is that every maid is a thief—that gives the mistress a migraine. And according to the mistress the boyfriends also steal things and spread various diseases."

Once I had said this I fell silent, as if I'd said nothing at all—and, as always when I came home from the ministry, I read the papers. Before long my wife came to speak to me about dismissing the maid.

"Of late," she said, "she's grown impudent; she scowls, and furthermore she's always out on the steps jabbering with the other maids. Once, when I went in the kitchen there were as many as four of them sitting there. In the courtyard she stands and gossips with the concierge. I believe it's high time to let her go."

I replied:

"Oh, let her stay on a while. She's talkative, but honest. She doesn't steal."

But my wife started to act terribly, I would say disproportionately, upset.

"Czesia, why were you laughing with the concierge's wife today?"

"It was nothing; we was just nattering."

"There's nothing to laugh at, my dear Czesia," said my wife sourly. "You probably think that you're quite clever."

I don't know what to ascribe it to, but my wife's nerves utterly refused to obey her. She came to me all set to create a scene: a moment ago she had gone out on the balcony, and the maid from across the way had said something to their cook; the two of them had looked at her and had burst out laughing; she wanted me to go and give them a talking-to. I stuck my head out of the window and cried:

"What's all this laughter! If you please! What's all this foolish laughter!"

But it truly seemed as if my wife was developing a persecution complex.

"Tell her she's fired from the first of the month. Her insubordination is growing worse. She's spreading rumors about us. I forbade her to associate with the other maids, and today I caught her on the steps snickering with the concierge and the cook from the first floor. I can't abide that foolishness of hers!"

"You want to sack her right away? Maybe she'll improve."

"Filip," said my wife with sudden concern, "I wouldn't have anything against rehiring our former maid, the younger one. Listen," she added with an effort, "what's the meaning of this? Czesia's laughing at me in this vulgar way behind my back—someone put her up to it—I sense it, I sense it for sure, that the moment I turn my back she makes faces and sticks her tongue out, or follows behind me. I sense it."

"I think you must be ill, my treasure. What could she possibly be laughing at, when there's nothing laughable about you?"

"How should I know what she's laughing at? At foolishness. Her own, naturally, not mine. She must have noticed something about me."

"Maybe she's amused by your manicure, the row of tiny little shining mirrors," I said pensively, "or maybe the fact that you wipe your nose on a handkerchief. God alone knows what might amuse an uneducated and uncultured maid. Maybe she's amused by your hair lotion?"

"Stop it!" she cried. "I'm not interested! It's not just her; the others are laughing too! Such inane, vulgar laughter! The insolence! Go to the landlord! Their heads have turned! It's going to make me ill!"

I gave Czesia a dressing-down:

"Czesia, why do you irritate the mistress? You know how delicate she is; she might easily fall ill!"

And I went to complain to the landlord about the disorder prevailing in the building—but the following day someone threw a rotting onion at me from a window. Indeed—it may have been—I also had the impression that amid the springtime noises of the courtyard I could detect a certain foolishness, a certain vulgarity, a certain suddenly excited, awful arousability—as if someone had tickled the heel of a mastodon with a feather. The maid from the back building had apparently had the impertinence to laugh in my wife's face; some awful drawings had appeared on our front door —Lord, monstrous jokes written in chalk, in which my wife and I featured in monstrous shapes and in a monstrous pose. On my wife's orders, the maid wiped these drawings off several times a day—my wife, driven to distraction, even lay in wait in the hallway and rushed out onto the stairs at the slightest rustle, but she was never able to catch anyone red-handed. All kinds of pranks were played.

"Police! Where's the police?! Police! How dare they! All the maids should be thrown out, and the concierge, and his children! The concierge's children are impertinent too! It's a mafia! It's a plot! You hear, Czesia?! Police! What are you looking at, Czesia?! I forbid you to look! Get out! Get out this second!"

But this shouting merely stirred up impudence and a terrible, insolent, hidden hatred.

"Filip," said my wife, shaking with fear, "what is this? What does it mean? Some kind of dirt is breeding here; something's brewing. There's something inside me—what do they want of me? Filip . . ." She looked at me then at once, ashen and extinguished, she crept away into the corner and sat down.

And I remained in my armchair, the newspaper in my hand, a cigarette burning down between my fingers, and thought for a long time. Doubtless it would have been possible to throw the maid out; we could also have changed apartments, even moved to another neighborhood; we could have—had I not been so feckless, so trembling and bashful. My wife asked me, what did this mean. What did what mean? For heaven's sake, who here was laughable, untamed, and monstrous? If my wife hated the maid, why then, the maid also hated my wife. I bent over this hatred, took it in trembling hands, and stared at it with the feeble gaze of an old man, listening intently to the insistent voice coming from the kitchen:

"So I says to the mistress, I says, if I was to tell you all the things they say, I think I'd drop dead first with embarrassment, and you'd burst a blood vessel."

I listened and said nothing . . .

Until my wife took off her wedding ring one day and put it on the dining room table, and I — oh, entirely automatically, after all I was quite lost in thought — I took the ring and slipped it into my pocket. And later I said to my wife:

"Honey, where's your wedding ring?"

My wife looked immediately at the maid, the maid at my wife; then my wife said:

"Czesia!"

Czesia replied:

"Yes ma'am!"

My wife exclaimed:

"Thief!"

The maid, her arms akimbo, yelled vulgarly:

"You're a thief yourself!"

My wife:

"Quiet!"

The maid:

"You be quiet!"

My wife:

"Get out! Get out this instant!"

The maid:

"Get out yourself!"

Oh, the things that happened! Heads had already appeared in all the windows, shouts, curses, insults were flying from every direction, and a terrible laughter was rising; then all at once I saw the maid grab hold of my wife's hair and tug, and tug, and as if through a fog I heard my wife's voice:

"Filip!"

The Rat

The terror of the entire established and prosperous neighborhood was a ruffian, roisterer, and brigand widely known by the name of Hooligan. He had been born in open country and on the boundless plain—had been brought up in forest, mountain, dale, and wilderness—he never slept in any enclosed space—and this gave him a characteristic massivity and breadth of nature—a boundlessness of soul—a swinging expansiveness of temperament. Yes, his was a broad nature that rejected cramped corners and was fond of drinking; and expansive gestures were the only kind of gestures fitting to him. Hooligan the brigand hated anything that was cramped, narrow, or petty, for instance pickpockets; and if he had to choose between pinching someone and smashing him in the face, he would smash him in the face—and he trod heavily and broadly across the fields, singing at the top of his voice: "With a heigh and a ho! A heigh and a ho!"

People got out of his way. And if someone failed to get out of the way in time, Hooligan the bandit would smash him right in the face with his paw, or lift him in the air and crush him—or he would simply maul him—then toss him aside and walk on. But he never perpetrated any hidden or petty killings; all his murders were noisy, bold, expansive and thunderous, committed in a grand procession with singing: "O Marysia, my Marysia!" . . . or: "With a nonny no, Marysia-o!" For he loved that Marysia of his more than anything else in the world; he loved her noisily, loudly, and broadly, with Cossack dancing, with vodka!

Yes, his was the broadest nature there could have been. He had no understanding whatsoever of quiet—and especially of quietening—the kind of quietening that, it could be said, is the principal thievish quality of people of our times—and he even slept sonorously, with open mouth, snoring, filling the valleys with his snores. He could not abide cats, and when he saw a cat he would chase after it for ten or twenty kilometers; whereas women he used to catch in abundance and bellow as he did so: "S-ing hell! S-ing hell!" Or he would shout: "With a heigh and a ho, hoo, hoo! Hup! Giddy up!" And that was exactly how he caught his one and only Marysia! Sometimes, however, he was oppressed by longing, and at such times the whole land was filled with his loud, sweeping elegies, which shimmered with dismal melancholy, and there rang out the bandit's croakings to the moon, outdoor, prayerlike, Ukrainian, Romanian, villainous, steppe-bound, or homegrown lamentations: "With a heigh heigh ho," he would sing, "O sorrow! O sorrow! Hey Marysia, Maryśka!" And the desperate dogs would bark down the lanes, howling dully and darkly. And in the end this howling also infected the people. And the entire neighborhood howled longingly, dully and blackly, straight at the pallid shining moon: "O sorrow! O sorrow!"

More and more songs multiplied and poured out around the bandit. He gradually passed into legend, and thus songs were composed about him too, either broad, outdoor ones or noisy, swaggering ones, though always with the same monotonous refrain: "With a heigh and a ho! A heigh and a ho! Ah ha, heigh, a heigh and a ho!" And there was more and more singing, rolling about, and killing. Yet in a crumbling and isolated manor house that stood nearby, for many years there had lived a certain old bachelor, a former judge, Skorabkowski, who was exceedingly irritated by the expansive exuberance of the neighborhood. He was constantly sneaking to the authorities to complain—all in the greatest secrecy, by the way.

"I don't understand how it can be tolerated," he would whisper. "Murders committed in broad daylight. . . . Rolling and sprawling about. . . . Roistering in the inns. And that singing, oh, that singing, that roaring, those eternal lamentations and howling . . . . And that Marysia, Marysia . . ."

"What do you expect?"—The chief of police was a corpulent man. "What do you expect, the authorities are powerless. Powerless," he repeated and stared through the window at the endless fallow fields, in which single trees grew here and there. "The people like him. They support him."

"How can they support him?!" burst out the retired judge, releasing his gaze through half-closed eyelids across the plain for many kilometers, all the way to the distant sand dunes of Mała

Wola, then bringing it back beneath his lids. "They're afraid to leave their homes! He kills people . . ."

"Yes, but only some people," the chief of police muttered in reply against the background of the endless plain. "The others just watch. . . . Don't you understand? For them it's fun—to see a decent murder. . . . Aha," he muttered and pretended not to see, for from a clump of trees not far away a corpse suddenly flew up in the air, followed immediately by a magnificent roar, as if thousands of buffalo were trampling the crops and the wildflowers.

The sun was dropping into the west. The chief of police closed the window.

"If you aren't willing to catch him, I will," the judge said, almost to himself. "I'll catch him and lock him up. I'll lock him up and constrict that broad nature of his. I'll constrict it and make it a little less generous."

But the chief of police merely sighed:

"Magnificent! Magnificent! . . ."

Skorabkowski returned to his deserted manor and, pacing through the empty rooms in his tobacco-brown dressing gown, dreamed up plans for seizing the ruffian. The miser's hatred of the rover gathered in strength with every minute. Catching him, seizing him, imprisoning and somehow quietening him became an imperative need of his rather constricted mind. In the end he decided to exploit the hellish straightforwardness of the ruffian, who would always assail his victims in a straight line, and—what was more—he also wished to exploit the excessive way in which the brigand had run rampant. In effect Hooligan had run so rampant that he was used to everyone running away from him, and the sight of a person who did not run away but stood still he took as a personal provocation. Accordingly Skorabkowski ordered his butler Ksawery to walk up to a tree on a nearby hill—and when the old servant carried out his master's command, the latter suddenly threw a chain around him and chained him to the trunk of the tree. After this, he dug a large pit with his own hands in front of the servant, set an iron trap in the pit, and hurriedly took refuge in his house. Dusk fell. For a long time Ksawery laughed at the "young master's" little jokes, but when the moon rose and illuminated the entire neighborhood as far as the distant woods on the horizon, the manservant slowly began to understand why he had been secured to a tree trunk on a hill and left so cruelly to the mercy of night's expanses. Dogs started to howl, and from the reeds there sounded the plaintive call of the brigand, who was beginning to yield to one of his steppe-wrought nostalgias. And gradually the great and terrible howling "Heigh ho Maryśka, Maryśka, Maryśka" began to surge through the night, plaintive and drunken, disheveled, limitless, seemingly unrestrained. First the bandit howled inexorably, wildly, without tremor or curb, giving free rein to his soul; after him the tethered dogs howled—and then the people howled, timidly and anxiously, through the casements of their bolted-up cottages.

"Young master!" Ksawery tried to call. "Young master!" But a shout would have attracted the attention of the bandit, and his anxious whisper failed to reach Skorabkowski, who was closely following the course of events from his casement. Ksawery cursed the fact that we humans cannot disappear, that we have to be exposed, though we do not want to be, though we cannot be, that someone else can put us on view and do with us in our stead that which is beyond our strength. The old servant cursed the *visibility* of our bodies, which is independent of us! But the bandit was already standing, already rising from his lair, and whether he liked it or not the old man had to catch his eye — irritate his pupil — via his optic nerve penetrate to his brain . . . and now Hooligan was already taking great strides to shatter his jaw, smash his nose and breast, crush his exposed and revealed neck! Haa! Ahaa! All at once he fell into the pit and was caught in the trap set by Skorabkowski, who immediately ran up and after a few hours' labor managed to transfer the thug's immense body to the secluded cellars of the old manor.

And so Hooligan was in his clutches! And so Hooligan the brigand had been dragged into a dungeon, locked up in a cramped space, gagged, chained to a hook, at someone else's mercy! The appeals judge rubbed his diminutive hands and smiled composedly, after which he spent the entire night thinking up appropriate tortures. He had no desire whatsoever to execute the roisterer — cramped, narrow and formalistic as he was, he wished to straiten and constrict his victim a little. Death was no tasty morsel for him; all he cared about was constriction. The retired man was in no hurry. For the first few days he did nothing but relish the notion that he had Hooligan in his cellar — that the brigand could not roar or make a racket, for he was *gagged*. And it was only when he realized that the noisy ruffian would be unable to make any noise, that he was *quiet* — it was only then that Judge Skorabkowski plucked up the courage to go down to the cellar and in absolute silence begin his practices, aimed at constricting and diminishing. Oh, how quietly! How powerful was the silence that rose from the cellars of the house and froze into stillness. There followed weeks and months of great quiet, the quiet of unroared roars . . .

And every day at seven in the evening Skorabkowski would descend into the torture chamber, wearing his tobacco brown housecoat, with little sticks or little wires in his hand. And every night, from seven onward, the appeals judge would labor in the sweat of his brow over the voiceless villain, silently, silently. . . . Silently he would approach him and to begin with would tickle him on the heel for a long, long time, so as to stimulate him to a spasmodic dainty giggle; then he would administer petty mortifications with the sticks and constrict his field of vision with the aid of boards; he would prick him with pins and show him peas, beans, and small beets. . . . But the brigand did not take it silently, but *in silence*. And his silence grew, surging and thrusting through the darkness, becoming equal to his most magnificent roars—and it was in vain that the judge attempted with his own silentness to vanquish the broad silence of the bandit—and hatred filled the dungeons! What was it that Skorabkowski actually wanted? He wanted to change the bandit's nature, refashion his voice, transform his broad laugh into a narrow giggle, reduce his roar to a whisper, shorten and diminish his entire figure; in a word, he wished to make him resemble himself, Skorabkowski. With the assiduity of a tracker he sought his weak points, subjecting him to particular and terrible examinations in order to find that point *minoris resistentiae*, the weak spot through which he could properly set about the bandit. Yet the bandit exhibited no weak spots, but only remained silent.

Time and again it seemed to the old gentleman that in the course of his strenuous operations he had succeeded in achieving a certain constriction—but every week there would come a time of truth, and for the torturer this was a terrible moment which the wretched, tight-lipped judge feared more than anything in the world. Because every week he had to take the gag from the bandit's mouth in order to feed him—oh, with what numb mortal terror he would stick mountains of cotton wool in his ears, place a bowl of food before the felled thug, and with a single convulsive gesture remove the cork from his mouth. And every time he would delude himself into hoping that despite everything he had succeeded in quietening the villain somewhat, that just maybe, this time he would not erupt . . . And every time the uncorked roisterer would burst out in an infernal orgy of shouts, curses, and roars! "S-ing hell! S-ing hell!"—he would roar. "You louse! Beat it! Beat it! Wait till I get my hands on you! I'll smash you in the mug, right in the mug. . . . Me, Hooligan, S-ing hell, S-ing hell, S- your mother! I'll kill you!" he would roar. "I'll kill you! Marysia! Marysia! Where's Marysia, heigh ho Marysia!" And he would fill the cellar with a roar that would spread throughout the neighborhood; he would spit curses, sing songs, vent his soul; and the miserly, shrunken torturer, white as a sheet, would thrust food into his gob . . . while he roared between mouthfuls. And the people in the local villages would repeat among themselves: "That's Hooligan roaring! Hooligan's still roaring!" After these sessions the former appeals judge would return upstairs paralyzed with fear and would go on searching for the point *minoris resistentiae*.

Till at last he found it.

It was a rat.

Oddly enough, a rat...

When one day a large rat chanced to visit the torture chamber and scuttled along the wall, the hitherto steadfast roisterer shrank.

Skorabkowski tore the gag from his mouth. The uncorked Hooligan did not burst out with a yell but, watching the rat, remained silent. His devilish disgust and fear were stronger than he was. And the only thing that happened was that as the rat passed close by his feet in the stocks, the brigand gave a convulsive laugh an octave higher...

At last! At last! How could God be thanked! He should drop to his knees in gratitude for this inconceivable grace! At last he had found a way! The appeals judge could not hold back his tears. For, by an inscrutable decree of Nature, even the strongest person has one single thing foreordained in this world that is stronger than him, that is above him and that he cannot tolerate! Some cannot tolerate primroses, others liver, while still others get hives from wild strawberries; but it was an astonishing thing that the murderer, who had not been enfeebled by torture with either little sticks or little pins, nor any of a thousand ingenious variations, who, it seemed, was stronger than anything—was afraid of a rat. He could not abide the rat! He was weaker than the rat. God alone knew why. Was it perhaps because the brigand, who murdered people like insects, was afraid to murder a rat—oh, he was not afraid of the rat itself—it was the rat's death he was afraid of; he was revolted by it more than anything else; a rat's death for him was infinitely loathsome, and he was unable to kill one, and no other death, of hog, or calf, or human, or worm, or chicken, or frog, was for him one thousandth part as terrible, repugnant, convulsive, slippery, rounded, and false as the death of a rat! And this was why the fearful thug was helpless in the face of the rodent—it was the only death that for him was unattainable, impossible. And thus at the sight of the rat he stiffened and shrank, growing visibly tighter and more constricted, and he trembled and shuddered. At last!

At last old Judge Korabkowski had become Hooligan's master! And from that moment on, he set the rat on him mercilessly.

With the rat on a leash he would draw close, shrinking the rogue and constricting him; or for a short second he would put the rat up his trouser leg and reduce his voice to a squeak; or he would make the brigand stiffen by holding the rat over him; or finally he would patter, hop and jump the rat around the ever-shrinking roisterer. The gag was no longer needed. The roisterer could no longer shout, let alone roar; and weeks, even months passed by in this fashion; and the old butler Ksawery, whose task it was to illuminate the pitiless rat with the aid of a candle, moaned and prayed quietly—and, his hair standing on end, with ice in his heart, the old servant begged the rat for mercy, cursing the absolute mercilessness of the rat, cursing the terrible and as it were irrevocable connections that are made in nature, cursing the boundlessness of the pitilessness. "Cursed be the rat and the young master and the house and the brigand's nature and the judge's nature and the rat's nature; oh, cursed be their natures and cursed be Nature!" Years passed. The torments grew ever more intense, and by means of the rat Skorabkowski tightened ever further, without respite—and the tension rose, and rose, and rose.

And all the time — the rat.

Without a break — the rat.

Only — the rat.

The rat, and the rat, and the rat.

Till Ksawery, at the very limits of tension, lowered his head and rushed after the rat, which had slipped off the leash with a squeak and run away, pattering off into the depths, into a crack, into a cavity. Then the rushing servant went astray and collided with the judge, whose head was lowered . . .

Skorabkowski, stretched to extremes of tension, had gone astray and lowered his head . . .

And he rushed at Ksawery with head lowered. The crash took place in the cellar; there was a shattering of brains — aha! So Hooligan the brigand was free after eleven years and four months; his torturers lay lifeless. And the rat was gone! The bandit swallowed and thought to himself that he should make his way out — and with tiny movements of his body he set about freeing himself. At dawn the ruffian got out of the stocks, opened the door leading to a small verandah overgrown with vines, and escaped into freedom — that once great strapping fellow, now mightily shrunken. From the verandah he immediately bolted for the bushes and began to move through them across the dike — and in the meantime the sun rose above the horizon. All at once a shepherd in the distance called:

"Cow! Cow-ee!"

Hooligan instantly crouched behind a bush. Oh, he would gladly have curled up somewhere, crawled into a cavity, a crevice, an opening, a hole; he would have burrowed into the undergrowth and hidden his back and the rest of the surface of his body. The ruffian looked down. A light breeze blew over him, but he did not delight in it at all, he did not breathe it in and sigh—he just cautiously and intently gazed downward. He was preoccupied by one thought—what had happened to the rat? What had become of the rat that Ksawery had flushed into a crevice?

But the rat was gone.

All the same, Hooligan kept his eyes glued to the ground. He had grown too familiar with dread of the rat, he had had too much of the entire immeasurability of the rat's horror, for the very absence of the rat not to be more important to him than all the sweetest voices and breezes in the world—no, the rest was merely ornament, only the rat or the absence of the rat was important! And the bandit's ears listened for nothing else but tiny rustles akin to pattering, and his eyes noticed only shapes akin to that of a rat, and every few moments it seemed to him that now, now he could make it out . . . now, now, he could sense it coming . . . he could virtually hear and see that hop hop, that jump jump, that patter patter . . .

But the rat was gone.

And yet it seemed impossible that the rodent, having been in such a close and terrifyingly painful relationship with his person for so many years, united with his person in a system of torment, accustomed to his person more than any animal had ever been accustomed to a human—it seemed impossible that the rodent (for one had to take into account the blind attachment of animals) could have broken away from him, disappeared, and abandoned him, just like that . . .

But the rat was gone.

Then suddenly something elongated scurried swiftly past near a large patch of sunlight, then took cover . . .

Could it be the rat?

The roisterer gazed around searchingly—he was not entirely sure—but again something pattered in the dry leaves.

And again—could it be the rat?

Almost certainly—it was the rat.

He stepped, while close behind him leaped
The faithful rat!
He skipped, and close behind him tripped
The faithful rat!

Hooligan rushed up to a tree and hid in a hollow, while the rat jumped into the brush and hid there. But the hollow did not offer sufficient protection; the unpredictable rodent, having emerged from the darkness of the cellars and blinded by the light of day, could have scampered under his feet and crawled up his trouser leg. For was it not so that the rat, scared and exposed, would desperately seek some hiding place, something familiar; and what could be more familiar to him than Hooligan's trouser leg? What hole was he more accustomed to? And the brigand realized that the crevices and cavities he created, the holes and nooks that, like it or not, he had in his body and between his body and his clothes —these were what the rat desired, these were his hiding places. And so he tumbled out of the hollow and, driven by fear, fled into open space, in any old direction, and behind him (almost certainly) the rat scampered across the ground. Oh, to find a cavity, a hole, a crevice, a fissure, to protect his back, hide his legs, cover himself on all sides, prevent access to those holes, cavities, and crevices of his that were so inviting—and the brigand, having come out from under the earth, dashed on and on and on through meadows, groves, valleys, hills, fields, and dales, fleeing with his cavities, and behind him (probably) dashed the rat. With his last remaining strength the bandit reached some cavity that presented itself to him; barely conscious, he crept into the hole, guarding his crevices, and wriggled into some straw. Only after a few minutes did he notice, half-crazed, that the hole into which he had crawled was a hole in the wooden wall of a shed—that he had crawled into a shed, or a barn. But at any moment the rat could crawl out of the straw and crawl into his armpit, or into a hole formed by the folds of his shirt; and so once again he poked his head out and looked around. But what was this? Was he dreaming or waking? Where on earth am I? Aha, this shed looks familiar! Who could that be, lying on the earth floor, on a pallet of straw, by the far wall? Heigh ho, it was Marysia, Marysia! Heigh ho, Marysia lay here, Marysia was resting, Marysia was sleeping, and breathing, oh, heigh heigh, Marysia, Maryśka! With a nonny no, Marysia! Shrunken, pervaded with rat to the core of his being, he fixed his eyes upon her, and could not believe it was her . . . The girl lay asleep, mouth open, and Hooligan jumped up—and was just about to start singing, start roaring, like long ago—like once upon a time: "Marysia, Marysia . . . heigh ho, Marysia, Marysia . . ."

When suddenly a rat crawled out from one side.

A generously proportioned rat peeped out from beneath a

beam, cautiously crept out onto the earth floor and gave a low hop not far from Marysia's skirt.

So again there was a rat.

By Marysia—there was a rat.

This time it was no phantom but an indubitable, palpable rat; it was hopping four paces away from him on the earth floor. The brigand froze. It was probably a different rodent—not the one with which he had been tortured, a different one—but rats are so alike that he could not be completely certain. What was more, he was also unsure whether all the years of such painful association with one of these rodents had not left him with something that attracted rats in general. But worst of all he was terrified that out of fear he might hop by accident onto the rat, for then the rat out of fear might hop onto him—no, no, it was necessary to act cautiously, to reveal his presence as delicately as possible, to startle the rat just a tiny bit so it would take refuge in its hole once again. For God's sake!—to avoid any violent movements, to resist panicking, not to succumb to that wild, subterranean, hopping-and-jumping unpredictability that is peculiar to those terrible, pattering, squeaking, long-tailed denizens of underground! The brigand identified the place where the rat's cavity was probably to be found and set about preparing to startle it delicately and quietly; in almost complete silence, with only a slight rustle or at most a cough—when suddenly . . . something enticed the rat to go up to the girl's right knee. He crawled in there—and Hooligan froze— for the rat had touched her, the essence of the rat had rubbed against his girl, his Marysia—against Marysia!

And all at once this touch, this rubbing of the rat against Marysia, more dreadful than anything, caused the bandit . . . to roar! He roared like long ago, at the top of his voice, to the entire world, he roared with his former, irresistible roar and flung himself on the rat; as he roared he leaped! He was no longer afraid; he leaped with a roar, with a roar he threw himself on the rat, with such a furious roar, so encased was he in his shout, that the rat would never in a million years break through that roar of his into his trouser leg! He no longer thought about the fact that he was cutting the rat off from its lair, but with a roar he flung himself on it from the front. Oh, Hooligan suddenly leaps, oh, the rat hops to one side, oh, there's a dodge and a leap and a skip and a bound— and the lightning certainty of the roaring brigand that the rat would not evade him, that he had caught the rat, that he would kill the rat and that it was devoid of any lairs or holes! . . . And I do not know if I should go on. Can my lips utter these most terrible things? Oh, they can, surely, for dread has no limits; on the contrary, there is a certain boundlessness of pitilessness, there is the fact that once dread starts to pile up, then piling up it piles up, it piles up piling up—without end, without limit, continuously; growing, it grows of its own accord beyond itself, mechanically. Oh, surely my lips will declare that the rat . . . that the half-blinded rodent, terrified and hounded, driven crazy by the blind and absolute need for a cavity . . . crawled into Marysia's mouth, scrabbled and hopped into the half-open oral cavity of the woman as she slept with open mouth. And before Hooligan could clutch at himself convulsively, he saw it: the rat pushing into the mouth, in a panic trying to hide in his beloved's oral cavity! O mechanisms!

While Marysia, half-conscious, awakened, entirely mechanically, at lightning speed closed her beloved jaws—and the mechanism of terror came to an end, the rat came to an end with its head bitten off from its body; the death of the rat had come.

There was no longer any rat.

But Hooligan was faced with the bitten-off death of the rat in the beloved oral cavity of Marysia his love. And with this he went.

He tripped, and close behind him skipped
A rat-death.
He leaped, while close behind him stepped
The rat's death in Marysia's oral cavity.

The Banquet

><

The meeting of the council . . . the secret meeting of the council . . . was being held in the gloomy, historic portrait hall, whose centuries-old power exceeded even the power of the council, overwhelming it with its magnitude. The immemorial portraits stared down dully and mutely from the ancient walls on the hieratic faces of the dignitaries, who stared in turn at the dry, ancient figure of the great chancellor and minister of state. Speaking drily, as he always did, the dry and powerful old man made no attempt to conceal his profound joy, and called on the ministers and undersecretaries of state there present to commemorate the historic moment by rising to their feet. For after many years of endeavors, the union of the king with Archduchess Renata Adelaide Christina was to come about; and Renata Adelaide had come to the royal court; and tomorrow at a court banquet the betrothed (who up till now had known each other only from portraits) would be introduced to one another—and this union, splendid in every regard, would intensify and would multiply into infinity the dignity and power of the Crown. The Crown! The Crown! And yet a painful unease, an acute concern, an anxiety even, furrowed the seasoned countenances of the ministers and undersecretaries of state, and something unspoken, something dramatic, lurked in their withered and age-old lips.

At the unanimous motion of the council the chancellor had called for a discussion . . . yet silence, a dull and mute silence, seemed the principal mark of the discussion that ensued. First to request leave to speak was the minister of internal affairs; but when he was given the floor, he began to be silent, and was silent throughout his speech—after which he sat down. Next to speak was the minister of the court; but he too, having risen, was silent through all he had to say, after which he sat down. In the subsequent speeches, one minister after another requested the floor, rose, was silent, then sat down again, and the silence, the obstinate silence of the council—multiplied by the silence of the portraits and the silence of the walls—continually grew in power. The candles drooped. The chancellor presided steadfastly over the silence. Hours passed.

What was the cause of the silence? None of the statesmen could either admit, nor even think, the thought that on the one hand was inescapable and imposed itself with an irresistible force, yet on the other constituted nothing less than a crime of high treason. That was why they were silent. How could it be admitted, how could it be said, that the king . . . the king was . . . oh no, never, never in a million years, death was preferable rather . . . that the king . . . oh no, ah, no, oh no . . . ha . . . that the king was corrupt! The king was for sale! The king sold himself! In his brazen, base, insatiable cupidity the king was a traitor more corrupt than anyone else in history. A bribe-taker and traitor was the king! The king would sell his own majesty for pounds and ounces.

Suddenly the heavily carved doors of the room swung open, and King Slothbert appeared in the uniform of a general of the royal guard, a sword at his side and a large cocked hat on his head. The ministers bowed low to the ruler, who threw his sword on the table and himself into an armchair and crossed his legs, looking around with his piercing little eyes.

By the very presence of the king the council of ministers was transformed into a royal council, and the royal council set about listening to the king's pronouncement. In his pronouncement the king above all expressed his joy that his marriage to the arch-duchess was to come about, and conveyed his steadfast faith and hope that his royal person would win the love of the daughter of kings—yet he also emphasized the burden of responsibility that weighed upon his shoulders. And there was something so extremely corrupt in the king's voice that the council shuddered in complete silence.

"We cannot hide the fact," declared the king, "that for us partic-ipation in tomorrow's banquet presents an arduous task . . . for we shall have to exert ourselves mightily to ensure that a favorable impression is made on the archduchess . . . nevertheless, we are prepared to do anything for the good of the Crown, especially if . . . if . . . um . . . um . . ."

The royal fingers drummed pointedly on the table, and the pronouncement became ever more confidential. There could no longer be any doubt. No less than a *bribe* was being demanded by the bribe-taker in the crown in return for his participation in the banquet. And all at once the king began to complain that these were hard times, that it wasn't clear how one could make ends meet . . . after which he giggled . . . he giggled and winked confidentially at the chancellor and minister of state . . . he winked and then giggled again . . . he giggled and poked him in the side with his finger.

In the most profound and, it seemed, solidified silence the old man gazed at the monarch, who was giggling, winking, and poking him in the side . . . and the old man's silence swelled with the silence of the portraits and the silence of the walls. The king's giggling died away . . . All of a sudden the iron-willed old man bowed before the king, and after him the heads of the ministers were lowered and the knees of the undersecretaries of state all bent. The power of the council's bow, rendered unexpectedly in that secluded hall, was terrible. The bow struck the king right in the chest, stiffened his arms and legs, brought back his royalty—to the extent that poor Slothbert gave an awful moan amid the walls and once again tried to giggle, but the giggle faded on his lips. In the quiet of the unyielding silence the king began to be afraid . . . and for the longest time he was afraid . . . until finally he began to retreat from the council and from himself, and his back, clad in the general's uniform, disappeared in the gloom of the corridor.

And then a monstrous and corrupt cry—"I'll pay you all back! I will, I'll pay you back!"—reached the ears of the council.

Immediately following the king's departure the chancellor

opened the discussion again, and again silence became the lot of the council. The chancellor steadfastly presided over the silence. The ministers rose and sat down again. Hours passed. How could the king, enraged by the refusal of a bribe, be prevented from committing some scandal at the banquet; how could the king be protected from Slothbert; and finally, what kind of an impression would this wretched, shameful, and embarrassing king make on the foreign archduchess and daughter of emperors, even if by some miracle a scandal were to be avoided—these were questions which the council could not acknowledge, which it rejected, which it regorged in silent convulsions amid the walls. The ministers rose and sat down again. But when, at four in the morning, the council submitted its resignation en masse, the helmsman of the ship of state refused to acknowledge it, and instead uttered these significant words:

"Gentlemen, the king must be forced upon the king; the king must be imprisoned within the king; we must lock up the king in the king . . ."

For it seemed that only by terrorizing the king with the hugely magnified pressure of splendor, history, brilliance, and ceremony, might the Crown be saved from disrepute. In such a spirit the chancellor issued orders, and because of this the banquet that took place the following day in the hall of mirrors glittered with every splendor, from splendor passed into splendor, from brilliance into brilliance, from glory into glory, resounding like bells in the loftiest and, it seemed, unearthly circles and regions of brilliance.

The Archduchess Renata, escorted into the hall by the great master of ceremonies and marshal of the court, blinked her eyes, blinded by the noble and immemorial luster of that archbanquet. With a discreet power, historically ancient names passed into the hieratic nimbus of the clergy, who in turn passed as if intoxicated into the white of honorable, wilting décolletages, which merged swooningly into the epaulettes of the generals and the sashes of the ambassadors — and the mirrors repeated the splendor into infinity. The murmur of conversation merged into the scent of perfume. When King Slothbert entered the hall and blinked, dazzled by the brilliance, a resounding cry of welcome immediately seized him as in a pair of pincers, and the bows of those gathered made it impossible to escape the cry of welcome . . . and the lane of people that formed forced him to move toward the archduchess . . . who, tearing the lace of her robe into shreds, could not believe her eyes. Could this be the king and her future consort, this vulgar little merchant with the mug of a shop assistant and the devious gaze of a small-time fruit seller and hole-and-corner extortionist? Yet — how strange — was this little merchant the magnificent king who was approaching between a double row of bows? When the king took her hand she shuddered with disgust, but at the same moment the thunder of cannon and the pealing of bells drew a sigh of admiration from her bosom. The chancellor gave a sigh of relief which was multiplied and duplicated by a sigh from the council.

Resting his royal, sacred, and metaphysical hand on the pommel of his sword, the king gave his other hand, omnipotent and consecrating, to the archduchess Renata and led her to the banqueting table. After him the guests led their ladies with a scraping of feet and a glittering of epaulettes and aiguillettes.

But what was that? What was that sound, quiet, diminutive, small, barely audible yet telltale, which reached the ears of the chancellor and the ears of the council? Were those ears mistaken, or had they indeed heard a sound as if someone from the side . . . as if someone on the side . . . was jingling . . . jingling coins . . . was clinking copper money in his pocket? What could it be? The stern, cold gaze of the historic old man passed over those present and finally came to rest on the figure of one of the ambassadors. Not one muscle twitched on the ambassador's face; this representative of a hostile country was, with a barely perceptible expression of irony on his narrow lips, leading to the table the Duchess Byzantia, daughter of Marquis Frybert . . . but once again there came the telltale, quiet yet perilous sound . . . and a presentiment of treachery, villainous, base treachery, a presentiment of a lurking, hole-and-corner conspiracy burst into the dramatic and historic soul of the great minister. Could there be a conspiracy? Could there be treachery?

A new fanfare on the trumpets proclaimed the commencement of the feast. At this irresistible command Slothbert placed his vulgar buttocks on the very edge of the royal stool; the moment he sat, the whole company sat too. They sat down, sat down, sat down, ministers, generals, clergy, and court. The king moved his hand toward his fork, took hold of it, and brought a piece of roast to his mouth; and at the same moment the government, the court, the generals, and the clergy brought little pieces of meat to their mouths, and the mirrors repeated this action to infinity. Afraid, Slothbert stopped eating—but then the whole assembly stopped eating, and the act of not-eating became even more powerful than the act of eating. Then, in order to put an end to the not-eating as quickly as possible, Slothbert picked up his goblet and raised it to his lips—and at once everyone picked up their goblets in a resounding, thousand-strong toast that erupted and hung in the air . . . until Slothbert all the more hurriedly put down the goblet. But then they all put down their goblets. So the king once again glued his lips to the goblet. Again a toast erupted. Slothbert put down his goblet, but seeing that everyone put their goblets down, he picked up his goblet once more—and once more the company, picking up their goblets, raised the king's mouthful to the heights in a thunder of trumpets, in the brilliance of chandeliers, in the repetitions of the immemorial mirrors. The king, terrified, took another mouthful.

The telltale sound—a quiet, barely audible chink, the characteristic sound of loose change in the pocket—once again reached the ears of the chancellor and the council. For a second time the noble old man fixed his intent and lifeless gaze on the conventional face of the enemy ambassador . . . and yet again, more clearly, the telltale sound was heard. By now it was evident that someone who wished to bring the king and the banquet into disrepute was in this clandestine way trying to tempt the monarch's unhealthy cupidity. The telltale jingling rang out once more, this time so clearly that Slothbert heard it—and the serpent of covetousness crawled onto his vulgar junkyard owner's mug.

The disgrace! The disgrace! The horror! So fanatical in its baseness was the king's soul, so trivially narrow, that he did not covet larger sums but precisely petty ones; small sums were capable of leading him to the very depths of hell. Oh, the most fundamental monstrousness of this matter was the fact that even bribes did not attract the king so much as tips — tips for him were like sausage to a dog! The entire hall had frozen in mute anticipation. Hearing the familiar, oh-so-sweet sound, King Slothbert put down his goblet and, forgetting everything else, in his boundless foolishness . . . licked his lips unobtrusively. . . . Unobtrusively! That was what he imagined. The king's lip-licking burst like a bomb in front of the entire banquet, which went red-faced with shame.

Archduchess Renata Adelaide let out a muffled cry of disgust! The eyes of the government, the court, the generals, and the clergy turned to the person of the old man who for many years had guided the helm of the state in his toil-worn hands. What was to be done? What course of action was to be taken?

And then it was seen that from the pallid lips of the historic old man, heroically, a thin old man's tongue issued forth. The chancellor was licking his lips! The chancellor of the state had licked his lips!

For a moment the council continued to wrestle with its astonishment; but eventually the tongues of the ministers issued forth, and after them the tongues of the bishops . . . the tongues of the countesses and marchionesses . . . and all licked their lips, from one end of the table to the other, in the mysterious luster of crystal, and the mirrors repeated this act to infinity, plunging it in mirrored perspectives.

Then the king, furious, seeing that he could not permit himself anything, since they copied everything he did, pushed back abruptly from the table and stood up. But the chancellor too stood up. And after him everyone stood.

For the chancellor no longer hesitated; he had already made a decision whose extraordinary boldness put convention to rout! Realizing that nothing could now conceal from Renata the king's true nature, the chancellor had determined to throw the banquet openly into the struggle for the dignity of the Crown. Yes, there was no other path—the banquet must, with utter relentlessness, repeat not only those actions of the king that lent themselves to repetition, but *precisely and above all those that did not lend themselves to repetition*—since it was possible only in that way to transform those deeds into archdeeds—and this violence on the person of the king had become necessary and unavoidable. For this reason, when a furious Slothbert pounded his fist on the table, breaking two plates, without a second thought the chancellor smashed two plates and everyone smashed two plates apiece, as if in honor of God; and the trumpets sounded! The banquet was prevailing over the king! Fettered, the king sat down and remained sheepishly in his seat, while the banquet waited for him to make the slightest move. Something extraordinary—something fantastical—was being born and was dying in the vapors of the abandoned feast.

The king jumped up from his place at the head of the table! The banquet jumped up too! The king took a few steps. The banqueters too. The king began to wander aimlessly around the hall. The banqueters also wandered. And the wandering, in its monotonous and infinite wandering, attained such dizzy heights of archwandering that Slothbert, overcome by a sudden dizziness, gave a roar—and with bloodshot eyes he flung himself on the archduchess—and, not knowing what to do, he set about gradually strangling her before the eyes of the entire court!

Without a moment's hesitation the helmsman of the ship of state flung himself on the nearest lady and began strangling her — and the remaining guests followed his lead — while archstrangulation, repeated by the multitude of mirrors, gaped from every infinity and grew, and grew, and grew — till it finally suppressed the gasping of the ladies. It was at this point that the banquet broke the last ties linking it to the ordinary world; now its mind was made up!

The archduchess fell to the floor — dead. The strangled ladies fell. And immobility, a hideous immobility, intensified by the mirrors, speechless, began to grow and grow . . .

And it grew. It grew unceasingly. And it intensified, it intensified in the oceans of quiet, in the boundlessness of silence, and it reigned, it, archimmobility itself, which had descended, had taken over and was ruling . . . and its rule was indivisible . . .

Then the king fled.

Waving his arms, with a gesture of the utmost panic Slothbert seized himself by the backside and without a second thought started to run away . . . He ran toward the door, to get as far away as possible from that Archkingdom. The gathering saw that the king was getting away from them — another minute and he would get away! And they watched, stupefied, for the king could not be stopped . . . who would dare to stop the king by force?

"After him," roared the old man. "After him!"

The cold breath of night blew on the cheeks of the dignitaries as they rushed out onto the square in front of the castle. The king ran away down the middle of the street, and ten or twenty paces behind him rushed the chancellor, the banquet, and the ball. And here the archgenius of that archstatesman once again reveals itself in all its archmight—for THE IGNOMINIOUS FLIGHT OF THE KING BECOMES SOME KIND OF ATTACK, and it is no longer clear whether THE KING IS FLEEING or whether, on the contrary, THE KING IS RUSHING FORWARD AT THE HEAD OF THE BANQUET! Oh, those rushing sashes and medals of the ambassadors, fluttering in the furious rush; the purple of the bishops; the ministerial dress coats and tail coats; oh, the canter, the archcanter of so many potentates! The common people had never seen such a thing before. Magnates, owners of vast tracts of land, descendants of the most splendid families, galloping alongside officers of the general staff, whose gallop was accompanied by the gallop of all-powerful ministers, with the rush of marshals, chamberlains, with the canter of most noble, rushing ladies of the court! Oh, the rush, the archrush of marshals and chamberlains, the rush of ministers, the canter of ambassadors in the darkness of night, by the light of lanterns, beneath the firmament of the heavens! Cannon sounded in the castle. And the king charged!

"Forward!" he cried. "Forward!"

And archcharging at the head of his archsquadron, the archking passed on into the dark of night!

Afterword

※

It was with the first seven stories of the present volume that a young and previously unknown writer called Witold Gombrowicz burst upon the Polish literary scene in 1933. Though many of the critics of the time were baffled by these bizarre works, others immediately appreciated the subtle humor, the brilliant literary and linguistic inventiveness, and the psychological complexity of the stories; virtually overnight, Gombrowicz's reputation was established and his genius recognized, by some at least. Thanks in part to these beginnings, Gombrowicz remains one of the most important (and enjoyable) European writers of the twentieth century.

In fact, the story of the writing and publication of these pieces is a curious one in itself. The first seven stories of *Bacacay* were written between 1926 and 1932 and first appeared in 1933 under the title *Recollections of Adolescence (Pamiętnik z okresu dojrzewania)*. *Recollections* brought Gombrowicz considerable renown, though few critics were capable of appreciating just how innovative his writing was. It was the publication of *Ferdydurke* in 1937 that cemented Gombrowicz's reputation as a master of prose.

The outstanding quality of these early stories may partly be explained by the fact that, though these were Gombrowicz's first published writings, they were not the first things he had written. On a number of previous occasions he had tried his hand at novels, but he had been deeply dissatisfied with the results and had burned the manuscripts. In his *Polish Memories (Wspomnienia polskie)*, written and published in the early 1960s from exile in Argentina, Gombrowicz recalled that after these failures he had decided to attempt some shorter pieces, and ended up being quite pleased with the results:

> *This time . . . these were not compositions abortive right from their botched conception; I engaged in level-headed work aimed at a concrete result. I set about writing brief pieces—short stories—with the idea that if one didn't work out I would burn it and start something new. But all of them came out well, in my view at least. During those university years, when on the surface I had distanced myself entirely from literature, a style was forming within me, and now from the first moment I discovered in myself a sureness of hand that I could never have anticipated.*
>
> *[...] One thing I do remember—that from the beginning the non-sensical and the absurd were very much to my liking, and I was never more satisfied than when my pen gave birth to some scene that was truly crazy, removed from the (healthy) expectations of mediocre logic, and yet firmly rooted in its own separate logic.*

It is also interesting to hear Gombrowicz's description of the method he developed as he wrote these stories:

A writer can, if he wishes, describe reality as he sees it or as he imagines it to be; this produces realistic works such as the books of Sienkiewicz. But he can also apply a different method in which reality is reduced to its component parts, after which these parts are used like bricks to construct a new edifice, a new world or microcosm . . . which ought to be different from the regular world, and yet correspond with it in some way . . . different but, as the physicists say, adequate . . .

Thus, for example, in my story "Dinner at Countess Pavahoke's" I invented a group of aristocrats sharing a series of exclusively vegetarian dinners in order to cultivate various kinds of sublimity and mental refinement; yet the swine of a cook serves them soup made from a little boy . . . and they consume it with relish. Nonsense, is it not? But it's nonsense composed of elements taken from life; it's a caricature of reality . . . how delightful it was to see this nonsense blossom beneath my pen, grow with its own inexorable logic, and lead to unforeseen resolutions.

Perhaps because of the critics' misinterpretation of the title *Recollections of Adolescence*—many of them, especially those hostile to Gombrowicz, took it to mean that the author was declaring himself not yet mature—when it came time to reissue the stories in postwar Poland in 1957 Gombrowicz decided to rename the collection *Bakakaj*, a Polonized form of Bacacay, the name of a side street in Buenos Aires on which the writer lived. This title, while striking, tells us nothing about the contents of the book; Gombrowicz explained in a letter to his Italian publisher that he named his book thus "for the same reason that a person names his dogs—to distinguish them from others."

The texts of the original seven stories of *Recollections of Ado-*

lescence were revised and in places shortened for *Bakakaj*; in some cases titles were altered. For example, "Adventures" was in the earlier book titled "Five Minutes Before Falling Asleep." In addition, Gombrowicz added two freestanding stories from *Ferdydurke* —"Philidor's Child Within" and "Philibert's Child Within"—and also three stories which had been published separately but had never before appeared in book form—"On the Kitchen Steps," "The Rat," and "The Banquet." The enlarged collection of stories was published as *Bakakaj* by Wydawnictwo Literackie in Kraków in 1957. This event was regarded by Gombrowicz as his postwar debut in communist Poland, but it also turned out to be the last time his work would appear in his home country in his lifetime. (His primary Polish-language publisher was the Paris-based Kultura house.)

Curiously, while *Bacacay* includes Gombrowicz's first works, it is the last of his writings to be published in English. Though individual stories translated by various hands have appeared in literary journals over the years, and *Bacacay* has been translated into numerous other languages, the present translation (made directly from the original Polish) marks the first time the whole collection has been made available to an English-speaking audience. The translation is based on the 2002 scholarly edition of *Bakakaj* published, also by Wydawnictwo Literackie, as the first volume in a definitive edition of Gombrowicz's collected works. This English version reproduces the "compromise" sequence of the 2002 edition, which broadly follows the chronological order in which the stories were written and published, with the exception of "On the Kitchen Steps," written earlier but omitted from *Recollections of*

Adolescence out of consideration for the author's father, who Gombrowicz was afraid might read an allusion to himself in the story. I have chosen to include my own translations of the two stories from *Ferdydurke*, on the grounds of stylistic consistency, given that Gombrowicz evidently considered them to belong with the other stories in the book.

I won't presume to suggest how these stories should be read. Over the years they have been interpreted from a psychosexual perspective as emanations of the author's troubled mind; as exercises in literary parody (the detective story, the adventure story, the folk tale, and so on); as sociopolitical critiques of the shortcomings of the Polish gentry and aristocracy; and as attempts at innovative literary forms. Justifications for each of these readings can be found in Gombrowicz's own statements about the stories, as well as the analysis of numerous critics. For those of my generation, in their combination of intellectual allusions and absurd yet po-faced humor they are reminiscent of nothing so much as the films of Luis Buñuel or even of *Monty Python* sketches. Others will no doubt find different associations and pleasures from their reading.

In this regard, it is interesting to note that in the very first copies of the first edition of *Recollections of Adolescence*, Gombrowicz included a "Short Explanation" addressed to his readers, in which he explicated "what the stories are about," emphasizing that the explanations were only necessary for readers who could not figure this out for themselves. Among his "explanations," he clarifies that in "A Premeditated Crime" the family loves the father, and he has not been murdered; and that in "Dinner at Countess

Pavahoke's" the soup is not actually made from the runaway boy, but that the association is purely linguistic, and that "the point of the story is that the hunger and suffering of poor Bolek Cauliflower make the cauliflower-vegetable taste better to the aristocrats eating it." He also explains that both "Adventures" and "The Events on the *Banbury*" take place in the minds of their respective protagonists only; he describes the latter story as "the dramatic tale of a mind, written with the aid of external events." And he warns the reader not to look for symbols: "There are no symbols here, only associations. It should be taken exactly as it is written. I am never symbolic." The "Short Explanation" was removed from the book after only a few hundred copies had been printed; it seems clear that Gombrowicz (rightly, I would argue) came to the conclusion that interpretation was the job of the reader, not the writer.

Whatever perspective one takes, there can be no doubt whatsoever that the stories in this book are brilliantly original works that deserve a permanent place in the canon of world literature. From the very beginnings of his writing career Gombrowicz was driven by an ambition to produce literature of significance on the scale not just of Poland but of Europe and the world. The stories collected here show clearly that from his first published works this ambition was realized. It has been a pleasure and a privilege to make *Bacacay* available to an English-language readership.

Bill Johnston